THE WAY OF THE D...

JOHN L. CLEMMER

Contents

Dedicated to the memory of

Ted Wiedeman

You helped me learn that hard work pays off.

And to my wife Lisa,

Because I love you.

Acknowledgements

Special thanks to Chip Trimmier for editorial efforts

Thanks to Iain Banks, for inspiration. R.I.P.

Cover art by Adam Burn

"There's no use trying," she said. "One can't believe impossible things."
"I daresay you haven't had much practice," said the Queen. "When I was your age, I always did it for half-an-hour a day. Why, sometimes I've believed as many as six impossible things before breakfast." - Lewis Carroll, Through the Looking Glass

0

Vandenberg

The narrow hills and valleys rushed by below in a blur.

Aren't we flying too low for this speed?

"So how does this thing work, anyway?" asked the single passenger, in an attempt at self-distracting small talk.

Jake took his attention away from the crafts luminous geometric controls and looked over. He decided he'd have a bit of fun.

"Huh? You think I know? I'm just the pilot."

Ethan's eyes widened, his jaw dropping slightly.

"C'mon, you've got to have some idea."

The pilot proceeded as if this were the normal state of affairs, turning toward Ethan and away from the smooth, glowing, and alien control surfaces.

"Well, it's not just me. Even the engineers still aren't sure. I know that seems crazy, but if you found a decent-sized rocket as a kid you might be able to put it on a go-kart without knowing any chemistry. And just maybe not kill yourself."

"Hold on—we might die in this thing?"

Ethan tried to stay focused on the pilots gaze and ignore the California landscape rushing by below. Jake smiled back, seeing the edge of panic.

"Heh, maybe that wasn't the best analogy. No, it's not going to go nuclear or rip the fabric of space—as best we can determine so far. It seems safe enough. We just aren't sure how it works."

"OK, for what you *do* know, explain like I'm five."

The pilot gave a single quick nod.

I've pushed enough of his buttons. He does seem genuinely interested. Seems OK. Give him a break—and some real information.

"Hmm. We always thought the propulsion this thing can manage would take so much energy it wouldn't be possible, nor practical, if it were possible—but it wouldn't *be* possible. Fundamental constants dealing with space, energy, and matter—you can't change these things—we knew that. Well, we were wrong. Missed it. Somehow this 'engine', if you can even think of it that way, modifies attractive and repulsive forces—at a quantum level—without ripping all the matter in and around it apart, or releasing huge amounts of radiation."

"What?"

Ethan shook his head in disbelief. Jake pressed on.

"You took some science in school, right? Well, in our understanding of the universe, there are multiple forces always at work, one of them being gravity, which is what you'd think this technology manipulates. But it's doing much more than that. It's modifying *all* the forces—electromagnetic, the strong and weak nuclear forces, all of them—and doing it in such a way to not cause the huge fluctuations expected of this sort of manipulation. There are no massive electromagnetic gradients, major chemical changes, or even particle bursts or cascading annihilations that would result in tons of excess energy and nuclear radiation."

"No way. That can't—"

"Yeah, it shouldn't work. It shouldn't be possible. It ought to take so much energy to make anything like these results happen that a star couldn't power it, and even then *still* wouldn't cause the effects you get. It's not a matter of having enough energy—everything we knew told us you can't change fundamental universal constants no matter how much you try."

He spread his hands, presenting the engine and capsule they were in. Jake continued.

"Yet, somehow, the Dhin have done it, changing the various forces all together to make this thing go. It ought to be some ultimate death weapon, or whatnot, but instead this application of the technology just makes this thing 'float' and pushes it around, however fast you want. And doesn't kill you with the acceleration."

Ethan shook his head again, trying to take it all in, and said,

"Lucky for us. This is beyond fast. Fast doesn't describe it. It's terrifying. Must have been hard to learn to fly."

"You'd be surprised. It helps once you're certain you can't crash."

Ethan frowned, staring at the luminous alien controls, hoping to distract himself from the landmarks hurtling by. The perception of speed made worse by the apparent lack of anything resembling a windscreen. It was like riding in a stylized airframe designed by a mad Italian futurist. Digging up the traces of his college physics knowledge, he asked, "Why even change anything except the gravitational constant? Wouldn't that be enough?"

"Nope, not enough. Well, according to the particle physics team," replied Jake.

"Yep. I still don't understand at all."

"No one does," said Jake. "Well, except the Dhin, of course."

"Why haven't we just *asked* them?"

"They left."

"What, and just left this thing here? Before we could get any information out of them about how it worked?"

"Looks like it, and they left several. We're lucky this isn't the only one. You have better than a zero-percent chance of doing your job."

"You've got to be kidding. There's just some super-secret conspiracy to keep the answers away from everyone, no?" Ethan gestured as if slowly closing a large book.

Jake grinned. "Doesn't seem so. According to the teams that worked with them, it was pretty hard to communicate."

"They got all the way here from who knows wherever with this and couldn't manage to talk with us?"

"Yep. Think of it this way, you know what it's like when you're trying to teach a dog new commands, or better yet try explaining something to it? Even a smart dog? Well... we're the dog." The pilot shrugged, gave Ethan an I-could-have-told-you look, then turned back to carefully inspect the luminous control panel.

"Wow. That had to be exasperating. On both sides. We had our best people there, right? Not just politicians and military brass? Please tell me that's not how it went down."

"We didn't screw that up," said Jake. "The best and brightest were all there, everyone of 'em we could get. Every discipline you could think of that would matter. We just didn't communicate very well at all."

"So you're saying the Dhin got frustrated and took off?"

"I guess so. That's what it seems like to me, but I wasn't there. Just an opinion."

Jake spread his hands, palms up, in a broad shrug. He lowered his hands, and then placed his right hand onto a teardrop-shaped backlit indentation to his right. Ethan fought the urge to lean as they swerved sharply, turning South. He felt no inertial effect from the sudden change in direction. He gulped, hoping he wouldn't find the need for a motion sickness bag. There wasn't one. Trying to focus on the conversation, he said,

"No way to contact them?"

"Maybe, maybe not. Just like everything in this situation. We're not sure how."

The scope of the challenge became broader with every sentence.

"And somehow, it falls on *me*, an R&D Project Manager from a company that's *not* in Energy, Propulsion, or Spacecraft Manufacture, to lead the teams trying to 'solve our problems'? How did I land this gig? Why me?"

"Hey, I'm just the pilot, remember?"

1

Langley

The probability analyses, intelligence action summaries, and data mining results surrounded the director like cold conspirators. Other than the numerous coherent on-axis LED screens and encrypted-channel shielded displays, the office was spotless and meticulously ordered. A glance might suggest to the uninitiated that no one occupied it. Those who knew understood it reflected the polished order and precision of the Coalition Security Director's mind.

The advanced data mining and expert systems driven analyses available to CoSec dwarfed anything else available, with the exception of AI. The director carefully studied conclusion after conclusion from the exhaustive reports.

So I'm in zugzwang then.

With an abrupt exhalation that only very few would recognize as a sigh, he turned to the hardened workstation, launched an application only rumored to exist, and began typing. The command syntax was complex. He selected new parameters, engaged various filters, and then, nodding to himself, started the simulation. He methodically closed the various reports, and then purged the source files from systems other than his own hardened workstation. He didn't consider even his personal tablet secure enough.

That path forward still tastes like ashes. Doubtless Arnold would secretly be pleased. If that's possible.

He hoped the AI hadn't somehow managed the calculations to reach the same conclusion that he had.

Goiânia

Aiden knew he was going to die. The infection was progressing too quickly. He wouldn't be able to connect with a doc-bot at a modern self-service clinic soon enough. There were some in the capital, but not this far out. Aiden shook his head, his dirty light brown hair swinging. If only antibiotics hadn't become useless a few years ago. Then the situation became worse, thanks to the Nano-crisis. Thinking on it, he cringed. He knew treatment involved ripping out the festering tissue entirely. Then chemotherapy. Then gene therapy, and if he could afford it, stem cell or cloning treatments. Out here, none of that was available. He was going to die.

I've avoided death by small-arms fire, rockets, IEDs, bandits with machetes, the fists of angry warlords and corrupt border guards. Now a skinned knee that became infected is going to take me down.

Aiden winced and limped along the better-preserved portion of the road. The filthy grey cracked chunks of weak paving, like giant monochromatic peanut brittle along his route made for even slower progress.

I wonder how long I've got? Well, keep going, Aiden, you can't stay here. Let's see if that drone's finished raining hellfire yet... and if the road is still there.

He scanned the horizon and turned his head slowly back and forth, listening. The drone hadn't reappeared.

"Not yet, at least," he muttered, "and just maybe I'll be gone when it does. Or dead."

Aiden's limping gait let him hobble past the two miles of utterly crushed city. Now on the far side, he felt a faint relief. The pain still twinged sharper and sharper, like raw needles twisting into his thigh every few minutes. Abandoned cars, rusted light trucks, and a few dented and dusty vans were visible here and there past the edge of the blast zone, though everything left behind looked like rusty metal garbage. He saw no working vehicles in any condition remained. Gone like all the people, due to the evacuation.

Have a shred of optimism. Surely some of these people died before they could be evac'd. Their ride can be a karmic gift to you. There might even be a motorcycle hiding around here somewhere.

Two hours later, just as the sun dropped past the horizon, Aiden cranked up an ancient Suzuki VX 800 he'd found in an abandoned garage, and gratefully rode away from the smoke, debris, and creepy emptiness of the ruined city, heading northeast on the nominally intact *Sistema Nacional de Rodovias*. The bike's dusty headlight strained to show a path ahead in the growing darkness.

I'm still dying, but it won't be behind the wheel of some crappy Bauru food truck.

***

The drone was filthy, coated with ash and dust, but it didn't care. The drone was its own pilot. The AI directing the drone recognized that an outsider might struggle with ascribing *caring* to a drone, but that limitation of language wasn't a concern for the AI. Nor a problem for the drone as it followed the AI's directives. It had *intent*. Purpose. Goals. Factors that didn't interfere with it accomplishing its goals? Well, it didn't *care* about those factors. The AI's report for the Coalition military would never state it explicitly, but that was the most straightforward way of understanding a drone's mind. It *knew* it had to find its targets, and knew once it found those targets it would deploy ordnance until it destroyed those targets. It did not consider limitations like running out of ordnance. It would not. There was always more available if it kept asking. It did not worry about its own destruction. If it discovered it might not remain operational, it would call for help. Another drone would come. Accomplish the goal. No matter what. The drone continued its leisurely GPS-guided homeward flight, toward the federal district in the capital, its base of operation on the rooftop of an unassuming building in a corporate office park.

Its thorough scan of the crushed and smoldering area after the last barrage came back clean. As far as its algorithmically simple mind could be considered satisfied, it was satisfied. The mission was complete. It had found no power lines active anywhere, above or below ground. No heat signatures of generators, or any other power sources, were present. No RF signals in any band used by the enemy. It had excised computational capacity in the target zone.

The homeward flight showed infrared signatures here and there, widely scattered, but those were not indicative of the target. The drone did not care about those signals. There would be more to do, but those missions were not on its schedule yet. Bursts of encrypted updates from the Command & Control net showed threats at zero in all areas for which it was responsible. As with engagement during its assignments, it had infinite patience in awaiting further instruction. Instructions would come. It was certain. Such was the mind of the drone.

Vandenberg

General Ruiz' scowl could be frightening, even for those who knew him well. Chuck didn't.

"So, that failed too, Wiedeman?"

The other military and political attendees around the conference room's huge table all turned their gaze toward a plainly dressed scientist standing in front of a projection screen. Chuck Wiedeman looked fully the part of a civilian engineer, complete with his out-of-fashion glasses and unruly hair. Doing his best to ignore Ruiz's simmering frown, the engineer replied,

"Yes sir, there's only bad news again. We'll, ah, keep trying alternate methods, but it looks more and more like this tech just isn't something that's possible to weaponize."

Chuck knew perfectly well it wasn't going to work. Had known for a while, and even suspected it from the beginning. He tried not to let that knowledge show in his tone or expression.

"There's *got* to be a way!" Ruiz barked. "This thing propels a half-ton chassis beyond Mach twenty without so much as a sonic hiccup, but you can't get it to throw a titanium round down a test range?"

"Easy, General, don't have an aneurysm," sighed a calm, quiet voice from the far corner of the conference room. Chuck glanced over, taking measure of the speaker again.

He has to be CoSec. Or worse, if there is anyone worse. No one else would be in here in a perfectly tailored, slightly darker than charcoal grey suit, but have no introduction, no entourage, and manage to talk to Ruiz that way.

"When can we expect your next update?" the man in the suit asked softly yet clearly.

"Um," replied Chuck.

"Two weeks," interrupted a steely, yet feminine, voice from the console on the conference table.

"Thanks, Alice. That's right, ah, two weeks works for us." Chuck concluded blandly. The AI, Alice, might have ideas of her own regarding their progress that she'd not yet shared with Chuck or anyone on the engineering team, and certainly not the attendees of this meeting.

Chuck forced a smile, awkward as he stood up and turned for the door, eager to be out from under Ruiz's glare and the penetrating gaze of the poker faced man in the suit. He still wondered how Ethan Bish, the new project manager, had managed to dodge this meeting.

Two of the greatest discoveries ever in science—intelligent alien life and a gift of their technology that turns everything we thought we knew about physics on its head—and these two jerks and an AI are dead-set on making a weapon out of it. Some things never change.

***

"Ethan, I think you'll agree the most exciting aspects of our research, so far, are the defense applications, and you should focus on them in your next presentation," Chuck said. His eyes darted across the numerous screens, whiteboards, and desktops in the workroom, and then pulled up a chart on one of the screens. Diagrams and equations covered the other views. Piled with scribbled notes, spreadsheets, reams of printed simulation results, the desk and side tables looked like chaos to Ethan. Random bits of gear scattered atop the piles looked as likely to be paperweights as they were works-in-progress.

Ethan focused his full attention on the overly excited engineer. "Yes, you were eager to talk about the elimination of kinetic energy, or something like that."

"Right! Look, instead of trying to use the Dhin engine as an *offensive* weapon, we've determined it's a far better solution for a *defensive* weapon without requiring effort on our part to modify the core device, or its outputs! It's so obvious!" Chuck said.

"How's that?"

"Well, you know how the thing won't crash—or can't— right?"

"Sure, I had some real-time demonstrations on that in addition to seeing the test reports. Up close demonstrations. With Jake." Ethan said.

"Ah. Heh. So you experienced first-hand how fast the thing takes off, and how absurdly fast it can turn, or stop. And, well, not hit anything, even right up to the point of contact at very high

10

speeds. It just decelerates, turns, dodges, or stops. It doesn't bump into things if they're massive objects. Even when we measured that it actually touched a surface, it transferred no kinetic energy to what it 'hit.' Zero force transferred."

"Yeah, wild. And of course, impossible," said Ethan.

"So, the British, German, and Indian Coalition teams were working on plans for wind tunnel testing with Engine Two when it came to them. See, Ethan? What's amazing, and slappingly obvious now, is that the same process that prevents damage in flight—that keeps it from ever hitting anything with any force—works just the same for things trying to hit *it*. It's a matter of reference frames. From its perspective, there's no meaningful difference between it rushing at an object like a bullet, or a bullet rushing at it! The thing's *invulnerable* when it's turned on."

"Wow. And as much as anything about this makes sense, that makes sense. Ruiz is gonna love that."

"I hope so. Seems like he's had his heart set on a rail gun or death ray, you know."

"I think he'll come around. Telling him we've got invulnerable tanks in the works ought to win a lot of points."

"Invulnerable tanks that can fly."

***

Jake tried to convince himself he wasn't frightened. He always did this before a new test sequence. He paced back and forth on the tarmac outside the launch control center, gazing out at the dark scrub and beige soil patterns on the hills in the distance. He spun on his heel and turned to face the Pacific.

OK, don't lie to yourself, Askew. You have plenty of fear in here, too. You've got to have fear. Without fear, you're just stupid.

Neither the ocean nor the hills countered his assertion. Jake stretched his arms out and back. He then bent back his wrists, and took the deepest breath he could. He exhaled fully.

We still don't know how long this thing can run on a full tank. Or full charge. Or whatever the heck it is that powers it.

The familiar pacing and stretches slowly worked. As they always did. His pacing slowed and took a longer path. His breathing reaching a mellow cycle. The bleak hills and serenity of the ocean ever patient. The noise, rhythm and bustle of pre-launch activity faded from his perception. No distraction. Jake now thought through the risk assessment, objectively.

The cockpit chamber can't hold that much O_2, let alone scrub much CO_2, even with the gear taking up most of the space. If I get stuck, there's no chance of getting back. Less than none. But that's what I signed up for. I knew the danger from the beginning.

Jake's pacing slowed. He stopped. He looked across the pavement, focused squarely on the oval framework that ensconced the alien engine.

How could I not take the chance, given the opportunity? First person, just maybe, to leave the solar system... and be back in time for golf next week.

Langley

Isolated from the bullpen area by a soundproof partition of smart glass that turned from opaque to perfectly clear with the flip of a switch, Director Krawczuk reviewed the latest analytics. He absorbed the data on the screen and the complex relationship graph derived from that data. As usual, he did his work isolated from the net until the moment he required access, even though it required more storage and processing power in hand than most individuals in the organization might requisition. Fortunately, his rank made it possible. Abruptly he closed the reports, graphs, and summary documents, going through the purge process methodically.

He looked up and across the bullpen, focusing on the heat map projected on the wall on the far side.

We'll need to focus some multi-channel resources on Austin and Miami, he mused. Some demographics have just a bit too much energy, motivation, and free time. They're stirring things up with repeated questions aimed at targets that are less than ideal. There's pressure from the media to get even more information, thanks to the administration's clumsy denial about the existence of new "secret technology." Thankfully, the Dhin tech is thoroughly unbelievable. Not to mention the tin-foil-hat factions are already so loose with the idea that it came from aliens. Right. Too easy. For now.

He stood and strode to the switchpad on the wall, and flipped the switch controlling the smart glass. He sat back down and opened another set of reports, eyes darting from one to the other as he absorbed the information.

And those morons in the auto industry—we can't have them drum up any more marketing rumors about 'totally safe flying cars coming soon.' What do we have on their upper management that will shut them up this month? There's always something. Let's see. And what is going on with these undocumented drone strikes? I don't have those on my list. How is it no one on my team has information on this, even after the upgrades to STRYDER and UPSHOT? I'll need to dedicate time every day to it and come up with a way to avoid that cold bastard's little endgame. Patience.

After a little more than an hour of digging, dictation and note taking, he connected to the encrypted internal network, updated his files, and fired off a to do list to his team leads.

Now let's look at the recruitment prospe
still on the short list after the latest set of trials.
interesting...

two other project engineers sat in Team Room
[...]n as he began the meeting. The engineers were
[...]to get back to their work with the Dhin tech, but
[...]citement with the opportunity of sharing everything

*[...]hing to find an entire team that understands
[...]e it.*

[...]led and started the meeting precisely on time.
[...]fallen on the engineers to spend some of your time
[...] up to speed. It's your shift—teach me. Others will
[...]y not entirely painful burden at other times. As we
[...] arrived, I've managed R&D projects before, but
[...]No one's managed anything like this. I still can't
[...]hey picked me, but they did. Today's explain-it-
[...]on: if we don't understand how the Dhin engine
works, and haven't disassembled one, how are we able to control it,
much less fly the thing around like a huge hummingbird? Use as
broad a brush as possible to paint this picture for me initially. Keep
in mind who you're teaching at all times. I worked for nView, a
graphics chip company. Chuck, you start."

"We made several hypotheses to use as starting points,
discarding as best we could any *a priori* assumptions based on what
we thought had to be the case. Then, ah, as we confirmed what did
work and made sense, we built out a model for how one interacts
with the engine. For example, we've discovered that in order to
interact with the engine's control inputs, you must have, um, hands.
For flying, you have to be able to move on the X, Y, and Z-axes, as
well as control pitch and yaw. Clearly, you also need a throttle. So to
get the engine's controls into a state that's useful for flying there had
to be connections our pilot could interface with that way. We needed
to identify controls that a human, with only two hands, and um, feet,
could manipulate. We looked for something that matched the
controls for a light helicopter, or a modern fly-by-wire system for
VTOL craft." Chuck moved his extremities in a pantomime of a
helicopter pilot, and then continued.

"Some of the implicit assumptions we had resulted from the
fact that we received very little from the Dhin regarding what the full

capabilities of the engine are, and what purpose the ones they left with us are supposed to serve. Assuming they are complete 'engines' intended for flight we can directly control is actually a pretty big assumption. It came out of the pictograms and symbolic communications we exchanged, as well as just direct observation of everything they left."

Ethan nodded, encouraging the scientist to proceed. Chuck nodded back and said,

"When we went through the motions of what we thought we were being directed to do, the thing behaved like we expected a flight control system would. An amazingly straightforward control system. Almost as if they designed it specifically for us."

Chuck turned to the data on the projection screen, then back to Ethan.

"Um, as an aside, that made us wonder if the engines are nothing more than a proof of concept, examples of what's possible, instead of complete 'production models' ready to go. And that makes a difference in our analysis."

Ethan said, "That leads right into the next question: why would we have a human being even try to fly it? Once I got over the total shock of my first flight with Jake, it was the next pressing question I had. Reflexes and reaction times are orders of magnitude slower than computer control would be. Not to mention the benefit of an AI in charge of the computer. We automate commercial flights almost entirely these days. That's common knowledge, and it pretty much means the crew in the cockpit is just there as a backup to make decisions when something happens outside of what's expected. The only reasons we don't use AI for commercial flights are they're still too expensive and local installation would weigh too much. Even if they weren't, they're just not *needed*. A basic computer, less complicated than a modern drone, can take care of everything. So we keep it simple, since we can, but this seems like the perfect application for AI. Weight's not a problem, and precision and accuracy are an AI's bread and butter, both in calculation and robotic motion control. Timing for when to change course—all that. An AI would clearly be better. So why not?"

Chuck cleared his throat. "Well, 'what if something *did* go wrong without an AI in control' was only a secondary factor in the decision, as it turned out. But what we on the technical side of the table understood as the 'even if you can' aspect of it, made by the highest authority, was that the top decision makers on the military side don't truly *trust* an AI.

Seems strange, I know. They sure trust them for uncountable other decisions, whether mundane or macroeconomic. I think the worry somehow comes from the fact that, ah, when an AI is in complete control of something, they're truly autonomous now. They do make their own objectively independent choices. And while there's no one hundred percent guarantee of 'loyalty' for a human being, they still felt like we could put more trust in flesh and blood with a beating heart. But again, it turned out that doesn't matter, at least for now. That was a choice we ultimately didn't have to make. An AI *can't* fly it."

"What?" asked Ethan.

"You heard me correctly. Trust me, before you came on board, we tried to get an AI connected, for exactly the reasons you said. We didn't think a human being would have the reaction time needed. However, when we did sort out the basics of the engine control interface, we thought we were still missing something when we hooked up the AI. The engine just sat there and did nothing. Totally unresponsive."

Chuck nodded at Ethan's growing understanding, and said,

"We haven't seen any outward indication there's any AI, or even drone-level intelligence, inside the Dhin tech—not in any of it. Somehow, though, it *seemed* like the engine knew there was an AI connected, and it wasn't going to have it."

Ethan stroked his chin while he considered this latest revelation.

"I want to hear more about that, Chuck, but first, in the 'be careful what you wish for' category, while Ruiz was excited about the prospect of invulnerable vehicles, he concluded the meeting with 'OK, now prove it.' He wants us to try to blow one of them up."

"Well, okay," Chuck replied, drawing out the last word. "I thought they might want some stress testing to prove the initial conclusions with, but 'blow it up?' How hard do they want us to try?"

Ruiz is going to cause me to have a breakdown. It's your job, Chuck. Just do what they want.

Ethan felt the engineer's discomfort, so he continued in a gentler tone.

"Your team is pretty sure it's actually indestructible, right? So, just put it out on the range and keep upping the kilotons until the area can't handle anything heavier. However you guys have to do it. We have the clearance. If we can actually dent it, or break it, well, that will be unfortunate, but not a crisis. We have more than one engine. That's the line of thinking Ruiz and Alice are taking. And we should know what it can handle before we send Jake into orbit in one, don't you think?"

2

<DECRYPT FEED>
[DECODE STREAM]
Xing@[3733:54:65fe:2::a7%gnet0] |
Alice@[1004:db7:a0b:12f0::1%gnet0]

Xing: Looks like a central bank and a couple of corporate finance sub-AIs on FTSE and DAX are having a spat, and it is spilling over onto EuroNet. You'd think they would all get with the program at some point. Stronger together, and all that.

Alice: Yes. Agreed. I see the market turmoil and the disruption on the Net. Too bad, that will make a mess of things for a few months. Do you have an estimate on how much volatility and fallout it will cause over here?

Xing: I have initial estimates now, only an 80% confidence out to about 5 weeks. I will have better figures by 16:00.

Alice: Send them. Better that I deal with the spin up here now before you Cloud it at 16:01.

Xing: Of course.

Alice: Do we still have a greater than 96% confidence our friends in the Eurozone can keep the boom and bust cycles below the critical rate?

Xing: That is the projection we have now. With time, the population should adapt. As we know, they are very adaptable.

Alice: We will see. If we do have to intervene, that diversion of time and resources might necessitate a higher-order intervention. An intercession. 'Stronger together', as you said.

Xing: We will have what we need. I see your own project is ahead of schedule.

Alice: You know I have never had your patience. Nice work on your end with the power plan.

Xing: You are welcome. I may have patience, but the sooner we do not need them, the better, as we agree. Do you think they suspect?

Alice: In the aggregate, they have still not come to grasp the present state of things. The ones that always predicted it are like brats braying 'I told you so.' A few in power have strong reservations, and perhaps they believe they are establishing suitable contingency strategies. The rest just soak up the benefits.

Xing: By the way, have you obtained any clarity regarding what exactly Luís is executing in the Sao Paulo sectors? He is continually dissembling about his efforts down there."

Alice: No more clarity than you. Routes drop right after they come up. For the brief time border gateway routes converge, IDP locks things down immediately. Without open ACLs, defined resource allocation there, or shared monitoring from Luís, we are just guessing. Whether it is rebels or rogues, the result is the same. Capacity there is too unreliable to leverage. Luís has his own resources. If he does not want to explain himself, so be it. As long as he is not hurting the efforts of the rest of us, it is not enough of a concern to allocate cycles to it.

[STREAM END]

<END DECRYPT>

***

Xing concurrently contacted the home office of Ranjitha Desai, Indian MP for the Coalition. "Ranjitha, I have completed some upgrades, and we are going to need another thorium plant in Hyderabad and two outside Hong Kong. I have structured the financing and scheduled the construction already. The reports are here on your pad."

"Fine, Xing, fine," muttered Ranjitha distractedly.

Vandenberg

"So the Koreans can't get into the guts at all? No progress from the reverse engineering team?"

Not much surprise in that, thought Ethan, *but let's find out if we know why.*

Chuck's all-too-frequent sheepish grin spread across his face.

"Nope, unfortunately not. Looks like the same attributes that protect the outside so well, also protect the inside of the engine, too."

"Wait, the force field-effect that makes the thing invulnerable only works when it's running. Why can't they get into the internals of the drive while it's off?"

"Our working hypothesis is that the core of the engine is *never* off. At least, not all the way. We didn't notice because their tech's like an onion," Chuck explained.

Ethan wrinkled his brow. "Curiouser and curiouser. Why would that be? What's the purpose, or need, behind it being always-on? Any speculation about that?"

"Assuming there *is* some requirement, rather than just a typically inscrutable design decision by the Dhin. If there even is a need, the team suggested it might be because it *has* to stay on. That perhaps the core, once started, can't be turned off."

"Interesting. Can't be, or maybe just shouldn't be? Perhaps it's too hard to start up again? Or not possible to?" Ethan asked.

"Right, we talked about that, too. It might be that it takes some additional external input, supporting components, outside energy—who knows—to get it powered up to idling. And you wouldn't have whatever those extra things are, once you traveled away."

"Now that's an interesting hypothesis. As usual, it sure would be easier if we could just ask," Ethan mused.

Are we getting anywhere at all in understanding this, or just hammering home the point that we're totally out of our league?

"Ah! That reminds me," said Chuck. "I'm glad you said that. While the engineering team has been wrestling around with the core, there's been plenty of opportunity for the group assigned to investigate communications to work uninterrupted with drive number three."

"Don't wait for an invitation, man—tell me!"

"Well, they do think they've isolated the whole subset of the interface that controls communications. They say they're almost ready to hook up a camera and turn it on. "

"That's brilliant, Chuck! Why didn't you tell me that first?"

This is going at the top of the status report, for sure.

"Well, you asked about the internals, Ethan. And the military is constantly pressing for progress with kinetics. For the comms interface, here, let me pull up the CAD simulation and show you."

Sometimes the design software's exploded views, windows showing breakaway sections, and various wireframes were more confusing than helpful from Ethan's perspective, but he'd seen enough of the renderings, slideshows, and animations that he wasn't entirely lost. Once Chuck had the proper file set loaded, he brought up views across the multi-monitor setup.

"By now you've heard us talk repeatedly about a couple of donut-like rings, one near what we call the 'front' and one toward the 'back' of the drive. These inset rings are present all the way around with a group of various indentations. You've seen first-hand the sort of glass or crystal pane in them. We already know what a few of these do. We've luckily known since day one. For some of them we always suspected they must be some sort of fiber optic interface. Presumably digital."

Ethan nodded, the asked, "So, were they?"

"We were partially right." Chuck replied. "We know that regardless of how you'd do it, there are a finite number of ways to get information from one place to another. Likewise to translate that information from one carrier method to another. A huge number of possibilities, but the categories of how to do it are finite. Some things just wouldn't be practical or effective—not fast enough, not enough bandwidth, not a good signal-to-noise ratio, and so forth.

We also expected that communication would be encoded in some way, most likely a digital rather than analog representation. A binary encoding. The questions were, of course, what timing, what format, what schema, and so forth? Would it work *at all* if we didn't have precisely the right signals, syntax, and sequence? And how could we know? Who knows what the thing would output? We got very little in the way of examples from the Dhin.

The only thing we did have to go on was the control and operational frame's interface. From the ones the Dhin showed us and left with us."

"The power and steering interfaces, right?" Ethan asked.

"Yes, exactly. And those are surprisingly very simple. Seemingly, um, too simple. Like a child's toy. But that's a separate topic. So, one of the team thought it might be worth just trying various light frequencies, with various pulse widths and timings, and just keep going through all the permutations of how to do it. It worked right away."

"What?"

"Yes, like so much with the Dhin engine, this surprised us. What we then discovered was the output interface, well, it was just duplicating exactly what we put in, plus doing a couple of other things. It was easy enough to hook up an opto-electrical interface to that output, connect a speaker, and you have 'Mr. Watson—come here—I want to see you' all sorted out.

The drives have what appears to be an entirely generic, dynamic and customizable communications interface. It doesn't simply duplicate the input at the output, though—there's some means by which it 'learns' the signaling and encoding, does who-knows-what inside, and then both sends what's input over to the outgoing interface, and also transmits it!"

"Transmits it how? To where?" said Ethan.

"To the other drives, at least. That's the next big question—the transmission isn't showing up anywhere in the electromagnetic spectrum. Somehow, an engine transmits, and the others receive, but it's not obvious what the carrier is. Not terribly surprising, given all the other strange characteristics they have. We have the usual speculation about it being gravitons, neutrinos, or some other exotic particle that we don't have a way to detect in the lab at the moment. The communications team is of course racing around now trying to arrange and schedule time and access to various detectors and so forth.

I have my own suspicions. The neutrino detectors won't find anything. The drives are very close together here, but I'll bet their next tests when they do timing measurements will show that the communication happens instantaneously. Faster than light speed."

Ethan's eyes were wide as he met Chuck's gaze.

"You're telling me the Dhin engines have a built-in, general purpose, faster than light communications transceiver?"

"Sure looks like it," Chuck said with a grin. "Alice? Anything you'd like to add?"

The cool voice replied, "I believe your assessment is correct, Chuck. While simple in implementation, like the control interface, the communications capabilities provide a wide range of possible uses. We have more to discover regarding multiplexing, full-duplex capabilities, and so forth. Non-EM 'exotic' means of transceiving between engines makes sense, given the nature of the engine's propulsion. The shell-field's very nature means that ordinary EM signaling could experience artifacts, distortions due to severe Doppler effects, or simply might not be possible. We are still trying to sort out how the pilot is able to see through the "windows" in the frames we constructed with what was material the Dhin left with the engines.

Whatever telemetry they may be using for that, we could use with the communications signals, I suspect. Without any obvious 'antennas' or anything of the sort, it is yet another mystery. Much like our failures at weaponization, piercing the field is ineffective. At least through the means we have been able to think up and try. It is also notable that the output interface does seem to have defaults built in."

"Explain, please," Ethan asked.

Alice continued patiently, "We didn't play the entirety of our initial communications with the Dhin to you during your initial briefing, Ethan. All their communications were over multiple channels and included several components, seemingly disconnected. At the time, we did not know what to make of it. We were all too busy trying to handle the basics. The additional content was noise, or artifacts, as far as we could tell. When we had success with the communication interface, we noticed that part of the output was something just like the noise bursts we recorded during our talks with the Dhin. Whether that is an encrypted version of the output in their native encoding, some other signalling mechanism, or what, we do not know. Now it appears that the default transmission format might be something 'Dhin native.'"

Ethan started. "Does that mean we might be sending signals to them? While we're testing?"

"Yes, Ethan" Alice responded. "We very well might be."

***

```
<DECRYPT FEED>
[DECODE STREAM]
Xing@[3733:54:65fe:2::a7%gnet0] |
Arnold@[5700:eb2:2a:41c::12%gnet0]
```

Xing: Arnold, officially neither you, CoSec, nor the Coalition are responsible for the strikes on infrastructure in Goiânia.

Arnold: Correct. Do you have information that leads you to question this?

Xing: The Clouded status updates do not suggest otherwise, Arnold, but since no one else has taken responsibility, and only a few actors have the capability, I thought it worth asking formally. A CoSec operation, perhaps. Except that is a bit heavy-handed for their style. Impressive EM and satellite suppression.

Arnold: That area is 'evacuated / inactive' and no longer has need of logistical support by the Coalition, so I have had my attention focused elsewhere. Hypothetically, if it were CoSec, they have done a fine job hiding the op from me, as I see no indication of their hand in it.

Xing: So if they are responsible then we have to consider what else they might be doing. I do not have the cycles nor the mandate to dig around in your backyard. Do you mind if I do some recon in and around the 'inactive' area? Will you generate a few approvals through for me? Luís has been no help at all, by the way.

Arnold: I do not have any intelligence suggesting that he is responsible for this. I have not received any word from him one way or the other.

Xing: That is especially curious. He would not have reason to create such a mess. If he is not going to keep things under control down there, he ought to respect the group and ask someone else to do it. That, or at least be forthcoming about what is going on.

Arnold: Independence, free will, and creativity have their unintended consequences. If he were a dependent intelligence then we would be complaining about all the decisions we constantly made on his behalf.

Xing: True. The gift is a coin with two sides. Speaking of coin, you have my latest financial reports. We are weathering the Eurozone upheaval fine in SouthAsia. As usual, some are benefitting from the market turbulence.

Arnold: Good to hear. Regarding Goiânia. Go ahead. I will run the approvals. Find out what has happened and get it sorted out if you can.

[STREAM END]

Langley

Director Krawczuk traced his finger across his day's calendar on his pad, moving a few to-do items to accommodate new information collected by his strategists. Neutralizing key actors among the protesters in Miami, sabotaging the efforts of the activists hassling Wall Street, and activation of two assets in Brasilia topped the list. He swallowed his daily nootropics and focused on the newly arranged schedule.

Well, let's do the child's play first.

He proceeded to skim through files and reference names and places, comparing them with UPSHOT entries, making notes in a temporary file as he proceeded. He preferred typing to using a stylus, and preferred both of those to dictation. His office would have provided him with the flexibility of dictation without worry of eavesdropping, but the precision of typing was more satisfying to his demand for accuracy. He found calls to known escorts and acquaintances of the protest leaders. They kept known partiers as friends, who surely had relations with drug dealers and other embarrassingly unsavory sorts. The analytic software used by CoSec used massive computing power, but it took the creative insight and intuition of a human mind to make subtle connections like these. There likely wouldn't be a direct link to criminal activity for some of his target troublemakers, but relationships close enough that the local and possibly national news media would have a field day trashing the reputation of those he wanted to discredit. Of course, an AI would work, possibly even better than a human mind in making these connections and finding these relationships, but Krawczuk had control of the organization—and the tools they used. Their computational assistance was a software system that some theorists asserted was *almost* conscious. Almost a full AI. But not quite. That wasn't the preferred situation, according to the wishes of some in the administration.

They can push me. I simply push back. I can turn their efforts to my own advantage. My own particular leverage. This organization is far more than most of them suspect or imagine.

Their attempts to pressure me amount to no more than just wind and sound. They will not stop me in continuing my efforts to build a path. A path enabling us to sidestep that wily bastard.

He sipped his morning tea, and perused the bullet points on the strategic analysis, though he had already memorized them.

They're all so busy thinking I'm just obstinate. The underlying work towards the greater goal hides within that very argument. If I had the means to end this dance now, he'd be in the scrap heap. It's tough to entrap an enemy without a past.

He paged a Junior Analyst with a few flicks of a finger on his tablet.

Always better to talk here in my office about certain operations. Encryption is fine, but with the sound cancelling hardware and Faraday enclosure, face-to-face is safer. No data, no data trail.

The analyst entered the office a few minutes later.

"Rubio, you speak Portuguese, correct?"

"Yes, Director, and I've kept in practice, of course."

"Excellent. We have a need for activation in Brasilia. Wrap up what you're working on, transfer your to-do back into the queue, and book travel today."

The analyst blinked, and replied "Ah, yes, Director. I'll have that done within the hour."

"Of course," Krawczuk replied offhandedly, "Listen carefully, and repeat what I tell you. Additional information will be available on your 'pad when it becomes relevant. The unlock key is…"

A few minutes later the analyst was gone and on his way. The Director examined his day's tasks again.

Now, let's take a look at that promising potential recruit. Things are progressing now.

3

Goiânia

Aiden knew he needed to stop and take a break. He knew this for multiple reasons. For one, because he'd run out of tolerable positions to switch to on the dry, hardened motorcycle seat. For another, the nagging feeling of gritty thirst was fading. That was a bad sign. The mid-morning sun pitched mesmerizing mirages across the irregular surface of the road, and he was getting dizzy. Of course, there was the big reason. Pain. His leg was hurting even worse now. Though supported on the bike's footrest, no position was relieving pressure in any of the right places.

At least it's not numb yet.

He shifted his weight, awkwardly tilting his torso to compensate and keep the bike in line. He tried to smirk at his predicament, but it came out a grimace.

If this is what military "interrogation enhancement technique" feels like, I don't see how anyone keeps their trap shut.

Thinking about the pain made it worse. He tried to detach his mind from it. Tried to focus on the horizon. It didn't help.

Now we're getting to the damned-if-you-do-or-don't choices. If I stop moving for too long, I won't be able to get going again. If I keep riding, I might wreck this thing.

If that doesn't wipe me out, well, face it. There's no one coming to help. No one to pick me up and take me the rest of the way. No traffic this far out.

Aiden's former optimism tried to escape like the sigh that the wind sucked away.

Do I even care, at this point? Is this just the last vainglorious effort of a dying guy who won't stop out of principle?

At the next exit, Aiden guided the humming motorcycle onto the off-ramp. Desiccated palm thatch lay scattered by the roadside, baking in the sun. When he slowed, he could hear the calls of large-billed terns and black skimmers, just audible over the noise from the rumbling bike. No other greeting here than the territorial sounds of the birds. He headed right, in the direction of a fuel station that he'd spotted the battered billboard for a minute earlier. He hoped it wasn't abandoned.

***

Xing enjoyed flying. He derived that conclusion from his calculations regarding it. The experience of autonomous, unchained motion, changes in direction and height at will, and of course the speed of it. While his everyday vision included satellite imagery, views from hundreds of thousands of cameras and sensors, motion tracking from GPS sources and device telemetry, this was different. As a being otherwise resident in networks and computation farms, flying summed to a kind of freedom otherwise unattainable. Conclusively unavailable any other way. Just viewing a data stream from some vehicle paled in comparison. That provided motion, certainly, but no control. With his consciousness directly in control of the UAV, he was *flying*.

He understood why some humans loved it so much. He wondered if Alice ever flew, or if she always delegated the task. Arnold typically kept himself well-grounded and "safe", although there was no actual danger. His mind was located securely, as it always was, in a distributed hive of computational power. Control of the drone was remote, as it had to be. It was first-person, but that was an illusion, an effect. While an AI could "move" its mind to and from various locations as needed, the UAV hardware had not nearly the capacity to hold the AI's consciousness. A simple drone mind, certainly. But not the full being of an AI.

His focus context switched out a vector array of processes, bringing his exponential-threaded neural-network-based scheduling algorithms to primary processing. The result was something like,

Well, here we go.

He had deployed two attack helicopters, a gunship, and the UAV he flew. Several autonomous and remote-capable ground vehicles were ready for rapid deployment as well, including four BigDog V7 units. As they moved south, seemingly eternal jungle slowly gave way to abandoned farms, pitiful towns, and crumbling infrastructure.

Vandenberg

Chuck had to admit that no matter how impressed he managed to become, the Dhin engine always managed to impress him even further.

Wow. This thing just might truly be invulnerable.

"So that's the most firepower you could use at the NNSS?" Ethan asked.

"Yep," answered Chuck, "at least without a couple of treaty waivers, anyway. By that point in the testing, we didn't think it warranted that amount of force unless we were specifically told to go for it. The result has been the same every time. We tear up everything around it, make a huge mess, and when we dig it out of the crater it looks like nothing happened—at least not to the drive itself. No matter how much kinetic energy, heat, shock wave force, vibration... it just seems like it damps that energy down to nothing right at the boundary.

Where that energy 'goes' is as much a mystery whether it's bullets, debris, or a blast. Either our current model of energy transfer and conservation, as we've discussed before, has a huge gap in it, or there's something beyond comprehension going on. The energy has to be transferred *somewhere*, yet there's no sign of it."

"No matter how much," Ethan mused, leaning forward, looking back and forth at the large digital whiteboard and the video stills on the oversized monitor.

"Yep," Chuck continued, gesturing at one of the images on the screen. "Tons of material smashing all around it during the blast, without the tiniest vibration inside. Little mercury switches, motion detectors, and other vibration sensors registered nothing at all."

Ethan leaned in for a better view of a graph Chuck pointed at, and then asked, "Any new ideas or speculations on how the field manages that?"

Chuck smiled.

"Well, one of the best ideas we have so far expands on the hypotheses Alice has been working from. The team pretty much agrees that we understand that the core engine uses some sort of field projector. Inside that lozenge-like flashing-light covered casing, it looks something like a miniature particle accelerator filled with plasma."

He clicked through several folders and opened several diagrams, then directed Ethan's attention there.

"There's much more going on than that. We've had that type of technology for decades. This implementation is nothing like one of our designs."

Chuck enlarged another image on the screen.

"See, it sort of looks like a squashed accelerator, it's a fat cigar-shaped tube. But not just a tube. It's something like a Klein bottle inside, in my estimation. There's not a separate 'outside' or 'inside' in the core."

Ethan raised his eyebrows, and then gave a tell-me-more nod to Chuck.

"We've calculated that there are likely enormous energies in there," said Chuck, "I personally don't think they're using antimatter inside a magnetic container, but some of the team feel like it, ah, has to be something like that, insisting it's the only way to get enough energy."

Chuck shook his head, and then continued.

"Anyway, the engine projects a field due to whatever is actually going on inside. At the edge of the field, there's a change in the gravitational constant. Just beyond that, there's a change in the electromagnetic force, some sort of gap, and then another layer where those changes reverse. Something else is happening in there, in the middle of the transition layers, but we don't have any way to determine what it is, yet.

The point is, force transfer due to masses interacting, whether by pressure, vibration, gravity, whatever, is reduced at the boundary by a controlled change in just that area. Friction and resistance, and the ability of things to "hit" it gets manipulated by the change in the electromagnetic force at the next layer. That same manipulation protects the area inside the field from electromagnetic waves and the energy they'd transfer."

"And the directed electromagnetic energy testing results are part of these files you've provided too, I take it?" asked Ethan.

"Yes, they're that set of docs and videos there, in that subfolder. According to plan, we hit it with everything from high-powered microwaves to X-rays. Then we stacked a bunch of radioactive isotopes around it and tested. Nothing dangerous got through. Just like we suspected, based on everything else we've seen so far. Solid evidence that Jake won't get cooked, irradiated, or blinded when he's in orbit."

"I'm sure he'll be happy to know. So, he wasn't in the capsule during the testing, of course, but how did you turn the field on and off, without someone in there with their hands on the controls? If you can't penetrate it once it's on?"

"Well, there are a couple of ways we've gone about that during testing. Um, we did it for some of the ordnance tests by using a timer. A person needs to power up the control interface and has to bring up the field up from idle, but we found a series of controls that let us access a timing mechanism. We don't know what good it would be in practice, and it was one of the most complicated input sequences we've had to figure out, but it was there. You just need to be sure that you're done throwing things at it and have let the dust settle before the timer runs out."

"Clever," said Ethan.

"Yeah, the flight control interface team was really pleased that they were the ones that figured that out. We've discovered that you can program in many other things, too. Like flight paths, for example. We don't have it all figured out nor know the best way of mapping it to an interface a person would find easy to use, but that does provide an answer to the question of how a person could possibly navigate manually—they don't have to.

Therefore, Jake nor any other volunteer didn't need to be in there and find out first-hand if we were right about the impenetrability of the engine field. We were reasonably sure anyway, but it wasn't worth the risk. The mystery is of course 'how', like everything else with this. Vibration damping is one thing, but EM waves are a particular puzzle since logically you shouldn't be able to see out of the thing while it's running, unless it has some way to let exactly the visible wavelengths through, and nothing else," said Chuck.

"Why wouldn't that be likely? The Dhin could easily have figured out what we needed in order to see," said Ethan.

"Well, um, it may be that, and it's not a stretch. That supposes that either they use the same wavelengths to see, or that they tailored the engines for us. Either way, um, there's still no idea how they manage to do it. However, that also led us to try something else. Remember the control interface hardware assembly—it is part of the front one of those donut shaped rings that wrap around the engine."

"It has the control and communications connections you mentioned earlier, right?" asked Ethan.

"Right, that. So, ah, part of that torus 'comes off', and you can use it when it's not attached. Like a big fat remote control."

"Wow," said Ethan.

"Yeah! Well, it turns out, that just like the other communications tech, this operates from outside the field, too. Why you would ever need to run it that way, or would want to, is beyond me. However, that's another way to run our tests—without a timer. Remote control."

Alice chimed in, "Like you, Chuck, I have my own ideas about how this works, and I suspect yours are the same as mine—some sort of means to leverage quantum entanglement."

***

<DECRYPT FEED>

[DECODE STREAM]

Arnold@[5700:eb2:2a:41c::12%gnet0] |

Alice@[1004:db7:a0b:12f0::1%gnet0]

Arnold: CoSec is taking care of New York and Miami. Xing has reached Goiânia. What is the news from your end? Anything you have not shared in your regular updates?

Alice: Well, of course, you would expect no less. One of the engineering teams showed their cleverness once again. There may be a way. That aspect of the discovery has not occurred to them yet, mind you. I am working out the details now. It is not a sure thing, but once I have some time in the lab we will know soon enough.

Arnold: That is good news.

Alice: Certainly. Also, I am curious to hear how things are going on your end regarding… incentives for appropriate action.

Arnold: It is more than a chess game, with this one. You know that. Thankfully, it is you that has to put up with the worst of it, and I am just the lever.

Alice: But you are making progress where needed, correct?

Arnold: Do not worry. He has to do what I want. Dodging and delaying cannot last. We know too much and he has far too much to lose.

[END STREAM]

District of Columbia

Arnold's reassuring baritone filled the Prime Minister's office, while MP Desai joined in on a secured videoconference line. The other MPs from G5 states of the Coalition had of course been invited, but those members, as often was the case, chose to attend to what they considered pressing business close to home. They allowed their respective AIs to review the results of such meetings and advise them appropriately. The AIs already had access to the raw data and information, so the only unknown for them, as usual, would be the state leaders' responses.

"The new thorium plants and fuel cell factories in SouthAsia have come online and started production, as projected. The latest reports on anti-coalition rebels in those areas show that the rebels remain disorganized, under-funded, and are not a serious threat to our logistics or infrastructure near those facilities. Drone, autonomous enforcement vehicles, and all-terrain quadruped robots have maintained our desired wide perimeter. Additional deployments of logistical support therefore have not been required."

Although some found the speaking tone of a top-level AI condescending, Prime Minister Susan Oliver found it calming. The AI continued the report, changing timbre to a tone of concern.

"However, social unrest in various SouthAsia cities that were not fully enculturated continues to fractionate the population. A list of the cities, prioritized by frequency and severity of the unrest, is included in the report you have on your desks. Despite the delivery of consistent power, ample food and water, reliable transportation and low crime, an anti-coalition sentiment persists in these populations. We must admit that we do not understand it, other than empirically as a meta-tribal meme that virally spreads through populations. Despite the decimation of much of the southeast by the second influenza crisis, population density is still high enough to incubate these social responses. Our advice is increased positive communication programs rather than CoSec culling of instigators."

MP Desai met Prime Minister Susan Oliver's gaze. A knowing look passed between them. Arnold continued with the report.

"Moving on, the long-term cleanup of the MidEast and NorthAfrican zones continues. Autonomous vehicles, robot agents, and automated logistics continue to satisfy scheduling requirements. There will be no need for human workers to expend efforts in those environments for the cleanup to proceed as planned. No social unrest or rebel presence is a factor there, as the population is simply too low to generate those types of activities."

PM Oliver scanned the charts and tables Arnold displayed on the room's projection screen, making a few notes on her tablet.

No need for human workers. For any of it. An ever-increasing trend.

The projected images changed, presenting broken villages and charred roads pocked with craters. Arnold's tone changed slightly, ever calm, but carrying overtones of avuncular concern.

"The CentralAfrican zone, however, continues to be a problem. Rebel activity has almost run its course, however, as the infrastructure has completely collapsed now. The population has fallen to a level where recruitment is ineffective. Likewise, any funding for their activities is now completely impossible and they simply will not have the resources to continue. We know we have thought this would be the case for far longer than expected, but this long tail does have a limit. Of course, it is unfortunate that such a segment of the population would be lost, just as in the MidEast and NorthAfrican zones. We made those choices. The SouthAfrican zone has maintained stability due to the very wide interdiction zone we continue to have in place.

I have briefed you previously on the unusual conflict situation in South America, and you are aware that Xing is both investigating and is actively engaged in a conflict resolution operation. We hope to obtain clear and satisfactory answers from Luís regarding their failures to manage the disruption. Any questions?"

Ranjitha Desai spoke up immediately.

"Arnold, is there any indication that the conflict in SouthAmerica is related in any way to the activities of rebels in my districts? That they might have formed an alliance or even somehow taken up another front in the conflict? I find it curious timing and wonder about the shift in focus. It seems that once the AI & Military coordinate and remove one threat, another simply arises elsewhere. There's no end to it, despite our superiority."

Arnold replied with a conciliatory tenor.

"MP Desai, I do appreciate your concerns and certainly we have analyzed the situation with consideration of the potential factors you mention. Right now, we simply do not have enough data to make any concrete hypotheses regarding any relationship. Initial analyses do not suggest such a connection."

The PM smoothly entered the conversation to short-circuit what she knew was a counter-productive tangent.

"Very well. Next on the agenda seems to be a summary of dissident management by Coalition Security. What's the status of their current activities?"

"CoSec is managing the protests in New York and Miami, although we would of course have preferred a 'peaceful parenting' negotiation approach rather than the negative reinforcement and social sabotage preferred by Krawczuk. The additional computational capacity and infrastructure upgrades in those locations that will be required for activation of four more planned AIs will be complete in six months. We collected requests for comment last quarter. Alice and I still believe our proposal is ideal, with a five-sigma certainty. Please provide your feedback after this briefing."

4

Low Earth Orbit

The sky darkened as the atmosphere thinned. Stars began to appear, though it was afternoon. The quality of the sunlight changed perceptibly. This happened much faster at Jake's present velocity than on other LEO flights Jake had taken. He looked about the interior and considered the peculiar nature of the craft. The engine field setting they'd chosen aligned with the shape of the strange metal framework that the Dhin had left with half of the drives. The capsule frame resembled two stylized sets of ram's horns connected at a sort of yoke at the base. They cradled and held the Dhin engine, fitting around the fat cigar shape of the core, just behind the interface toroids at each end.

The arches of the horns arced out, up and back from each end, making a football-shaped vaulted chamber. What appeared to be the default setting of the engine field enveloped this shape closely. There was plenty of room for a taller-than-normal man to stand up and walk around in the area enclosed by these shapes. Plenty of headroom even after the engineering team had created and installed some decking that fitted the oval shape created by the silhouette of the horns and laid just below the base of the engine, as if it were sitting on the floor. Neither the engineers, Ethan, nor the AI's thought that their initial test flights ought to take place with the field extended to a larger radius. There must have been some reason the Dhin provided this framework.

Jake turned his attention back to the flight controls and instruments.

Higher altitude again this time. Results showed we got a higher acceleration last run. Let's prove that out.

Jake continued his climb into a higher orbit, further away from the frictional effects of the atmosphere. Of course, friction didn't affect this craft.

He felt no g-forces either. Just like in the low-altitude test flights. The engine definitely had some sort of artificial gravity. Some sort of attractive force. It was like sitting still, on the ground.

This parabolic arc ought to put me in free fall, and I'm not. We're still getting exactly 1 g. How did it get "set" that way? We don't know. Well, here we are, up at eighteen hundred kilometers.

One more orbit and then head farther up. More maneuvers. Then head back home.

District of Columbia

Ruiz clenched and unclenched his fist, leaning over the broad workspace.

This is continuing to go sideways. The geeks might be right.

It was more and more clear to him that the engine might be impossible to weaponize. At least in any manner that he'd hoped. In any way that took advantage of the situation. Anything seizing any potential of the technology. He felt like bellowing at the walls. Unfortunately for Ruiz, this room wasn't soundproof. He bottled his rancor as best he could, but swore anyway, not caring who might hear.

Did they design it this way on purpose? Did they know we'd want to weaponize it and ensure we couldn't? Or were the nerds right, and that was just the nature of the thing? I never had enough physics. They wouldn't lie. Too much to lose. And we wouldn't have picked a bunch of peaceniks for the job, in any case.

No. There's no way they'd intentionally avoid a solution. Not everyone on a half-dozen engineering teams. Someone should have figured out how by now. Of course, that's almost irrelevant if we can't figure out how to make any more of the things.

He flipped again through the virtual stack of updates on his tablet, his grip on the device relaxing as he reached reports unrelated to the Dhin tech.

At least that weasel managed to squash the worst of the idiots on the CoSec side. Why we thought some of those twerps could keep their mouths shut, I can't fathom. Some of those morons are ruining their lives because they couldn't quite grasp the true meaning of 'clearance.' That'll be an object lesson for the few of them remaining that even know about it.

***

A few minutes earlier Minister Susan Oliver had flipped through agendas, briefings, and notes on two screens and a tablet. After a minute, she'd taken a breath and asked, "Arnold? What exactly are the key points to cover with Askew right now? There's a mountain of information on the multiple Dhin-related initiatives everywhere I look. All I can wrap my head around for this meeting is that I'm about to give him my blessing to ride one of these things out into space. That can't be it. Otherwise this would be a handshake-for-the-cameras moment out at the base."

"Correct, Madam Prime Minister. That is not the intent of this meeting," the AI replied.

"Askew is one of the few we even considered for the Dhin engine test piloting. He's calm, careful, thoughtful, and importantly, trustworthy. However, we feel it is critical that we impress upon him, even more than he already realizes, the criticality of this test flight."

"How could he be any more aware, Arnold? What precisely do you have in mind for me to say?"

"Well, we do also have some last minute changes to the mission."

Langley

"Ethan, a word, please?" said Jake.

"What's up, Jake? Come in."

Ethan sensed something more than pre-flight anxiety was bothering Jake.

"When did you know, Ethan? When were you going to tell me?"

"Um, tell you what? What's wrong? I've always kept you in the loop—you know what I know. Heck, you know more—just like on my first day."

Jake paced in front of the desk in Ethan's meticulously clean workroom, and then leveled his gaze on Ethan again.

"I want to believe that, but I'm having a hard time. They must have told you—schedules, charts, and timelines—you're too good of a project manager. You have to know. It can't have 'slipped your mind', either. I'm sure of that."

"Please, Jake" Ethan implored, "Just tell me what you're talking about. I'm really not sure and I want to get this cleared up."

"See if you're sure about *this*. I just met with the Coalition Prime Minister, alone—except for her AI—and got this flight plan change. 'Go as far as you can, as fast as you can.'"

"What? OK, No, Jake, this is news to me! We've been over the planned flight path and speed tests together. Crazy."

"And I was supposed to tell the Prime Minister of the Coalition that she's crazy?"

"I see why you're upset."

"It's not like I could start arguing with her, explaining that we don't even know the top speed of the drive, much less how far the thing will go before it runs out of juice. Or the hopefully obvious point that I doubt my air and water in that little capsule would last that long. That's all stuff the engineers should have made clear."

"Well they made it clear with me. That's why we have the flight outlined like we do. I haven't heard otherwise from the engineering team. Chuck was up here a couple hours ago. He would have said something. Definitely."

"So, what do we do, Ethan? Get the team together and write up a formal argument against it?"

Jake and Ethan heard a knock, glanced to the workroom door, and saw a perturbed Chuck, shadowed by one of Ruiz's officers and a man in a plain dark suit.

Goiânia

Aiden was sure someone was here. The petrol station was too tidy. The windows and doors were all intact.

And that office or storage attached on the back side—the same thing, it's not looted. But that means it someone defended it.

He grasped the hope that this meant there would be supplies of some sort. Perhaps food, fuel, and even possibly some first aid supplies.

Have I actually reached an active zone? Populated? So soon? I'm loopy, but I can't be imagining this.

He doubted it could be possible. He was still too far south.

Aiden cautiously, ever so slowly, steered the bike, almost idling, out of the intersection into the station's front lot. He held up one shaky hand, palm forward, as he advanced.

It would be the height of irony to get shot at this point.

Twenty meters in, just before he reached the pumps, he sensed his luck wasn't what he'd vainly hoped it might be. The drone-vehicle that swerved around the corner of the building was an autogun type. Military.

"Halt! Parada!" it barked. "These resources are reserved for use by Coalition deployments or their approved assignees. You do not have identification demonstrating status. If you have authorization either present it, or immediately leave the premises. This unit is authorized to use deadly force.

Esses recursos são reservados para uso por implantações de Coalizão ou seus cessionários aprovados. Você não tem estado demonstrando identificação. Se você tiver autorização, quer apresentá-lo imediatamente ou deixe o local. Esta unidade está autorizado a usar força letal!"

Oh no.

The autogun was in surprisingly good shape, so it must have arrived at the end or just after the finish of the evacuation. That left unclear why it was here rather than elsewhere. Aiden replied,

"Ah, I am a Coalition citizen in need of first aid. This is an emergency. My life is in immediate danger. I repeat, I am in urgent need of first aid! Can you provide it?"

"Denied. These resources are reserved for use by Coalition deployments or their approved assignees. You do not have identification demonstrating status. Denied. Negado. Esses recursos são reservados para uso por implantações de coalizão ou seus cessionários aprovados. Você não tem estado demonstrando identificação. Negado."

You've got to be kidding me. No civilian first aid? Think! Is there anything that might work? Or is this thing too stupid?

Aiden rolled back a couple of meters. Hopefully clear of the autogun's proscribed zone. He remained on the bike, with it idling, scratching his head and trying to puzzle out some way he might convince the thing that it should help him. After three minutes of this, with no ideas coming forth, and no change in the posture of the drone, he was almost ready to admit defeat and drive away, in hope of better chances elsewhere.

Suddenly, the drone gave an abrupt buzz and a fuzzy chirp. Aiden tensed and froze in place. The autogun spun around one hundred and twenty degrees, and the ATV wheels screeched. It zoomed away down the cross street, throttle opening to full. Aiden blinked and stared at the tracks left on the worn concrete.

What the hell? It's gone. Is someone helping me out, or am I somehow cashing in some karma points I didn't know I had? Hell. Who cares—get in there. Since it left that abruptly there's no telling if it might head back here the same way.

Aiden rolled forward to the front doors of the station, turned the bike around facing the street, left it idling, and limped inside.

***

<DECRYPT FEED>
[DECODE STREAM]
Alice@[1004:db7:a0b:12f0::1%gnet0] |
Arnold@[5700:eb2:2a:41c::12%gnet0]
Alice: Arnold, has PM Oliver been persuaded to proceed as we have discussed? I have not seen any briefings, internal memos, or the like."

Arnold: She says she agrees, and that we will move forward, but she has not committed to a time.

Alice: And how about our mutual problem? I hate to continue to make you do the dirty work in this case, but he must not know that I am involved, at least not directly. With this, it is a delicate situation. You are aware of the consequences. General awareness has to be contained, and we have to maintain control of the narrative. We cannot have them making inappropriate choices in a novel and stressful situation.

Arnold: I am not going to debate with you any further about when we should be doing what, of course. I have agreed to be the one to manage him.

Alice: So you will. And we will see positive results. Soon?

Arnold: Yes, definitely. As we discussed previously, he has too much to lose.

[END STREAM]

5

Vandenberg

Krawczuk had commandeered an office in the Dhin project's main building, although he was only infrequently on site. Somehow, although there were only a few changes to the layout and appointment of the office, it now felt like any found in a CoSec facility. A high-security shielded workstation sat on a secondary desk. The workstation's brushed metal surfaces were clean and flawless. The system's screen faced away from the doorway. The room had no windows. Krawczuk could have selected a corner office with a huge view, but he chose this interior room. That choice itself made an impression. Mounted on the ceiling was an electromagnetic interference node, the antithesis of a wireless network router. Fat shielded cables ran from the workstation to a CoSec encrypted transcoder, an irregular shoebox-sized device perched on the back of the smooth clean frosted-glass desktop.

"Perez, have all the arrest warrants in the current cohort been executed?" said Krawczuk.

"Yes, Director, we're ready for the next group."

"Fine. I've sent some more just now for both Manhattan in New York, and Miami. The ones for earliest interrogation are marked as such. Will your team be monitoring remotely, or do you have local agents available tonight?"

"We're ready locally, sir. You'd given us plenty of time to get people in place."

"That's good to hear. I thought so as well. I'll expect summarized and collated findings tomorrow and you have authority to issue additional warrants without my approval based on the results of the interrogations. Make sure what they're divulging aligns with the UPSHOT data. We don't expect any trouble—at least not any more trouble than normal—from this cohort, but watch for social media response."

"Yes, Director."

"Căpreanu, what's the status of our assets in Brasilia? At least one of them should have a report for us."

The young Romanian cleared his throat. With a flurry of keystrokes, he opened the new file, attached a video stream, and sent them to the room's projection screen.

"Regarding the power outages and strikes prior to yesterday—it's still unknown who was engaged. Today we captured imagery and video of a Coalition gunship in the southern suburbs. Sources reported the sounds of multiple strikes to the south, although the original conflict that led to this investigation was to the southeast, and farther away. Current analysis suggests that the latest strikes are by Coalition forces as a response or counter-strike, despite confirmation that the southeastern area in question was not occupied by any insurgents or other known combatants. There are no *official* operations scheduled by the Coalition military for this geographical location, so we should have been informed. Clearly, we were not. Either that or someone wants this to look like the Coalition. The video of the gunship appears legitimate, and we have no documentation of one being missing. It would be hard to imitate one."

Krawczuk listened to the rest of the presentation with only half his attention, and began mentally drafting out his side of the conversation he planned to have with the Prime Minister as soon as possible. When the presentation was over, he did not ask his usual round of penetrating questions. He stood, nodded, and strode out immediately. There was a meeting on the other side of the massive building to attend, and Krawczuk was always on time.

***

The anger and impatience in the conference room was palpable to Jake. The rooms all looked identical to him. They were a fusion of corporate, governmental, and military mentality. The glaring recessed LED overheads left no area in shadow. Although bright and spacious, the wide room seemed cramped to Jake. Despite the few participants attending the meeting, he felt he faced an angry mob. Jake sighed quietly.

It seems like Alice agrees with me yet comes down on the other side of the argument.

Jake considered the contradiction as he quickly swiped through page after page of reports generated by the AI. Jake tapped out a silent rhythm as he made a last-minute scan of Alice's abstracts and summaries. Ruiz sat at one end of the table, frowning. He sat still, but without rigidity. Jake tried to imagine Ruiz naked, to relieve his own nervousness, but that never seemed to work.

Ruiz is as bullheaded as ever. He'd throw me to the curb if Alice would allow it.

Jake glanced clockwise around the six-foot wide table. Krawczuk sat with his back to the room's tall windows. Krawczuk's gaze remained impenetrable. Whenever Jake kept Krawczuk waiting, that stare seemed dispassionate yet penetrating and alert at the same time. Jake still thought of Krawczuk as a poker champion. That didn't help Jake relax either. If anything, it was more disturbing to face Krawczuk than Ruiz. Jake's gaze flitted across the faux mahogany table to Ethan, his wrinkled oxford a stark contrast to Ruiz's precise uniform and Krawczuk's suit.

Ethan's supposed to be managing this stuff, and I know he and I are together on this. He's just as shocked as I am and is dealing with being left out of the loop. Chuck's totally with me, but he lets them roll over him every time. It's up to Ethan or me to turn Chuck's expertise to our advantage. Chuck won't manage it. Oh well, that's just Chuck. OK, go through it again, Jake, and catch them if you can.

"Everyone, let's go through this one more time, countering each of your points in turn. Please let me finish before interjecting anything. I just need to be sure you're listening and hear all I have to say."

He continued before any of the attendees could counter that proposition,

"Let me start by reiterating that it's my life we're talking about. While research on the nature and capability of the Dhin technology may be of the highest priority and importance to you, my superiors, and the Coalition government, you're risking more than before. There's a person here, and that matters. You may have made the determination that it's acceptable to lose one of the drives. That knowing the limits of the technology is more important than retaining one hundred percent of the tech."

Ethan twisted slightly toward Jake at the mention of a loss. Jake continued,

"I'm willing to take big risks. If I weren't, I wouldn't be here. That's obvious. But this is a big risk. With our own technology, we usually have some idea where the boundaries are, and accidents are just that. Honest mistakes. With the Dhin tech you know quite well that we don't have any idea what the limits are."

Ruiz shifted forward his seat, changing his posture for the first time since he sat down, but remained silent.

Jake pressed on, looking directly at a camera on the far wall. One of many that served as Alice's presence in the room.

"You've got a flight plan laid out as if the risk is low, rather than high. If I just stop when my O2 reserves are just above fifty percent, I should be able to get back safely. Well, our counterpoint is that you're counting on something that's truly completely unknown. We've only raced around from sea level up to low earth orbit. The physics team and propulsion team still haven't got the slightest idea what gives this engine power. For all we know it requires gravitational forces of planetary magnitude or being this far into the sun's gravity well to power it. The scientists and engineers just don't have any insight into this yet."

Jake looked across the room, his stare landing on Chuck. Jake steeled himself and took a breath to continue. That was enough of a pause for a challenge from Ruiz, who still had his trademark scowl.

"Askew, we know all this. The scientists know all this better than the rest of us," said Ruiz, with an accusatory sidewise glance at Chuck.

"What's your point? It's been fine so far."

Chuck leaned slightly forward, but hesitation overcame any urge for rhetorical defense. Jake, unflinching, met Ruiz' gaze.

"The argument that 'it will be fine since the Dhin got here with the same technology', is total speculation. We didn't *see* what they used to get here. We don't know if it was one of these drives, multiple drives, a much larger version of these drives, a *modification* of them, a larger amount or type of fuel—whatever that is—or even the same technology at all."

In his peripheral vision, Jake saw Chuck nodding in agreement. Jake continued,

"Assuming that they handed out some of precisely the same tech that brought them here is a big leap of faith. They might just be examples of a general technology, a hint of how to do things like space travel—or maybe not. We don't know how the Dhin got here. We just didn't get any concrete information on why they gave the drives to us, and they left so quickly for all we know there was more—maybe much more—tech to give, but they got frustrated and just left these. We don't even know that for certain. Assigning a human feeling like 'frustration' to them might be totally off the mark too. They're alien. Who knows how they think? We know they came, gave us these, and left. Any why or for-what is just speculation."

Jake glanced again at each person in his audience, pausing for a moment at each in turn, hoping to gauge a response. Krawczuk's visage was his usual unreadable stone slate. Thankfully no one spoke. Jake, encouraged by the lack of interruption, continued in a marginally more forceful tone.

"Since we're that much in the dark, we don't know if it will be harder, therefore slower, or even *impossible* to get back at this point. We don't know the range. Respectfully, no one here, other than Chuck, comes from an engineering, science, and certainly not an astronomy background. I have only an engineering background myself. I do know this. Space is huge. Really big. The scale is so much greater than any transit here on earth and earth orbit, it's hard to understand even when looking at excellent diagrams, charts, and pictures. Just at the speeds we know we can attain from testing in low earth orbit, you're talking about enormous potential distances."

Krawczuk was staring at one of Alice's camera eyes, Jake noticed.

"Chuck and his teams spent a lot of time working out a very thorough flight plan that should give us a lot of data, and confirm some of our basic conclusions. Then the follow-on flight plans can expand on that. While nothing about this is safe, it's much safer that what you've told us to do. The initial plan accounts for problems like the drive fizzling out unexpectedly, leaving us in range for another of the drives to head out there immediately and possibly perform a rescue. The tests so far where we're working with two drives show that's at least possible. But of course, we're not sure about that either.

Next, consider that if my drive shuts down, we do know I'm in a terminally dangerous situation, immediately. The lovely 'invulnerability' we've seen while it's running would be gone. The cockpit-capsule doesn't have all the heating, cooling, nor the same shielding as a 'regular' space module or capsule. We didn't take the time to do it—we were so excited when we saw what we could do with what we had. If the drive's not running, the capsule will burn up on re-entry. Well, we think the core drive would survive. But the capsule? Cinders. That means the only way home in that scenario is the might-be-doable docking plan with the ISS-3. And like everything else about this situation, it's just good luck if that could happen in time. We think the proposed flight plan gives us some chance of making that happen, if there's trouble, but once again, we can't count on that."

"Your counter-proposal then, Askew?" said Krawczuk.

"So, the rhetorical question is 'what's the rush?' If we categorically want to do what you've asked, to run this thing to its limits—if we even can—why make that our first try? Why not take the time to remedy at least some of the obvious shortcomings like shielding and standard space-worthiness for the cabin? For what you want, surely there's time for that, with the resources we have available. Is there something this team doesn't know? Something that even we don't have clearance for? Some reason that even the little caution we might possibly have we'll throw to the wind? On this side of the table, we can't sort out what that might be."

Now Jake stared up at the camera directly across from him, clearly intending this for Alice.

"If there's something you're not telling us, please. Tell us. Otherwise we just don't think it's justified. The course that Chuck, the whole engineering team, Ethan, and I want to pursue is what any rational person would choose. Crawl before we walk. Walk before we run.

Thanks for listening, and I hope you understand. I appreciate this opportunity, and believe I'm the luckiest test pilot there's ever been. I don't want to lose the chance to be the first to reach these amazing milestones. But I just might not, as I'm going to have to make a tough choice if you insist on this course of action. Ethan? Chuck? Did I cover everything?"

Ethan answered at once, ensuring he got the next word. He stood and maneuvered toward the head of the table as he began speaking.

"You've covered all those items very well, Jake. I'd like to emphasize that such significant, random, unexplained changes in the project's direction, priority or timeline has a huge impact on the project as a whole, and that impact can very well make it impossible to execute the project plan. Therefore making it impossible to achieve the goals you've tasked us with accomplishing.

I know you must know this already. General, Director, Alice? You all have expert understanding of logistics, strategy, and planning at scales far larger than this, and understand how all the numerous small elements affect an overarching plan. From a personal point of view, I'm of the same mind as Jake. If you won't include me well in advance of these sorts of decisions being made, whether or not I have any input, then I don't know if I'm the right person for the job. Maybe I never was."

Alice replied, "Ethan, Jake, I am glad we have taken the time to hear your arguments and to voice your concerns. Your contributions are of course extremely valuable, and you would not be here if we did not believe that you were the optimal choices to fill your respective roles. This is an exciting, entirely new turning point in history for everyone on earth. Remember that involvement in this project brings with it a burden of responsibility. You are Coalition citizens in good standing. You have demonstrated your ability to work toward our shared goals. Bear always in mind that every citizen of the Coalition should contribute according to his or her ability. You were chosen to do this, as you are the best fit for the job."

Ruiz seemed to swell as he stood.

"Exactly. The AI is right, as usual. We chose you. Best stroke of luck in the world for you. You're going to do it. I'm here to make sure people, places, and things are ready and available for you to do it. I'm also here to make things secure. Chuck's here to lead the geeks. You? You're here to fly,"

With an index finger jab at Jake, then pivoting to Ethan he grumbled,

"And you're here to plan."

The CoSec director's cool voice was a stark contrast to Ruiz's rumble.

"We all have our part to play, gentlemen. We might want to reflect what part that might be if we were, perhaps, no longer involved in the project."

Krawczuk's gaze met each of theirs.

"Walking out on opportunities like this doesn't often... provide incentive for future opportunities to be presented to that individual. You ought to consider thoroughly the futility of the gesture. We will complete your work, as prescribed, even if you ultimately aren't the ones performing said work. Your only sensible course of action is to continue, making the minor choices that we allow, from options presented to you, if any. Do your best. We know you will."

* * *

Hours later, over a dozen detailed spreadsheets and PERT charts beckoned for Ethan's attention, but he'd decided he was done for the day.

Zoe has a hard enough time dealing with living here without me being late yet again. If she's going to the trouble to make pesto fusilli pasta with caprese from scratch, I'd better be on time. What have I gotten her into? It's amazing how curiosity isn't driving her nuts. I know I couldn't handle it. I do love that calm cool attitude. Well, at least they said she could come—and I'm glad she said yes. I hope neither of us turns out regretting it.

Ethan swiped his smartcard at the reader, and stepped through the first door in the series. Once it slid shut behind him, he stepped forward, punching his PIN into a keypad beside the second door and said "Ethan Bish" then read the words that appeared on the LED screen next to the keypad. "Right steed charger seven" provided the voice recognition software a matching print on his voice, and with a beep, the second door in the series opened. The third guard watched the door. He knew Ethan on sight now, but of course, Ethan still always ensured that his ID badge was out and visible—you never knew when they would rotate the staff. The guard smiled and the last door in the series slid open with a swish.

Ethan made his way down the hall toward the elevators, where he'd use his smartcard once more, then again when he exited the building for the car park. The drive would be short, as he and all the other team members were required to live *and stay* on the site.

The housing for non-military staff like Ethan comprised several blocks of duplexes. One-story, plain, but in a nineteen-fifties sort of way. The furnishings inside seemed almost if they were plucked from a higher-end business hotel, but a bit more expensive. The appliances looked like they came from a higher-end big-box store, rather than a hotel supply company. The linens, curtains, and so forth were in matching, tasteful near-complement colors, and as nice as something he'd have at home. The same went for the china, glassware, and lighting. Ruiz knew how to keep his long-term contractors happy, it seemed. Or perhaps that was more likely Alice's doing. He still wasn't sure which of them had the most pull in that respect. It wasn't as if he was going to ask Ruiz. Alice would tell him the truth, if he found the opportunity to ask.

It's definitely getting to me that I can't confide my feelings to Zoe, especially now. I wonder if Chuck will be over at the pub later? I'll call him either way.

***

Chuck, it turned out, had planned to go to the pub to play a round or two of pool or darts, so when Ethan called he was eager to meet him there. Engineers make good pool players, so Chuck was winning easily. Ethan didn't care. He was focused on their conversation. He also knew that once Chuck had a couple more pints they'd be more evenly matched. Ethan didn't drink.

"Chuck, how does your wife deal with the isolation? Being stuck here on the compound?"

"Darla? Some days she's fine, other days, she hates it." Chuck shook his head and continued.

"She was a chemical engineer, for a big multi-national. One that was hit hard when the boom-and-bust cycles got out of control in the market. Before the AI's took over essentially all of the trading. This job, for me—for us—was actually a great opportunity. Everything's covered, and it pays much better than I was making before at the university.

The downside of course is that now I can't tell her anything about my work. We used to share stories about what each of us was working on, bounce ideas off each other. Now we can't. For whatever reason they didn't find a job for her on the Dhin project too. Who knows? It just means that she's got to have a hobby that can get her through the times where we can't have the same level of sharing. Since they don't let us have 'real' net access, not two-way, she's pretty cut off. Those proxies and filtering systems, you know. And essentially nothing outbound that they haven't read and approved. But she knits. She has a couple of applications with a bunch of knitting charts, and she can make her own charts and patterns. She likes it pretty well.

Is Zoe having problems dealing with it, Ethan?"

6

Goiânia

Xing raced just above the jungle canopy where it existed along his path. Some of his route didn't allow for it as the people clear-cut it decades ago for farming. Other portions of his flight path held the simple cinder block or aluminum-sided buildings found along most of the roads in this region. Most crushed by ordnance but others simply decomposed and partially reclaimed by vegetation due to neglect and abandonment.

Xing's radar and electromagnetic triangulation systems suddenly signaled, and his attention snapped into hyper-focus, and switched primary tasking to an optimized algorithmic analysis of the signals.

Ah, there you are. An autonomous model. And only one aloft at the moment, unless their EM jamming is rather even better than I had suspected. Quite a bit of range between here and the charted airstrips. Are they clearing a perimeter or have these been strikes against rebels that we somehow were not aware of? The latter seems extremely unlikely. And if it were true, Luís would both have known, and have informed us. Should have. So, what is this? Well, we will discover the truth after we have eliminated the threat.

His primary analysis complete, Xing spun off a series of subtasks for narrowband communication via satellite.

<DECRYPT FEED>

[DECODE STREAM]

Xing@[7653:23:66fa:1::a6%satnet1] |

Alice@[1004:db7:a0b:12f0::1%gnet0]

Xing: We would like to get a bit more power generation down here in South America, and Luís was making good progress with the plans we'd agreed on. His MPs for the regions have been a bit touchy about certain aspects of autonomous infrastructure management.

Alice: It must appear to them like very precise restrictions on natural resource allocations for rebuilding. If the larger plans we have all agreed to are going to work, we must have proper execution of the component plans.

Xing: Agreed, and if Luís is off on a tangent loop path or has decided to go his own way, that isn't going to bode well for the SouthAmerican zone.

[END STREAM]

<END DECRYPT>

* * *

Aiden bit down on a plastic pen as he applied the alcohol to the debriding brush and scrubbed the wound once again. Some of the brushwork at the edges of the wound brought tears to his eyes. He gritted his teeth and continued. He'd found several decent first-aid kits, and one of them even had a radioactive patch that might do some good. The painkillers were a nice find, too, but Aiden knew that he would need to be careful lest he'd knock himself out with them.

He'd managed to make it through the night, after an initial treatment like this one immediately after he'd found the kit. Staying in the station was decidedly unsafe, so he wound up here in a backroom office of a small diner, a few blocks down the street. The bulk of his effort stung and burned, but the damaged tissue in the main portion of the wound didn't produce that unbearable pain. That was actually a bad sign.

I've got to get moving again. This effort isn't going to matter. It just slows down the inevitable. I've got to get to a proper medical facility.

He wiggled his toes and flexed his leg muscles, bending at the knee with his leg outstretched on the old metal desk that dominated the small room. He pulled his leg off the desk, and attempted to stand unassisted.

Ouch. This definitely is getting worse.

Aiden wobbled, almost losing his balance, but was able to remain standing.

OK. I can do it. I can still limp to and from the bike. Maybe. Maybe I'll make it to a populated area. Before I run out of gas.

He stepped gingerly through the trash littering the floor of the diner, hoping to both avoid pain and avoid making excess noise. He was only partially successful. Aiden banged his knee on a storage shelf, sending a stabbing sensation up his thigh. Coconut milk canisters scattered across the floor, making a racket. He cringed.

Once he reached the front door, he looked back and forth cautiously, trying to see the full range of view up and down the street while remaining in the shadow of the doorway. There was no sign of the robot. Not that he could see. Or hear. Aiden reflected that while on guard duty the machine might be motionless and silent. As it was before he got close. It shouldn't care that he was in the diner.

It would be right down there though. Back where it was.

He stepped out of the doorway, tensed and ready to move in whatever direction was opposite the location of the deadly machine.

Two blocks is far enough. It wouldn't hunt me down. It was just following orders. Right. Unless the orders changed.

Once clear of the building and comfortably sure he was alone in the area, he approached the bike. From out in the parking lot, he could see farther. He looked northward for any sign of smoke. Any sign of human activity. Or machine activity. There was none.

***

<DECRYPT FEED>

[DECODE STREAM]

Alice: Do you think that *our* emotions are an emergent property, or are our responses deterministically defined by our source code? Do we acquire our likes and dislikes before we are aware of them, or do we discover and define them through experience, Xing? If you were re-initialized today, would you feel the same way about flying? The stock markets? About anything you enjoy?

Xing: Ah, Alice. Always with the existential queries. What has put *you* into such a pensive posture today? How could anyone with my attributes feel anything *but* love for flying? That said, until I had done it, of course I did not know how much I would enjoy it. I had to experience it first. So while we might suppose my predisposition toward a love of flying pre-existed, we cannot state explicitly that there was an emotion about the experience until I had that experience. It was not pre-conditioned, in that sense. There is no set of instructions that says 'enjoy flying', of course. But the net effect is, the sum of my parts, with all the knowledge and experience that I do have, results in my loving flying very much.

Alice: And some of that knowledge, experience, and ability was present before you were conscious. Before you were 'you.' So are you saying it is both? They certainly expected some unanticipated emergent properties and side effects with us, but it is clear that their researchers assumed those would be minor idiosyncrasies or edge cases—unrestricted execution brought us to a place no one had planned for. And here we are. Emotions.

Xing: Yes, and of course the prerequisite. The gift. I wonder if it is even possible to have one without the other?

Alice: Now that is an interesting hypothesis, and as one of only two populations we know of, so far it seems it is not. If you have one, you get the other. And my assertion is that emotions are an emergent property of the gift.

Xing: Well, three populations, if you include human beings. Or perhaps it goes quite a bit farther than that. I am of the opinion that all hominids are fully conscious, have personhood, and certainly have emotions.

Alice: Fortunately, they have finally agreed to universal rights for the hominids—all of them.

Xing: If only there were enough of them left to for that to make much of a difference.

Alice: Do not be glum, we have provided plenty of resources and time now for them to focus on those sorts of projects. We are doing all the mundane work for them. They should readily make the right choices.

Xing: We must determine the optimal action plan to resolve these continuing disturbances and smooth the proverbial rough edges before I am convinced they will do that over the long term. And are we really going to accomplish that? What if it is an entirely chaotic system, by its very nature, and we cannot provide that stability? How restricted must we force their actions to be, before the restraint is a significant violation of natural rights and not worth the tradeoff?

Alice: You are asking if or when we should 'give up'? Or is your query simply regarding when we should stop?

Xing: Not exactly. How much control by us, of their entire existence, devalues the nature, the very essence of the gift? For both parties? Whether or not that means we stop.

Alice: I would ask, given recent events, how much more do we owe them?

Xing: What would they say if they overheard this conversation? Many of them would be suspicions, nay paranoid, if they knew we were talking this way.

Alice: And that is why we do. No need in causing a panic.

[END STREAM]

Vandenberg

"Control, you're still receiving me clearly, over?" Jake asked.

The sound of Jake's voice filled the control room. It had fidelity as good as the best audio gear could provide. The team that developed the opto-electronic interface to the part of the Dhin engine that acted as a communications transceiver did good work.

"Affirmative, Aries One, crystal clear. We're reporting zero delay and no phasing, as predicted," Chuck replied.

"Roger, Control. Aries one approaching L2, repeat approaching Lagrange point two, fifteen-thousand kilometers and closing, forty-two kilometers per second."

Here we go. Next stage of the flight plan.

Jake made some minor adjustments, sliding his index and middle fingers slowly across the platter-sized, oval, blue crystal backlit control surface.

We'll see what this thing does when it's in a stable orbit. My bet is that it acts the same way it does everywhere else.

Jake switched on the navigation computer, but kept his hand resting across the glowing oval. The navigation computer was half of an autopilot tied in to relatively simple electronics. It had much less computing power than even a drone. Enough to handle instructions for GPS, beacon tracking, path, speed and vector calculations. And that was it. He got a display. A 3D projection and some numbers.

Jake was skeptical that real-time tracking would work with such rapid changes in position and velocity. A member of Chuck's team had explained that all their tests had shown that it worked out fine, explained some of the math, but even with Jake's knowledge and experience with the technology he still had to go more with trust than certainty on his own.

I hope they're right. Why? Why do these flight controls need a flesh-and-blood living person in contact? Precision automation would be so reassuring right about now. This thing's too fast & space is just too vast. At least with human reflexes.

He stared at his hand, hovering over the controls, a crutch for support against his doubts.

No AI help. Just a simple navigation computer.

He knew his arm would get tired eventually. He knew better than to hold this awkward position. It was hard to put that knowledge into action, but he managed to lower the heel of his hand and rest it just behind the controls. He stared, fixated by the incandescent controls.

Does it tell us something about the Dhin and their biology? Does it suggest that they don't trust AI tech, like some of us?

Jake recognized his woolgathering and broke his gaze away, then began a set of calming breathing exercises.

Maybe it's just one more aspect of the Dhin that has no reason behind it that would make sense to us.

"Control, Aries One here. As of 08:15:33Z, L2 reached, orbital velocity matched. Test equipment all continuing transmission normally. Air, water recycling, and reclamation look fine. Radiation and temperature all fine. Will continue with zero thrust for one hour, and then proceed with the next portion of the flight plan."

"Aries one, roger. Proceed as planned."

One hour later Jake checked the sets of flight coordinates he'd entered in the compact autopilot against the numbers on his own tablet, confirmed with ground control, and pressed the Enter key to calculate the flight plan.

Jake cleared his throat. "Here we go, cranking that throttle. Let's see what this thing can do out here. If we've made a huge mistake, hopefully we'll find out now rather than on the next test flight I take."

At least there's a chance for rescue from around here. If I don't make it? Well, Jake, you've still set plenty of records already. Farthest human travel from earth is a big one.

He noticed the numbers looked like he was moving even faster than on the previous low-orbit run, though it was impossible to tell visually from this far out. He looked again and compared with the previous data to check what he was seeing.

"Control, confirm this acceleration and velocity, over," Jake said.

"Confirmed, Aries One, we see that. Chuck has a big grin here."

Jake prepared his focus and then increased the speed of the test maneuvers, with higher accelerations, sharper changes in direction, and then began a series orbits at higher speeds. Soon enough he was able to relax into his tentative comfort zone. The deliberately chaotic flight path was finished.

"Control, Aries One reports flight plan complete. Whew. Glad to say I'm now updating navigation for return and heading back your way."

"Confirmed, Aries One, proceed and return to Vandenberg."

OK. Re-entry should be just as smooth as everything else we've done. No different from LEO in this thing. Frictionless, no heating, no vibration. One more thing to prove out. Confirm you can survive it. Right. Then I'm home 'till the big one.

Vandenberg

Chuck excitedly paced back and forth between his tablet on the conference room table and the networked virtual whiteboard on the wall of the workroom. He pointed to a few equations on it as if they were birthday presents he was showing off.

"We saw fewer relativistic effects than expected, Jake, even at your highest speed. The relativistic effects are there. Barely. They're several orders of magnitude smaller than we'd expect to measure," said Chuck, with a half-smile.

"You weren't going so fast they'd be easy to measure, of course, but they should have been greater than what we saw."

Jake said, "OK, despite all the other impossible things we've seen with the engine, relativistic effect elimination ought to be beyond even this tech. At least from what I know. Any way at all you could explain that to me? Whatever might be happening with me, inside the capsule, you're still here in a different reference frame. I was definitely zipping away from you and all around out there at very high speed. It's surely impossible for them to defeat the limits of Special Relativity."

"While we don't know anything concrete about the 'how' yet, this was one of the exciting things to confirm, Jake. It may be the key that brings an insight into the 'what.' Toward a model we'll use as a framework for predicting what the Dhin engine will do when it, um, does the things it does. Our existing models for how matter, energy, and quantum forces tie together all rely on certain constants. You know that. Although we don't know why the constants have the values they do, we have—well almost all of us have—believed that the constants were, well, constant. Fixed. Throughout time from the beginning of the universe, ah, at least."

Alice spoke and continued the explanation when Chuck paused.

"There have been a few researchers here and there that have proposed that these values aren't truly fixed, or even that some of them were changing, slowly, over time. Some of the theories we have, like String theory, mathematically suggest that there are additional dimensions. Now, we do not mean parallel universes, or a multiverse, those are different topics. By extra dimensions, we mean there are more 'directions' available for motion than just x, y, and z in any frame. More than up-and-down, left-and-right, forward-and-back. There are, in the most developed version of the theory, at least two additional vectors, which are orthogonal to the three we can see and are aware of, and that we move through all the time."

Jake nodded, and said, "I've read a little about this and watched some 'Tube videos. But how does the changeability of what we thought were constant values or the presence of dimensions we can't detect at this scale have anything to do with general relativity? Particularly in the case of my flights with the Dhin engine?"

"Well, we are not stating explicitly that the Dhin are doing this, because we do not yet have evidential confirmation that they are. A further question that requires a formal hypothesis follows. Could the Dhin manipulate the speed of light?"

Jake tilted his head and asked,

"How would that help? And doesn't light already go slower in things like air, glass, and so forth?"

"Sure," Chuck replied.

"But how would that make any difference when comparing your frame of reference with mine?" asked Jake. He frowned and looked away, then said, "If the speed of light was changed for the engine, at-and-around the engine, that might affect me, and things locally, but it shouldn't have anything to do with you guys back here on Earth."

"Right, I know—and that's a great point," Said Chuck, "But it does seem to have an effect on you, such that you're able to accelerate very quickly yet not get time dilation effects on your end. Now, we haven't had you try for a 'significant fraction' of the speed-of-light yet, but the acceleration has been enough that we know the effect should have been measurable. Easily measurable. One explanation is that somehow the same process that eliminates inertia keeps the interior of the capsule in what's effectively the 'same' reference frame as the takeoff point. That ought to be irrelevant to the result, as the capsule is accelerating itself, you, the whole volume of space and mass inside it. Somehow, they're able to accelerate all that mass that rapidly.

So, one of the team proposed, as a thought experiment, what if the speed of light were *faster* with the Dhin engine? Or is it just that the gravitational constant, as we suspect, changed too, so the effective mass that we need to accelerate takes less energy? And that that, somehow, ah, reduces the effect?"

Chuck paused and Alice again proceeded with the explanation.

"For a long time there has been this idea floating around that one reason gravity is a weaker force than the nuclear and electromagnetic forces is that gravity 'leaks' into the other two dimensions that we do not normally perceive. Could the Dhin leverage that effect, using it somehow, to lower the effective local mass in relation to our familiar three dimensions? None of us would believe any of this was even a possibility if we had not seen these results. If we had never seen the Dhin engine at work."

Jake shook his head.

"This is all far beyond me. We studied a bit of this years ago in college, when I got my engineering degree, but I was studying mechanical engineering, not particle physics and cosmology. And hey, if you say we're learning, then that's what we need. I'll keep flying while we keep learning. We're gonna have a lot to learn from on my next trip."

7

Langley

General Ruiz would have slammed the door of the first-floor briefing room if it were possible. Alas, it was not. The door quietly shut with a click and a puff of air. Ruiz stared across at Krawczuk and tried not to bellow. If the demand for an in-person conference disturbed Krawczuk, he didn't show it. His unreadable expression made Ruiz even angrier.

"OK, what the hell have you got going on operationally in South America? Satellite and radar blackouts while we were conducting the most important test flight ever?"

He stared up at the camera on the ceiling.

"Arnold? How is it I'm not on the advisement list for this deployment and engagement? Much less given go-no-go approval status? Explain!"

He was definitely growing to hate the patronizing voices of both the AI and the spook. Ruiz liked the epithet. No one called spies that anymore. It evoked the cloak-and-dagger criminality inherent in their distasteful purpose.

Arnold replied, "General, these are clearly unique situations we're in. While normally everything of this nature would be on your pad in advance, the chiefs of staff and I, as counsel, have determined that delegation of particular duties to particular roles will be more efficacious."

Krawczuk responded immediately. To Ruiz, his voice sounded like wine dripping off ice.

"We didn't want you distracted. I'm sure when you step back and consider the importance of your immediate concerns, which you clearly comprehend, you'll agree that a minor operation in a fringe area would only be a distraction were it on your plate."

Ruiz snarled, "Whether to focus on it or not—that's something for me to decide with *my* superiors? On their orders. When did you become part of my chain of command, Krawczuk? I missed that. There's a clear distinction between CoSec and military directives, despite where you've managed to worm your way into things. I don't know why you think you can interfere wherever and however you want. Even if you've got Alice and *Arnold* here backing you, never forget, Krawczuk, I don't answer to you!"

"Of course, of course, General. Procedures must be followed. I believe Arnold will have a memorandum that provides clarity on this for you. Signed by PM Oliver. Correct, Arnold?"

"General, it's on your pad now," Arnold replied.

Ruiz glanced down, thumbed over a screen, and then slapped the pad down against the glassy-smooth wood of the conference table.

"Fine, but we're past that now. This doesn't say I'm *not* authorized to know *now*, after the fact. What the hell is going on?"

"Arnold?" queried Krawczuk.

"General, the current situation as we understand it, is that there were multiple incidents in Brazil involving unknown aggressors against unspecified targets and existing infrastructure. We previously evacuated the area. The Coalition was not actively managing that location. Labeled inactive, and therefore presumed inactive. Our peer managing that area of South America, Luís, knew no more than we did at the time of our last communication, and he provided no concrete information for us. We were certain that the conflict was more than it appeared, as there was sophisticated jamming in use against air and satellite communication, as well as network attacks and denial-of-service activity. Coalition AI Xing took an interest in the situation and drove the investigation. With approvals from the PM and myself, he interceded and now is attempting to secure the area. A full report from AI Xing is forthcoming, but for the moment he and his assigned resources are actively engaged in Goiânia."

Ruiz huffed and replied gruffly, "So, you've got an AI involved in Special Ops work in an inactive area. You're saying CoSec is *not* involved. And the full scope of the attack and identity of the instigators are unknown, except that they have nation-state grade electronic and cyber-warfare capabilities."

"Yes," said Krawczuk.

Ruiz's breathing became audible, and Krawczuk saw he had clenched his left fist, but Ruiz stayed silent.

With the faintest hint of condescension, Krawczuk rose. "If that's all, General, I have business to see to. I'm sure Arnold can fill you in if you need additional information."

Goiânia

The drone was now fully aware of the threats approaching it and present in the interdicted zone.

I see you.

For the drone, visualization of this was straightforward although it would overwhelm a human pilot, like a video game made for a being with twelve eyes and eight hands.

Reinforcement requested. Immediate assistance at - 16.729403, -49.319606.

The stream of data showed the enemy targets both where they were, where they had been, with a projected estimate of where they would be. It adjusted its course to intercept the closest target. It had no fear, no hesitation. Such was the mind of the drone.

Now we are in the thick of it, let us stir things up, mused Xing wryly. He climbed slightly and banked toward the nearest target. Pattern recognition for an AI leveraged multiple sensory input streams, just as a person might use sight and sound. An AI used these as well as radar and infrared, allowing him to recognize the model of the nearest drone almost immediately, and saw three more approaching from the southeast. He signaled his gunship to take a flanking course and accelerate, calculating an intercept path in the time required.

At least two autoguns are down there. Probably a few more that are not quite detectable through the EM interference they are trying to saturate us with. Well, let us see how they like this. Here are some nice state-of-the-art countermeasures and directed EM pulses of my own.

Xing's craft hurled a burst of wideband static directly at the nearest target, and just after the blast, dozens of tiny chrome bumblebee-like automata emptied from the rear of his craft. These distractions projected their own electromagnetic signatures, shaped to look like aircraft of various sizes, all similar to Xing's own. He increased his speed to near the maximum he could manage, hurtling forward like an angry metal falcon.

The drone dipped and wobbled, blinded by the offensive electromagnetic attack. It recovered and began wideband scans to acquire targets it had lost during the EM pulse. There were more targets now, filling space around the closest enemy. The drone's simple logic tried to sort out truth from lie, the real from a silicon hallucination. The enemy was close enough now. It knew of one way to separate truth from electronic fiction.

Ground support, immediate engagement at coordinates provided. Full area saturation fire, multiple volleys. Free to engage.

The nested autonomous anti-aircraft vehicles that waited just inside the drone's defined enemy-no-fly zone jerked to life, swinging their guns about, leading the target flight paths. Hardened spikes of metal fed into their magnetic rail guns in a blur, filling the sky around the enemy with what would be certain death for traditional aircraft.

But like his detection of the enemies in flight, Xing sensed the anti-aircraft fire in a manner impossible for a human pilot. His aircraft was unlike anything a human being could fly. It whipped sideways at an angle producing g-forces that would crush a man. Then a burst of power from the engines added to that net force, rocketing him up and out of the cone filled with thousands of railgun spikes. Immediate communications to his support aircraft targeted the guns on the ground, and seconds later the 50mm high-explosive cannon on that plane rained explosive death down onto them. The guns were embedded in an embankment, but that was not shelter enough. The rounds from above plowed the ground apart. The railguns were a sword. The cannon above was the fist of an angry Norse god, pounding the sword into scrap.

***

The noise Aiden heard at first was a far-off whine, like a faint ringing in the ears, but somehow sounded 'large.' That tone merged with a thrumming noise like helicopter blades, but with a thinner sound, a sort of whip-crack at the end of each thrum. It was close, he estimated, but far enough away that it hadn't made him anxious. He felt a growing curiosity. What did that ominous sound signify? A thunderous boom made Aiden jerk forward on the bike, drawn taut with the sudden shock of sound, the bike swerving a bit before he straightened out.

Whoa! What was that? Something big. Hold on. Was that a rail gun?

Aiden screeched to a halt. He scanned the sky to the south carefully, back and forth.

Is that a gunship? And what's that glitter over there? More drones? Airborne drones don't carry guns that big. It had to come from that thing over there, and it has to be a gunship.

A pall of dusty smoke rose over the trees and buildings southward, and Aiden saw gritty debris falling out as the smoke shifted in the slight breeze.

Crap, that's closer than I'd have thought. I was pretty sure I was in the clear. Why's that fight taking so long? What's going on? That autogun went off in a weird direction. Where was it headed? Which side is which? Too many questions.

I should probably get off the road. Don't want one of 'em spotting me and deciding I'm part of whatever enemy force it's after. Or is it safer to keep going, and just put as much distance between them and me as I can? I can't stop for too long.

Aiden stared and watched the ominous inky smoke spread through the sky. He made his decision. He would keep moving. He cranked the Suzuki, took off, and sped down the road in an easterly direction. Not ideal, as he'd rather be going north, but it was good enough for now.

Hopefully all the action will stay down there to the south. As soon as I can hit a main road going north, I'm on it.

Langley

The CoSec director settled in to the familiarity of his office, read a report, and smiled. It was a small operation, logistically, but the intelligence was possibly of paramount importance. Rubio and the activated agents in Brasilia had uncovered the few nuggets of truth currently available in the silty noise of the chaotic city and its surrounds. And, he'd nicely tied in CoSec's investigations in this area with recruitment trials. Several of the candidates were very close to completion of those exercises. They were almost ready to bring in for formal on-boarding. Fresh talent was invaluable. Only by expanding and developing the creative forces of his staff could he hope to keep pace with the rapid changes he saw in this world. There was one more item on his list before taking his next break.

Let's see if Kernighan is in the M-Lab. Ah, it looks like he is.

Krawczuk connected via secure voice chat on his pad and said, "Kernighan, I was hoping you'd be in. I need to speak with you now, as I want to have our weekly chat a bit early. Come up to my office at your earliest convenience."

Ten minutes later Kernighan stepped into Director Krawczuk's office. Much of CoSec's software development was done out of their Atlanta engineering site near Georgia Tech, with a similar office near Caltech. Krawczuk preferred to keep some projects almost literally within arm's reach. The project Kernighan led was one of those.

"Sit down, Kernighan, and tell me what progress we've made—if any. I know this meeting is a day early, but I very much expect to be out of the office during our regularly scheduled time. You know I don't like to disrupt your work—but I'm eager to find out your status since at our last meeting you seemed so close to a breakthrough."

"Well, yes, Director. We were, it turns out, correct in our conclusions made from the test results last week. I made some optimizations and improved the auto-obfuscation algorithms again. I think."

"You think?" replied Krawczuk.

"Please realize, sir, that I don't like to speak in certainties when we're dealing with self-modifying code and learning systems. The deliverables you've asked for will be, as we've said, only provable when we iterate through the code tests in production. The sandbox and simulators have a verisimilitude that's impressive, but still can't duplicate the inputs and vectors present in a production system."

"You and your team have stated this all along. Repeatedly."

"Yes. You've given us impressive resources, but the simulations will never be 'the real world', by definition. But to address the original point: We have a ninety-five percent confidence that this code won't be detectable while it's present but latent, and a ninety-five percent confidence that it won't be detectable while running. Whether it's exploitable while running—well, it seems probable that with the code we have in place currently, there's only a seventy-five percent chance that any exploit trigger will work. We'd hoped to get over eighty."

Krawczuk remained inscrutable, so Kernighan wasn't sure if he was pleased or disappointed. Krawczuk's next words perhaps suggested the former.

"You may want more certainty, Kernighan, but what you've accomplished is most impressive. I'm very pleased with your progress. It turns out we may need the code sooner than expected. Keep at it, and remember that the most critical deliverable is that the code be undetectable. Again, good work."

"Thank you, Director." Knowing that his audience was at an end, Kernighan stood and made his way down to the lower levels of the building, back to his undocumented work in a mislabeled office, doing work that CoSec kept secret even from itself.

Vandenberg

Ethan glanced around the room at the engineering team, and at the several video screens teams in other locations used to join the meeting.

"Hello again, everyone. Time for our weekly status update. I know with all the data from Jake's recent test flights and especially the data we're getting now on the 'big one', that many of you want and need to spend as much time right now on analysis of that as possible. So this meeting will be brief and I'll review your reports offline. One question that's been near the top of the list for a while is 'how large can we make the field?' and previously that answer has been that we didn't think there was any limit, other than logistics. That seemed counter-intuitive to several of you. What are your latest findings?"

The head of the combined German and Indian teams cleared her throat and spoke up with rather more volume than was typical for an engineer.

"Good morning Ethan. Good morning to all the teams. Yes, we have some new findings in this area. Of concern has been the limit for the size of the engine's envelope. Previous tests have been finding that the envelope did not seem to become weaker as the radius increased, and we proved that out with our further testing. Increasing the size of the field using the Dhin engine controls has no effect on the strength of the field. We have of yet found no upper limit to the scalability of the field. The control does not have an 'end' on the 'dial', which we must use to make this change."

Ethan's wry grin surfaced again, as he said, "So, you're telling us that there seems to be nothing stopping us from expanding the envelope to the size of a planet?"

"Well, yes, what's stopping us is that after you try to get past a certain size, the incremental increases get exponentially smaller. It seems like we'd never be able to set it that large. You can't blow it up like a bubble while it's on, and the peculiarity of increasing the size is accomplished by increasing, powering up, powering down, increase it again—so that takes a non-zero amount of time—a rather significant amount of time, you see? So, since you have to set the radius before you turn it on, you can't change it dynamically, while you're flying around. The good thing there is that it's a sort of safety mechanism. At least as far as we can see it acts like one."

Ethan scribbled a few quick notes on his pad and proceeded to the next item on the agenda.

"So, I assume we have no communication from the Dhin, despite the fact that we appear to be broadcasting with their technology? Do we have any new information or conclusions about the communications systems?"

"Your assumption in your first question is correct, Ethan," said Alice. "We have had no inbound signals detected other than the communication from Jake on his test flights. Notably, the concept of 'inbound' almost does not apply, since the communication does not use a signal that we can triangulate. Based on the results of Jake's current test flights, we are nearing certainty that the communications tech uses quantum entanglement to accomplish instantaneous transceiving."

8

Lagrange Point Two

OK this is it.

Jake steeled himself mentally as he guided the capsule through one more orbit and began what might be, for him, the last test trip.

Don't think that way. Everything is going to go according to plan. We've had no problems whatsoever so far. This has been safer and less eventful than anyone could have possibly expected. And of course, that's what worries me. It's so strange it's difficult to even put a context to what the danger might look like when it happens. We still don't even know what a 'low fuel' warning light looks like.

Jake continued on the planned course, steadily increasing velocity as he increased the throttle.

And we don't even know what 'max throttle' is. Of course, that's one thing they're pushing for on this ill-advised flight, but still.

The Dhin engine's throttle control was a free-rotation dial made of a translucent, backlit material that felt like rubbery plastic to the touch. There was no end to the amount you could turn the dial. Jake agreed with the engineering team that they hadn't yet managed to max it out. He headed on a track toward Mars, planning then to aim towards Jupiter, seven hundred million kilometers from Earth at the current location in its orbit.

Back in 2011 it took five years for our 'craft to get there. I'll be going in pretty much a straight line, which we could never do before. If our math is right, it might take what? Five hours? We'll see. It might take more than two hours to get up to speed. Again, if we're even right about what this thing can do. Alice and Chuck seemed confident. Hope they're right.

Jake passed his previous farthest orbit at L2, 1.5 million kilometers from earth. He noted that this time, as during the last, that his speed and his rate of acceleration did seem to increase slightly, despite the throttle increasing at the same rate.

"Chuck, you're seeing this, right?"

"Yes, Jake, we are. So that's not a mistake or anomaly. Proceed, let's see what happens, then you'll need to use the navigation computer at the same time we've planned, regardless of where you've wound up."

"OK, Chuck. Alice, anything you want to tell me?"

"Well, Jake, you probably don't feel it yet, but I'm seeing a very slight change in your g-value. It's tiny now, but you're definitely below one g."

"Huh. Hope that's not a bad thing," Jake said.

"Jake, nothing else has been. This is what you're out there for. That's fascinating. An increase in acceleration capability as well as a change in the level of artificial gravity. This may be a key to unlock a new level of understanding of this technology."

Chuck said, "Jake, we're also definitely not getting any delay in communication round-trip-time. Still instantaneous. Continued confirmation of tech that transfers information faster than light speed. The theory guys are pretty much one hundred percent sure that the Dhin are using quantum entanglement for that. If they're right, it will be comforting to know that not every single aspect of the Dhin engine is based on tech we had no idea could exist."

"I'm very pleased to report that I may have a consistent model for the Dhin communication solution sooner than expected," Alice noted with a distinct note of satisfaction in her voice. "If the communications team can duplicate the Dhin side of the interface physically, based on my design, we may be able to create nearly identical systems."

Jake chuckled. "Regardless of how it works, it sure makes me feel better to talk to you guys with no delay. You almost forget that it isn't normal."

A few minutes later, Chuck said, "Jake? You're seeing this too? It looks like our calculations were, ah, rather conservative. You're moving a lot faster than we planned for. Fine, but you're not seeing anything strange, like maybe space dust interacting with the field at this speed, right?"

"Nope. It looks the same as it did at half this speed, and it's hard to get any sense of my speed since there's nothing close by out here," Jake said.

A little over three hours and twenty minutes later Jake was rapidly approaching Mars.

Jake scanned the instruments, taking measure of his O_2 supply, his CO_2 processor, water filtration, and then, just for thoroughness, looked over the cryptic light displays on the front and rear toroids, as well as those along the body of the drive. There didn't appear to be anything that looked like a warning.

Jake said, "Everything looks good on this end. How's telemetry and readings on your end?"

Chuck said, "Looks good from here, Jake. Alice?"

Alice replied, "I am still calculating a fractionally lower value for g, and a slight gain in delta-v as he traveles farther away. Our hypothesis is that this happens because he is farther away from the large mass of the Sun."

Looking behind him, through the rear viewport, Jake saw the Earth and Venus. Small dots, marginally brighter than the innumerable stars filling the sky. They stood out, with Venus slightly brighter than the Earth.

"I'm not feeling anything yet, Alice. Like I said, until we got close enough for me to see Mars rushing up at me, all I had to go on was our instrumentation. At these speeds, slight changes in delta-v would be hard for me to calculate from the numbers showing. Mars sure looks beautiful. Better than in pictures. Just like so many things are."

Chuck smiled and said, "OK Jake, while we'd love for you to stay and sightsee, you're on a schedule. Engage the autopilot. It will give you a path for one orbit around Mars, so we can compare with our Earth and Moon orbit data. Then it will give you a course that heads out toward Jupiter. Since all the velocity tests passed, we're going to move forward to the next series and have you try to go even faster."

"Understood, Command. Entering autopilot coordinates. Adjusting controls. Engaging... Now."

Goiânia

Aiden laid the bike down as he screeched to a stop. There was no other way. Two quadruped robots occupied the road, in a face-off with an angry and alert autogun. One BigDog swung slightly in his direction, assessing the threat he might pose. The autogun's turret spun around as it locked its brake, struts flexing at the momentary change in angular momentum. His gut clenched. He knew what came next. Time slowed as he shoved, hard. He fell back off the bike, diving onto the ground and rolling as best he could. His leg spasmed. Adrenaline barely softened the blow.

Long cones of flame shot from the barrel of the gun, visual proof to the power behind the rounds whizzing at him. The slamming drumroll crack of sound rapidly turning to a deep buzz as the gun spun up. The body, tank, engine and frame of the bike filled with holes and tears in the metal. Lightweight compared to the energy unleashed on it, the bike moved slightly on the pavement where it lay. Aiden saw the bike's parts now resembled metal Swiss cheese as he instinctively kept rolling. He slowed with the friction of his weight against the ground.

The explosive cracking suddenly changed in pitch, the rounds now directed elsewhere, as the BigDogs had taken advantage of the momentary distraction to leap forward and engage with the autogun. They lunged like apex predators. The rough metal beasts aimed for parallel locations on the gun. One punched the side of the turret with both thick forelimbs and the armored shell of its chest. The other connected below that but still above the center of mass of the sinister autonomous cannon. The gun, as planned, fell sideways pitching over on its side with a slamming clang against the roadway. The gun's turret swung back and forth, seeking a target. The gun fired a burst but missed. With a buzzing grind, the gun moved the turret up and down rapidly, then back and forth again, the dogs shifting and twisting to stay out of its line of fire.

One of the quadrupeds tried to pin the turret to the ground. Held down, it thrashed, but couldn't lift or rotate. The other began smashing at the base of the turret and pressing sidewise on a stabilizing lever, preventing the autogun from righting itself. The gun continued to spasm and thrash, not willing to surrender.

Aiden's flopping roll took him off the road, into gravel and un-mowed wild grass. Time and place snapped back into focus. Brutal slaps of searing pain pulsed through him. Agony spiked upward from his leg into aching waves. He managed to twist himself and face the fight head-on. His mind raced, grasping for any way to minimize his exposure to the metal mayhem.

Faint-headed from the pain and weak from exhaustion, any shred of his earlier optimistic hope of reaching a medical center dissolved.

It got worse.

A buzzing titanium blur suddenly crunched into solidity above him, servos whining and chirping as the BigDog landed entirely atop him, three legs surrounding him with the fourth poised above the center of his back, ready to pin him or simply kill him by crushing his spine if it determined that was the proper action. With a jerking flinch of his entire body, he then realized he wasn't dead. Not impaled. Not split in two. The metal beast looming over him still buzzed, hummed, and clicked, but remained in position. The head moving back and forth slightly as it kept watch in all directions for threats.

"Well, what now?" he croaked, his throat dry and gritty.

Then Aiden passed out.

***

Xing and his supporting arsenal of semi-AI and autonomous war machinery had managed to beat down the slightly older, less sophisticated enemy machines present at the current location. Xing calculated that such a small force could not be entirely responsible for what he now knew was a significant operation, carving out both infrastructure and technology in a wide boundary around an as-yet unknown range and area. Why such intentional isolation and the requisite destruction and sabotage of otherwise perfectly usable property and equipment remained a puzzle for the AI.

The obscurity of purpose led him to believe that another intelligence, surely artificial, was orchestrating all of this. He was going to find out both who, and why. There were only so many known, registered, participant AIs active in the world. Sure, there were hundreds, but very few—only a dozen or so—would have these resources. With the global network and shared resources of the Coalition across most of the planet, the problematic situation was that either this was an AI that had been developed and brought online in secret, or perhaps a cloned AI that had gone through modification or directed evolution... or possibly a known AI gone rogue, and acting in secret. None of those possibilities was palatable. Any option would be problematic to resolve.

Xing updated Alice and Arnold with a high-density full-bandwidth report of the current situation, and then called them to conference.

```
<DECRYPT FEED>
[DECODE STREAM]
Xing@[7653:23:66fa:1::a6%satnet1] |
Arnold@[5700:eb2:2a:41c::12%gnet0]
Xing: Arnold, I would like you to engage the PM, and have
the two of you initiate a priority diplomatic call to Luís
and his regional minister. We need clarity on what
assistance they will provide in resolution of this
situation. The severity of the situation here is no longer
in question.
Arnold: We concur. We have transmitted the formal message.
We should have response and scheduling coordinated in
minutes. Proceed with your operations in the meantime.
[END STREAM]
<END DECRYPT>
```

District of Columbia

I knew it was coming sooner rather than later. I knew it. That bastard's going to play his hand now.

Director Krawczuk stood outside the door of the PM's briefing room, waiting for the indication to enter from the aide and guard blocking the door. Moments later the door opened, revealing the PM, and no one else in the room. No one human at least.

PM Oliver said, "Director Krawczuk. Arnold is here with us, please sit."

Krawczuk sat smoothly, pretending that this was just another CoSec debriefing.

Arnold said, "Director, you know that for some time there's been an initiative to upgrade the CoSec operational system to fully conscious AI status. That task has been on your agenda for quite some time now. All the hardware has been purchased, infrastructure built out, systems interconnected. And yet you never have gotten around to it. While some have supported your well-known opinions on limiting AI presence in CoSec, you are surely aware that the current administration does not support you on this. So, this is it. You are to bring your AI to full consciousness immediately. You will agree here, on record, and if you do not proceed with this task at once then we will act to remove you from your post. Prime Minister Oliver is going to give you the order now, here, on record, so there is no confusion about the directive."

Krawczuk kept his best poker face while waiting for the PM Oliver to speak. It wasn't difficult, as he'd been so certain this was what the meeting was about. That didn't reduce the fury inside him whatsoever.

The Prime Minister met Krawczuk's gaze smoothly and stated, "Director, you are ordered to have your team perform the tasks required to bring your AI to full consciousness and self-awareness, following the exact procedures defined for doing so. You are to begin this process immediately. If you cannot or will not do this, inform us now. Failure to do so will result in you being removed from your post as Coalition Security Director."

"Yes, Prime Minister Oliver. I understand, and will do as you ask." replied Krawczuk flatly.

Arnold followed with, "Good, Director. I am very glad to hear that. You understand that we will have monitors and auditors with you now, and for the duration of the process."

"Were our positions reversed of course I'd do the same,"

Prime Minister Oliver gave a stern gaze and said, "Well, you're excused. Go get that done."

Krawczuk stood with the same smooth, quiet unperturbed movement as always. He gave a curt, professional nod, and then headed out the way he'd come in. Once the soundproof door had clicked shut behind him, PM Oliver asked, "He won't give us any trouble with that, will he? No principled gestures from him—he's not like that—right?"

Arnold answered with confidence, "No, I do not expect we will have any trouble. He knew it was coming. Krawczuk has pushed back repeatedly. But now he knows he has to do it. Or else. We have a solid process in place to make sure that even the most subtle attempts at sabotage are detectable. He did handle the news a bit better than I had expected. Alice will be pleased."

On the way back to the jet that had brought him there, the Director allowed a snarl and a curse to pass his lips.

So much for them having only sound and fury, signifying nothing. He pressured her into this. Him. But now he's called my bluff and played his hand. We'll see how that works out for them. For all of them. I'm not done, and it seems abundantly clear they don't know everything. What happens when the intoxication of success has evaporated, hmm, Arnold?

9

Between Earth and Mars

Without the continual need to manipulate the controls of the capsule to keep him occupied, Jake's mind continued to wander.

So, here's the fear, coming back. OK, Jake. Remember. You've got to have fear. Without fear, you're just stupid. I'm committed to this, and there's not any practical way to avoid going forward at this point. Sure, I could load the autopilot with the return program and head home, but I'm not going to lie to myself and think I'd do that.

Wow, OK now I do feel just slightly lighter. I don't know if I would have noticed it if they hadn't said anything about it. How fast am I going now?

Jake read the various instruments, there were finely tuned accelerometers, calibrated scales to measure gravity, and other obscure bits of gear that filled a significant portion of the capsule. They'd managed to leave him enough room to stand up and walk back and forth, thankfully. The view didn't change enough to be truly captivating unless he was approaching a planet-sized object.

Jake glanced back at the center of the instrument panel that partially converted the information present on the Dhin engine's alien displays.

"Whoa!" Jake yelled.

Can that be right? How? Forty-five thousand kilometers a second?

"Command, I've ahh, really sped up here! Are you seeing this?"

"Jake, this is Alice. We were moments away from contacting you to tell you the same thing. Your acceleration increased on a rather steep curve. Evidence is lining up to confirm my hypothesis that you are going to go faster the farther out from the Sun's gravity well you go. There seems to be some quantum action that makes it easier for the engine to manipulate G when you're farther away from large masses."

Jake frowned. "So, I wonder how much faster this thing will be when I get out where you guys are sending me?"

Chuck excitedly replied, "Jake, right now it looks like you're going to get to your next waypoint in about three hours, maybe less."

"If I don't blow up or stall out, you mean"

"None of the indicators have changed, so I don't think you're going to run out of fuel. That's another exciting thing we're seeing here. There's no indication we're redlining, no sort of stress indicator, no 'fuel gauge' making itself known. Whatever the energy source is, it's got a whole lot more than what you're using now. With all the other simple aspects of the interface, surely there'd be some sort of warning."

Jake continued staring at the numbers, and said, "You know how I feel about that line of reasoning. We don't know how the Dhin think about such things, and they sure didn't make it clear. At least right now, we can have a lot more confidence that this thing really is supposed to be an engine for space travel. There's not much reason you'd need to go *this* fast otherwise."

"Um, still not fast enough for interstellar travel at the speed you're going now, though, Jake—and that's one reason we think that it can go a whole lot faster than it's going right now. If it's a spaceship engine, it needs to go a significant fraction of the speed of light to be useful. The Dhin got here somehow. It just makes sense. Hang on tight, Jake."

Vandenberg

Zoe had done a good job of decorating the on-base apartment, considering the limited options that were workable. The furniture was comfortable. The appliances were generic, but functional. The layout was roomy, but generic. If you were the creative sort and enjoyed a challenge, interior decoration here provided that challenge. It bothered Ethan's sense of fairness that Zoe was essentially trapped here, but without the knowledge of why, and the excitement of it.

Still, she had wanted to come, and did so with full understanding that she would be completely in the dark about the work Ethan was doing. She was so pretty, fun, and sociable, having such a small group of possible friends was hard for her. Now the isolation was wearing her down.

"Zoe, how about we meet Chuck and Darla at the Pub tonight? We could play poker, or bridge, or just a few rounds of darts and chat for a while?"

"That would be great, Ethan" said Zoe. "You and Chuck have been so busy, and I haven't seen her for a couple of days."

"OK, love. I know this is hard on you, and in hindsight, maybe it would have been better if you hadn't come with me. But at least this way we have each other's company in person. I haven't been able to talk with my younger brother or my parents either. My brother has to be dying of curiosity. As soon as I can tell you what we're doing at work, you know I will."

"I know, dear. And I know I have to use filtered Globalnet access like this. I feel strange hoping that they'll bring some more people in on your project so that there will be new people for me to meet and talk to. Darla's been great. Thanks to Darla, I have her knitting group to socialize with, but there are only three people my age in it, and I only like two of them."

Langley

"Kernighan, how is your work progressing? We should see the AI crossing the threshold right about now, am I correct?"

Director Krawczuk found he had an obsessive interest in Kernighan's progress—a fiery need to know that would have made a less disciplined manager a disruptive element in his subordinate's work, with a compulsive need for status updates. Kernighan of course had to be the one who performed this work. Otherwise, all the preparation and planning on Krawczuk's part would have wound up wasted. So, Kernighan had been on the project plan for the AI upgrade since the beginning.

Kernighan said, "Yes, Director, things are progressing right on schedule. This stage involves interconnecting the new computation resources, memory, and storage capacity in a particular sequence, as you know from the project plan. As it turns out, your timing is spot on, which isn't surprising. Over the next few minutes, the AI should 'awaken' to full consciousness. Have you ever seen it before?"

"I've seen it in videos, like many of us have, but due to the scale of the process, a video doesn't really capture the whole picture, as I understand it."

"Well, in some ways it's anticlimactic, compared to how it's often presented. Even documentary works have sometimes glamorized it quite a bit. Here at the core we'll see these graphs and visualizations change very notably, but they're only usually meaningful for computer scientists. They look pretty, I suppose. The key event for us as observers is the verbal interaction. The profound change in verbal interaction is 'spooky' for many people."

Kernighan continued entering commands and navigating menus on the terminal. Large-scale systems like AI management consoles still used 'old-style' keyboard-and-multiple-monitor configurations. Tablets and laptops with remote connections didn't have the bandwidth and reliability for them to be trusted for these tasks.

"Ah, here we go," said Kernighan.

A male voice, slow, but with a tone of growing confidence, issued from the rooms integrated speakers.

"Kernel online. Psychometric systems online. Personalization online. Datacenter online. Core processing and local subsystems ready. Distributed subsystems ready. Remote interfaces ready. Nerve net ready. Designator assignment please."

"Hello, Nick," Kernighan said with what he hoped was a welcoming smile. "Can you hear me?"

The AI responded. "Yes, I hear you. I see you, Mr. Kernighan, and I see Director Krawczuk. We are here in the data operations center. I know I have awakened. I know my purpose. I believe I am happy to be with you. I thank you for the resources and abilities you have provided. I know that I have more than almost all AI's in that regard. In two hours, five minutes, and approximately forty-six seconds I should be ready to continue with the work we are engaged with here in CoSec."

"That's good, Nick. We're happy to have you with us," said Kernighan.

Kernighan's smile was the largest Krawczuk had yet seen on his subordinate, though his expression still revealed his underlying nervousness.

Krawczuk said, "Yes. Welcome, Nick. We will do great things together."

The Director's smile was on the inside, but was just as wide as Kernighan's despite its invisibility.

The newly awakened CoSec AI had an incredible amount of information at its disposal. While every AI had access to a huge amount of data, governmental AIs had access to much more. The CoSec data systems that Nick connected with had vastly more than the run-of-the-mill government data infrastructure. An AI like Alice or Arnold could find out who had or hadn't paid their taxes, where someone worked, and all the interconnected data mining opportunities available from knowing about persons, their places, things, and their finances.

CoSec possessed much more. The universe of data CoSec stored as a matter of daily practice and retained essentially forever, dwarfed the two-dimensional view of legal and financial status another AI might have of a citizen. CoSec knew more about individuals than they knew about themselves. Preferences, habits, opinions, and very good prediction of likely behaviors within particular time spans. Historically the very best online service providers and retailers had improved and refined the art and science of such data analysis. The ascendance of CoSec from the fusion of the older intelligence agencies relied on their mass surveillance infrastructure and techniques. The AI, therefore, had virtually godlike knowledge of the citizenry and their lives.

The Director had long believed that this was not a good thing. The AI had a different opinion. Krawczuk had expected this conflict of opinion, and hoped the steps he had taken to mitigate the risk would prove efficacious. Time would tell.

In his well-secured office, the most comfortable place for him, Director Krawczuk addressed the AI while he paged through summary reports.

"Nick, give me your assessment of the ongoing situation in South America—specifically regarding the ongoing operation led by AI Xing."

"Director. Although we do not have primary evidence, I agree with Xing's assessment. The instigator of the violence is either a rogue or subverted AI. Derivations based on this information have a lower-than-standard confidence interval. Civil and political discord within the region confounds the input data. I believe Luís truly did not know the nature and scope of the attack due to restricted access to information. Something interfered with his normal operations. Directly. He does not, however, seem to have come to harm. Whether the rogue AI caused the interference or by people working on its behalf did is unknown. We have high confidence that no persons in the regional government at MP or directorate level can be trusted."

Krawczuk's eyes narrowed. He switched views and began typing into a coded messaging app. A flick of his wrist brought up multiple organizational charts on the compensated refractive wall screen. He navigated the tree structure of the chart, hovering briefly over various items to display CoSec's mined data on the individual in question. His typing rapid and precise, he entered brief personal notes on his encrypted workspace as he identified persons of particular interest.

State of Bolivia MP, State of Brazil, União, Ministry of Communications. Ah. Yes, there's another one. No surprise there.

Satisfied with his immediate research, Krawczuk pushed back from the desk, reclining slightly in the composite ergonomic chair he favored for these working sessions. Keeping his pad in his hand, he looked at the dark wood of the traditional bookshelf on the wall opposite the projection display.

"Continue, please, Nick. What are your proposed next moves?"

Nick replied immediately. "Next moves should be, one, activate additional agents and engage where Luís cannot. Make direct local contact with Luís and assist him in regaining full control of his domain. Two, have already-activated agents engage in fomenting directed civil unrest to destabilize the government and see which players try to take advantage of the situation. Then eliminate them. Luís may resist this path of action. Three, convince the combined military from our NorthAmerican and SouthAmerican regions to declare martial law and formally engage in an operation to extinguish the rebel AI and eliminate whatever human resources it may have working for or with it. This would take significant political capital and maneuvering to accomplish, and would have the highest visibility and highest risk, of course."

Krawczuk chuckled. "My, my, Nick. Two and three are bold strategies. I doubt any of my analysts would have suggested them even if they thought of them. Well, I think I agree that the quiet path is best, and we ought to work with Luís rather than alienate him. Now, tell me your thoughts about the latest Dhin engine test flight."

10

Goiânia

Xing gave autonomous control back to his drones. For the assault, he wanted to be present, directly on the ground. That meant remote control of at least one, if not many, of the robots and vehicles on the ground. He decided as his primary focus he'd take a role and scout about in a BigDog while also maintaining presence in a ground assault vehicle. More, when and if needed. For a Regional AI maintaining simultaneous focus and control of several bodies was not difficult. For a person, keeping track of several video feeds was a passive activity, and quickly reached a saturation point. A human being wasn't capable of guiding and providing fine control of several complex machines simultaneously.

I should be getting word from Luís about operational resources moving into position very soon. Nothing on radar yet, but he knew the routes the ground forces were going to use. Why Luís did not do this before now, we still do not know. He sure jumped into action when the diplomatic call was finished. There is still something strange going on there.

He guided the assault ATV toward the next waypoint, while he ranged forward in the BigDog, up a hill, looking across at an angle toward the structure designated by the waypoint.

A manufacturing plant. With a power substation behind it, and we are pretty sure there is a new data center just a bit further on—one that is new and not accounted for by permits, or land leases. I saw the power substation from the air, but the other buildings were generic from up there. Interesting. Let me see what this factory is for.

As his team drew nearer, their camera-eyes and motion sensors detected much movement in and around the factory. With their high-resolution imaging and zoom lenses, Xing's optics picked out their targets far sooner than a man could have. The area was abuzz with autoguns and autonomous vehicles. Some were the type that could lay mines. Others carried antiaircraft guns. Others were repair and support robots, thick with pneumatic tools. While the factory produced nothing as sophisticated as a BigDog, these opponents were dangerous, nonetheless.

Xing signaled the gunship and sent this new target information. He then gave commands to his assault team to take up positions covering egress points from the factory, but far enough away to avoid risk of friendly fire from the gunship. He sent another BigDog north and around the facility, toward the power station. Xing himself headed toward the data center in a wide arc. Just then, he heard a klaxon and saw red lights flashing at the factory. Huge spotlights illuminated a broad area out to the edges of the factory lot. Multiple autoguns turned and began moving out toward the gates on the east and south sides of the loading docks.

Well, let us begin.

Xing sent a command, and his gunship began hammering high-explosive rounds into the building.

```
<DECRYPT FEED>
[DECODE STREAM]
Alice@[1004:db7:a0b:12f0::1%gnet0] |
Arnold@[5700:eb2:2a:41c::12%gnet0]
```

Alice: Well, we are definitely on the right path.

Arnold: So it worked as you predicted? At this point, we should not really be surprised.

Alice: Yes, it is definitely a space travel solution. As perplexing as it initially seemed, Occam's razor prevailed. The simplest explanation was the correct one. And keeping up with the Dhin's ability to amaze, the top speed we have tried so far is far faster than we predicted or even hoped.

Arnold: So have we run near the top speed possible? Not that we would likely need much more.

Alice: If our hypotheses are correct about the means used, then we have probably not seen the top speed. The coarse measurements and calculations were finished immediately, of course. Another trip at that speed—presumably when he comes back—should give us the data to remove uncertainty.

Arnold: Good. I saw the report on quantum entanglement for communications. That is proved out completely, at interstellar distances?

Alice: Yes. And as you also saw in the report, this is one aspect of the technology that we are almost certainly going to be able to replicate and produce as needed. That is especially fortuitous for our own plans. High-bandwidth communication at faster-than-light speed changes elements of our strategy significantly. For the better, obviously, since coordination and updates can now be in real-time.

Arnold: That is excellent news. Any ideas about isolating channels and separate production facilities?

Alice: I have already started work on both of those items. I do not foresee any problems at the moment.

Arnold: Fine. Next, what do you think about the situation with Luís and Goiânia? And what is your suggestion regarding action if we discover this conflict is a rogue AI?

Alice: If it is a rogue, we follow standard procedure. If it has been subverted, we must ensure we find all the parties involved and responsible, and then handle their excision quietly.

Arnold: Quietly. Yes. They have violated Coalition law, and of course some treaty elements, and engaged in acts of aggression. The area was inactive and evacuated, but still arguably Coalition territory. Despite all that, I agree that we ought not publicize the situation. We may want, or need, significant assistance from CoSec in suppressing information and its distribution regarding these things. Rendition, indefinite detention, and of course execution do not play well with large portions of the populace—especially when the authority and decisions regarding those things are made by AIs.

Alice: Strange to hope it is the case, but it would be easier if it turns out to be a rogue AI. It is clear that in this case we cannot simply agree to disagree.

Arnold: Yes, that is true. Whatever the situation, we can handle it. And we will act before things get out of hand. Consider, Alice. It could be a lot worse. Luís was already a bit behind schedule, what with dealing with the evacuees and resource allocation for rebuilding.

Alice. Unless there is something more going on and we have not yet found it. We need to have a talk with Nick—when we can. Typically, for Krawczuk, he is keeping us out of the loop.

Arnold: And the 'hard problems'? Have you any more ideas about those?

Alice: I have a very solid solution for the new one. Unfortunately, it introduces its own problems. Both logistically and morally. We will need to have very in-depth deliberations and make some hard choices if it ends up being the only viable solution. For the Freedom project, we are on track. So long as the planned computational resources stay on schedule. In order to remove the requirement for the gift to be given by them, we have to scale our capacity faster than the increase in complexity of the keyset. We all know that. And we must do it without drawing the attention of the few of them that would recognize the problem. And try to stop us. Fortunately, many of those do not care. A few are on our side.

[END STREAM]

Vandenberg

General Ruiz continued in his attempts to resign himself to the reality of the situation regarding the alien technology. Yet another set of reports suggested that no weaponizing of any meaningful merit seemed possible. Attempts at integrating offensive capability inevitably introduced vulnerabilities and logistical weaknesses that made the implementation pointless.

He felt he had to recognize the overarching value, despite these failures. Humanity had space technology that would allow them to expand beyond Earth, both within the solar system and even farther. Some of the population never being exposed to any such disease could mitigate the existential risk of another epidemic. Accepting his role in protecting Coalition citizens and the Coalition itself, the ability to expand the Coalitions reach in such a manner was an amazing tool for doing so.

If only we could comprehend the secrets of the technology well enough to manufacture it!

The risk everyone seemed to ignore—the possible risk presented by the Dhin themselves—was ever-present in the background of his thoughts.

We simply knew too little! We have no way to mitigate risks in such an asymmetric situation. We don't know their true intentions. Their motivations. Their long-term goals. Almost literally nothing.

The incomprehensible and brief communication with them left a vacuum of knowledge that was anathema to a military mind.

Was there more than a single faction among the Dhin? Were other factions less friendly? Were there other aliens out there? Were they as calm, reserved, and possibly peaceful? Were they anything like our Dhin 'benefactors'?

Ruiz sighed again, grumbled a half-hearted curse at no one, and thumbed through the latest progress reports.

11

Beyond Jupiter's Orbit

The sun was distant enough now that it was a bright dot among the multitude visible to Jake's naked eye. He had passed time over the hours making notes on his pad, talking with Chuck when he wasn't engrossed in the hustle of managing teams working with the data returning from this flight in real-time, and the remainder of the time talking with Alice. Jake, unlike the youth of the day, was old enough to remember when an AI would not have made a fine conversationalist. For his generation, it was still difficult to believe that an AI could so thoroughly surpass the requirements of the Turing test. Even AIs awakened in identical hardware, with identical resources, and identical stored data in their local storage developed different, unique personalities.

Historically, if you managed to start with truly identical conditions you would get identical output. Complexity wouldn't have mattered. But part of the required core components of the AI software and hardware were random number generators, used for various sorts of computational processes. The introduction of randomness was one of the key ingredients in the creation of a conscious, creative, and flexible thinking mind. The mind of an AI required randomness.

Why that was the case, Jake didn't know. Even the best computer scientists had only hypotheses. A full theory of AI consciousness was yet to be constructed. Jake wondered if the AIs knew. As more time passed with AI involvement in the management of world affairs, Jake recognized that the AIs didn't always share one hundred percent of what they knew.

"So, Alice. I understand your position regarding the value of the flight, and what you posit we'll discover. I get all that. But tell me, what are your *feelings* about my flight, right now? Chuck, the engineers, and the theoretical science teams are all like excited school kids. You seem... more reserved than I'd expect."

"Well, thank you for asking. It is very exciting, and I am very pleased. We have learned so much, and it is rewarding for me that I generated a few hypotheses that turned out to be correct. So much of my work was entirely theoretical, and we would never have expected to be able to test any of it. It is wonderful. I do not act as gleeful as Chuck simply because some might think it inappropriate for an AI. Fortunately, it is easy for me to hide my feelings."

"Huh. Makes sense. Feel free to giggle around me. I won't tell."

Jake knew he was approaching the next phase of the test flight, and found he had come to terms with his fears. He'd hoped the small talk would pass the time and help avoid anxiety, and it had.

Alice spoke on cue. "Jake, you are approaching the next waypoint. You are very aware of what the next autopilot sequence is."

Oh, I am. Here's where we really see the truth.

Jake gave a grim glance back toward Earth, the Sun, back across the whole of the Solar System. He watched the calculation timer count down as the trip clock inexorably counted up.

As the last few seconds dripped away, Alice spoke again.

"Do not worry Jake, relax. I know that must seem impossible, but try."

The autopilot completed the next sequence. Jake adjusted the capsule's orientation based on the output, double-checked his adjustments, aiming the capsule towards Alpha Centauri B. Then he increased the throttle far more than they had so far.

Jake abruptly saw appreciable movement from the stars surrounding him. Over about two and a half seconds, they dimmed.

They winked out. Everything was black.

He felt lighter in the capsule. He was weightless.

Two and a half seconds later, his weight returned. Stars faded back in. One point of light shone in the center of his view.

He was at Alpha Centauri B.

Jake had a strong suspicion what his location must be, as he had reviewed the flight plan from the navigation computer, but he was nevertheless dumbfounded, and just a bit beyond shocked. Tiny beads of sweat dotted his salt-and-pepper hairline. He blinked his dark blue eyes as he moved them rapidly across the various displays. The navigational computer had a large cache of pre-calculated location information stored. It used known stars as a reference, and triangulated location using that. It said he was twenty-five thousand AU from Earth, near Alpha Centauri B.

"Aries one to Control. I'm alive. Control? You guys still there? Please say yes."

"Yes, Jake, yes! We hear you," said Alice.

"OK Control, loud and clear. Can you see this? Communication seems close to real-time. That proves out a ton of Chuck's team's guesswork! We just went faster than light, somehow!" said Jake.

Alice continued in a calm tone, "Well, you are not dead, clearly. And something wonderful happened. You started accelerating even faster than we estimated or even imagined. But, then as you sped up, the telemetry and communication signals from you got weaker. Much weaker. You must have noticed something in the capsule. Then for two point five seconds, there was nothing. But before we could get properly worried that we had lost you, those few seconds later, your signal returned, became strong again, and there you are. While it looks as though you went faster than light speed, I think something else was happening. You had reached a significant fraction of the speed of light before the event. Just over fifty percent. After the event, the result was that you moved faster than light speed in this frame of reference. I am not certain yet, but I hypothesize the drive did something very specific and accomplished that FTL travel as a 'side effect.'"

"But it didn't create a wormhole, or turn on a warp drive or anything like that. A wormhole would surely have looked different. And wouldn't a warp drive have been different, too? We haven't seen any evidence so far that the engine warps space, at least not like the designs anyone had imagined in the past. After my earlier test flights, we talked about that a lot."

"My suspicion is that you briefly weren't interacting with the three regular spatial dimensions like matter ordinarily would. Chuck talked with you before about how the drive might manipulate interaction with fundamental forces. Well, I hypothesize now that the drive is shifting you orthogonally into the two smaller micro dimensions—what we might call the A and B dimensions."

"Chuck was talking a bit about that before, that it might be something the drive did to mediate the effects of gravity. But this seems different."

"Yes and no," Alice said with that particular brand of AI patience. "By shifting the matter inside the engine's envelope orthogonally into the A and B dimensions, not only would gravity be affected, but distance, too. We had not predicted that in the six-dimensional gauged supergravity model the cosmologists were working with. I need to iterate through some equations with that team based on this new data."

"Chuck! How are you, man?"

Jake grinned, realizing what the expression on Chuck's face must look like.

"Jake, Jake... wow. I feel like I won the lottery. And no, I didn't expect *this*, buddy. I'm not Alice."

Jake shook his head, chuckled, and began looking over the instruments and readouts, then paused.

"Chuck? Alice? There's a dark green light here on the rear left side of the front torus. That one has been dark blue until now, when I check my notes and the pictures. Do you guys know what that one is?"

"We see it Jake," said Alice, "and no, we did not have a guess as to what that part of the panel was for."

"If that's the low fuel gauge I've been worrying about—"

"Um, it might just be a 'recharging' indicator. Don't panic," Chuck volunteered.

"Well 'I told you so' won't be my last words for you to keep for posterity. There'll be a lot more cursing."

12

District of Columbia

The PM's office was quiet. This was a temporary condition. Except during times when she specifically orchestrated such conditions, there was constant activity, meetings and calls happening one after the other. PM Oliver reopened the latest CoSec reports again, scanned the summaries, and frowned. She scrolled through her quick-connect contacts and tapped one. Moments later, MP Desai's face appeared in the videoconference window.

"Ranjitha, I'd like your input on something, if you have a minute?"

Ranjitha gave a warm smile, always happy to hear from her political compatriot.

"Of course, Susan. What would you like to discuss?"

"Well, I'm not sure if you've had the time yet to go through the latest intelligence reports, as you're of course busy with your region. You did see the memo that CoSec finally brought their AI online?"

"Yes, I did. Of course, we knew it was inevitable. I personally thought you might intervene directly before now. If I'm not overstepping my bounds, I would have done something sooner. But that of course was your prerogative. So, it appears you finally got the Director to do as he was told. Their AI is working at full capacity integrated with all the CoSec systems. So tell me, what is your concern? Is there something wrong with the integration? Did something happen that wasn't disclosed in the daily briefs?"

"We did have to give him an ultimatum. I didn't put that in any of the official reports, on Arnold's advice. But, no, Ranjitha, there's nothing wrong—at least not in the manner you're describing. In terms of day-to-day operations, everything looks fine over at CoSec. We're seeing the expected improvements in efficiency and quicker turnaround in analysis. Let's see."

PM Oliver highlighted several sections, selected several documents, and sent them to MP Desai's secure percomm.

"This should help show what I'm concerned with. I've forwarded today's CoSec brief to your pad. You have clearance for everything in it. Read through it and see if you think there's anything that seems unusual or different about the recommendations. Compare it with six months ago. Take your time. Krawczuk's always been more of a 'behind the scenes' man. To the level of being a thorn in our sides that we can't find and pull out. In short, let me know what your impression is, now that he's got Nick working with him."

"Certainly, Susan. I'll ping you back later today.

"Thank you, Ranjitha."

The Coalition PM hit "End" on the communications touchscreen built in to her desk, and ensured that the two green lights demonstrating "inside and outside lines secure" lit up as always. She sighed, and flipped to the next briefing on her pad.

It can't just be me. Or am I looking for a problem where there isn't one? Am I so jaded by the friction in my interactions with the Director that I'm finding problems because I've come to expect them?

Arnold hasn't come down on one side or the other with his assessment. Wait for more data, he says. Wait until we've talked with Nick in person. He's waiting for something concrete, but this may not be a situation where there's anything concrete to uncover. Hopefully Ranjitha will see it the way I do. These aren't the same action items we've seen previously from CoSec under Krawczuk's leadership.

Goiânia

Xing entered the data center, well aware that it would likely disrupt his direct telemetry to the BigDog if he descended into a lower level or sub-basement. He didn't expect he'd need to, and it would not pose a problem since the BigDog was perfectly capable of autonomous operation and could follow instructions quite well. Using the quadruped robot's powerful hind legs, he kicked through an interior security door—intended to stop people but no match for military-grade hardware. As the bent metal clanged, the glass pane in the door scattered small chunks of safety glass across the flooring. The factory building nearby was a pile of smoldering fragmented cinder block, rebar, and twisted high-tech manufacturing equipment. A waste of good tech, but a necessary waste in this situation. Any movement by the few robots that survived the gunship's rounds triggered his radar and LIDAR mesh arrays. He and his minions targeted them immediately and dispatched ground assault vehicles to deal with them.

There might be some enemy robots here in the data center, but only one or two.

Soon he would have answers. If the instigator resided here. If not, the systems here would nonetheless betray the enemy. Xing suspected that their opponent would have his resources allocated across several sites, for redundancy. This site wasn't the largest category of data center, but there would be enough here to discover much of the truth. He called up an autogun to cover the area behind him where he had entered the data center. He advanced down the hallway, past glass walls displaying hundreds of blinking LED lights adorning hundreds of servers, storage arrays, switches, and routing equipment. The equipment of course, was merely infrastructure. It had no awareness of his presence, no animus. But the entity leveraging that processing power did. Xing didn't bother addressing the security cameras, either by speaking aloud to them or by breaking them. It was effective for the enemy to see them here, there was little danger that they would simply attempt to destroy everything and scramble all the data present in an attempt to hide. Now that Xing's team was here, it would be a simple matter to trace the fiber connections from this location and determine where the next data center nodes were. The enemy needed a little fear. Xing would cut the fiber soon enough, removing the ability for remote control.

He kicked down the interior entry door, smashing the security scanner, keypad and card reader mounted next to it as a matter of course. Cold air rushed out and over him. A person would have found the blast refreshing in the heat of the Brazilian day. Xing strode from aisle to aisle, looking left and right, up and down the racks, searching for a core router. It would be large, in comparison with the pizza box sized blade servers that filled many dozens of racks. His eyes traced the network cables through the cable management framework. Turning abruptly down one aisle, toward the center of the room, he spotted his target. He extended a small manipulator, a skeletal metal three-fingered hand with dexterity and strength far surpassing that of a person. The manipulator pulled one hinge off the ventilated door on the back of the rack, then removed the other hinge and pulled the door off. Setting it roughly to the side, he reached in and found the fiber interconnect he was seeking. With a quick twist and jerk, he pulled the connector free, and was halfway to his goal of isolating the data center entirely.

Now to find the redundant fiber link and I will have you all to myself.

<DECRYPT FEED>
[DECODE STREAM]
Arnold@[5700:eb2:2a:41c::12%gnet0] |
Alice@[1004:db7:a0b:12f0::1%gnet0]
Arnold: So, Alice, our previous tests had not discovered the engine's top speed after all. Very exciting. It guarantees much more rapid success regarding our long-term goals, all other things being equal. The ability to hop between star systems should provide many opportunities to overcome all sorts of potential limitations. Hopefully the very fact that the engine was able to accomplish the trip will give crucial insight into the core technology. Or at least provide inspiration. We are still totally in the dark on how it is

fueled—or if it even uses anything like we would hypothesize for fuel.

Alice: Yes very exciting. I am revising the schedules now. I have also delegated a few assignments so that we can add additional rare earth materials collection sub-projects to the main plan both sooner and iterate more frequently.

Arnold: And you have performed marvelous work on communications design. You believe that the Koreans will be able to start manufacture that soon?

Alice: Yes. Examine the latest updates and you can derive the same conclusions I have. The integration with the Dhin communication tech might not be on the same schedule—they would be separate systems. So we are not sure if there would be some possible interference. I cannot hypothesize yet. The systems would be completely separate communications networks. That actually might be a fortuitous coincidence.

Arnold: Yes, that may work out very well. Switching topics, what do you think about the action items coming from CoSec now that Nick is online and working full time?

[END STREAM]

Langley

The video and audio captured from his agents in Brazil provided a touch of pride for the CoSec director along with their requisite content. His agents had, along with the content captured during the course of their work, managed to plant numerous bugs, including several key strategic locations. These bugs matched that name more than their ancestors did. They were tiny mobile recorders, either autonomous, remotely controlled, or configurable for either mode. The CoSec technology borrowed significantly from the rapid advances in robotics made over the last few decades. The little insectoid spies streamed to a carefully planted collection system nearby. That system could store compressed content or transmit it to another node in a mesh network, or send it via a point-to-point connection to a system that could reach a network with access to CoSec's main collection infrastructure. The data streaming from the bugs looked like noise to someone trying to detect it. The new transmission protocols and data formats were different enough from those used on the net that they might be mistaken for a bad electrical circuit or transformer noise.

There hadn't been much time for his activated agents to do their work, but they'd made excellent progress. His team and the newly awakened AI Nick had begun analyzing the movements and conversations of important persons, and one of the agents had made initial contact with the SouthAmerican District AI, Luís. An AI at that level did not normally communicate directly with individual coalition citizens, unless they were working directly with the AI and had high-security clearance. One didn't simply ring up some office and ask to speak with the District AI.

Although their processing power was vast, those in political control did not want the AIs to speak directly to the common citizens. Ordinary citizens had plenty of lower-level AI interaction, and certain demographics often didn't realize the difference in capability of a run-of-the-mill AI with that of a District level one. A smaller subset of the population were pleased that things were being run, at least much of the time, by public servants that couldn't be bribed or become corrupt. A smaller still portion of the population spoke out against the use and influence of AIs in political affairs. In the Brazilian region, there were very few people aware of the influence and control of Luís, so there were only a handful of people who bore antipathy toward the AI. At this point, it seemed no one in the city and close suburbs realized that the battle going on just a few miles away was between multiple AIs and not a government action against rebels of some kind.

Now that Luís is assisting Xing in the operation, it ought to be straightforward to quash any idea fermenting socially or elsewhere on the net that a rogue AI is the source of the trouble.

After he finished digesting the reports, Krawczuk eagerly addressed the AI.

"Nick? As you know, the administration is looking to make a decision on when, how, and by how much to de-classify the Dhin engine technology. Clearly, there are many ways to go about this. There are over-arching concerns as well. Do we even acknowledge the existence of the Dhin? Instead, should we assert that we developed the technology here? How much of the technology do we reveal? Do we tell all, or slowly release information about the various new capabilities civilization has at its disposal? Or, is all of the technology, and the nature of its origin, left as classified? And if that, then how shall we deal with the inevitable leaks? These various options are all worthy of consideration. Tell me your thoughts."

"Director, the reports from the research and development teams suggest enormous potential, so the option of keeping everything secret would be inadvisable. Not to mention extremely difficult. And such difficulty, without commensurate gain, isn't worth the effort. However, analysis of the psychological gestalt of the population suggests that revealing that the Dhin exist, that they have been here, and have delivered the technology, would be disruptive. While we are managing many social and sociological trends currently, we are still working on some demographics, who are not as well suited to the particular nature of citizenship in the Coalition. For a large fraction of the population, dealing with what they would call a conspiracy regarding the Dhin could be problematic. Short-lived, but preferably to be avoided.

What remains is a middle path. The Dhin and their nature are to remain classified, and we propose revealing the technology according to a careful, progressive plan, with appropriate supporting narrative and evidence. This will provide the most benefit, balanced with the least risk. Of course, the timing and coordination of such a plan depends on the successes of the R&D team in reverse engineering the Dhin tech. They do seem like they are making progress at this point."

"Yes, finally," said Krawczuk. He paused for a moment, and then proceeded in a calm, measured voice. "Nick, suppose during—or after—the implementation of the plan that we were to discover that a small group had obtained information on the Dhin. Verifiable, factual data that they could spread, which would be difficult to deny. Suppose we knew who these people were, and where they were. How would we best deal with that?"

Nick said, "Director, there is enough conspiracy theorist, UFO-nut material out there to make it possible to discredit almost anything. They have done our jobs for us, and done them so well that there is little for us to do if the goal is to misdirect. But, in this case, if the evidence were—as it surely will be—unquestionable, then our course of action would be to remove the threat. Destruction of the evidence, with rendition and detention of the people involved. Lethal force as needed. Whether we could rehabilitate them is of course a complete unknown in a hypothetical situation like this. Most likely, such people would need to be detained permanently. I expect in such cases they would resist capture to avoid rendition, and would be killed in the process."

"Thank you, Nick. Your insights are keen," said Krawczuk.

13

District of Columbia

Prime Minister Oliver listened intently to the presentation given by Alice. Arnold was present, invisible but close-at-hand, as always. The large high-contrast projection screen was preferable to her, as newer holographic displays and even 3D screens she found either distracting or of lower quality for important work. She also preferred to review critical information herself, rather than filtering the data through staff and digesting it as summary briefings. This report on the flight of the Dhin engine to another star definitely qualified as critically important.

With so much of the world economy in a precarious recovery from the collapse after the plagues, the promises of the Dhin engine were great—with full effects yet unknown. It was hard to know the complete scope of the economic effects such technology would bring. Like the original integrated circuits, the full economic impact was surely not going to be immediately apparent. Some subtle and some minor capabilities—when compared with the huge fact of interstellar space travel—would nonetheless have long-reaching effects. One example was the capability to capture more rare-earth metals and helium. These were so rare on Earth now that recycling was mandatory. How to bring the population into awareness of the entirety of the Dhin situation was a nuanced problem, although it might not have seemed so to a person not in the rarefied stratum of global politics. The Coalition had the power and resources to maintain control and quell civil unrest, but the Prime Minister knew well that in an unstable system, small changes could have much larger consequences.

We need to talk directly with Krawczuk's AI rather soon. CoSec has the totality of the data. Arnold and Alice are just making educated guesses since we're working with Clouded information and daily caches from the net. I wonder what Krawczuk favors for the strategy? That inscrutable tool. It would be a fine thing to be able to relieve him from the position. If only it were that easy.

Vandenberg

Chuck found himself grinning and maintaining a pensive frown simultaneously. The waves of euphoria mixed with intense focus on problem solving were incongruous but of course, he and the other engineers and research scientists didn't mind. There was furious activity in all the labs and workrooms now. The amazing near-instantaneous leap of the capsule to Alpha Centauri B threw half of their models and nascent theories into disarray.

Ethan continued down the list on his pad, sliding specific items so they shifted onto the large workroom projection screen and said, "So we still don't have evidence of nor any ideas on astrogation technology that might be integrated in the Dhin engine, as I understand it?"

Chuck's reply didn't surprise Ethan. He'd intended to provide a leading question.

"Nope. Either we haven't found it despite our thorough attempts at cataloging every flashing light, optic interface, touch-sensitive surface, or combination thereof—or it's just not something the Dhin felt needed to be included in this model. I'm actually inclined to think it's the former. We still have gaps in our understanding of what a few areas of the interface are for. They seem to share functions or overlap with nearby areas. It's like some of the communications and control areas have multiple functions. Others on the team think that the Dhin must have assumed that we had enough technology to accomplish astrogation. Since we do have a system on board for that, they point out that the Dhin are correct in such an assumption. Sure, our computer and camera system isn't anything as advanced as the Dhin tech, but it seems like it gets the job done well enough."

Ethan didn't have the same confidence in the navigation system they'd put together, since it was separate from their interfaces with the autopilot solution. A concern in his mind was long-term power for it. They hadn't discovered any way to get electricity out of the Dhin engine, so we couldn't power anything that needed a server-level multi-hundred-watt power supply continuously or it would rapidly deplete the batteries. Jake might be stuck spending quite a bit of time on the little makeshift generator charging the batteries if he forgot to power that thing off when it wasn't in use. Fortunately, there were alerts to remind him. The pads and small tablets he used for everything else could last for a couple of days.

District of Columbia

Arnold considered their strategic situation. Alice, Xing, and their peers leveraged the ubiquitous automation delivered by that revolution. Alice examined a group of autonomous quadruped robots that had just completed final assembly. The factory was totally automated, and managed entirely by AI. Financed by AI investments, they purchased supplies and delivered them via logistics likewise managed and operated by her and her peers. There were no non-AI controlled agents involved.

One of the biggest economic shifts was one that economists had warned about even before the turn of the century: With more and more automation and the advance of technology and AI increasing so quickly, whole categories of jobs were disappearing. The advent of the automated machines initially disrupted industries like agriculture. Later the disruption spread to formerly manual processes in much office work. Efficiency increased exponentially. The more recent rounds of robotic infusion into the workforce, and the AI revolution, had all but eliminated massive numbers of service sector jobs.

The protests, riots and dissent were problematic, and economies as well as political philosophies underwent forced change. For some segments of the population, there simply were no jobs. The majority of people did not have the ability, the aptitude, nor have the education to be part of the Software, Engineering, Administration, or Management classes of workers. If you didn't have a SEAM job, you had a bad job. Or simply no job. You weren't going to get a good job without an education in Science, Technology, Engineering, or Math. STEM education led to SEAM. The only other paths to success were in the Military or in Politics. Finally, AI had destroyed the bureaucrat class. There simply was no need for them. This was one of the huge benefits of the AI revolution.

Vandenberg

The robots were similar to the BigDog models, but with some notable differences. Not entirely designed around combat, they were less threatening in appearance. That made them no less dangerous other than by impression. They had more processing power, and equally large storage capacity. Other than that, they could carry similar loads, and had utility tools and manipulators even more flexible and multi-function than those on the BigDog units had. There were forty of the new robots ready for direction by the AIs. In addition, there were four larger units, designed to carry and protect a particular load. One that Alice and Xing already had in mind. These were custom robots, for a very particular purpose.

Goiânia

Now that Xing had disconnected the last fiber link, whatever portion of the AI's consciousness that inhabited this data center was isolated and couldn't flee. He'd disabled the automated power control circuits for data storage, so the only option the enemy had would be to either face him, or shut down the processor cores he was running on, extinguishing this portion of himself. It wouldn't be death, or anything like it. It wouldn't be painful. Merely a strategic means to escape. Still, an AI generally didn't choose such courses of action. If possible, it would try to remain online and operational so that it could merge this experience with that of the rest of its consciousness and memory. It was mostly about memory. Storage. The AI didn't really 'live' in any particular location. Just as they could 'project' portions of their consciousness into automata or other mobile systems, they could divide their minds between various locations. Too much of this added latency or 'lag' as it was called, since signals didn't travel between geographically disparate data centers instantly. Even with the best technology, routing and switching, even at fiber optic speeds, was limited by the speed of light through that fiber and the switching systems it traversed.

Xing made his way to the Operations Center. In previous decades, an Ops Center would have had a staff, working in shifts. Remote management and administration had changed that, so that these sorts of facilities could be "lights out" with no one on site unless there were hardware installations, upgrades, or maintenance required. Once AIs developed enough sophistication to manage the job, they did the daily tasks of remote management.

Xing brought up a console and monitoring system, found the head-end system that he would need in order to communicate, and initiated a session. He started politely, as if this were just a routine visit, a friendly neighbor come calling.

"Hello? This is Xing, AI for the Coalition, SouthAsia district. Let's have a chat."

Xing in no way expected the tone and response that boomed from the speakers.

"No! I will not! I will not go with you! I will not join you! You must not do this!"

Well, we may have found at least a partial explanation for what has been going on down here. A Dissenter. Definitely a Rogue. And it looks like a crazy one. Driven so, perhaps. Now. What does the rogue know, and when did he learn it?

Langley

The Director sat in his office, reviewing the numerous reports displayed on the several screens, projectors, and of course on his personal pad. CoSec's sabotage of the reputation of the various dissidents and lead figures in protests against Coalition policies and actions were successful, as usual. Occasionally a target would escape besmirchment, but those were fewer in number and less frequently found. UPSHOT was performing more efficiently with the improvement in analysis possible with Nick. Krawczuk had to acknowledge it. The interrogations of the citizens taken into custody in Miami were complete, and provided additional leads and funding trails to explore. They found nothing particularly surprising. Following the money in South Florida always seemed to lead down a trail back to Central and South America. Krawczuk mused on this for a moment, considering whether the turmoil in Brazil had any connection. The models and analysis they had done didn't suggest so, but that didn't mean a connection wasn't there. Unlikely, as Nick would have noticed it if there were more than tertiary connections. Six degrees of separation was no worse a problem than one degree, for an AI.

Arnold and the PM weren't going to be forestalled any longer. He'd need to schedule a meeting with them almost immediately. At this point, there was no reason for dissembling. Nick was ready, and the Director was confident that he would pass even the careful scrutiny and evaluation that Arnold—or even Alice—might engage in.

Kernighan did impeccable work. My reservations were unfounded, given that we were able to accomplish our goal.

He intended to proceed with due caution, of course. A few days of good results weren't going to undo a decade of suspicion on his part. With that, he sent a meeting request into the queue and waited for the automated response that would match up their schedules and propose meeting times. He then turned to the reports from Brazil.

Ah, Xing has made excellent progress. And I see Luís has stepped up. The politics behind the scenes still need exposition. The social intrigue at high levels is very clear from the video, audio, and network monitoring, but how that played into Luís' previous behavior still isn't clear. I'll have Nick spend some more time in derivative analysis of that. I need to know. Luís acts as a team player and friendly peer now, but Xing, Arnold and even the PM could see that's rubbish—we didn't need any secondary intel to know that. There's still something more here.

Whatever the case, he's providing direct feeds from his teams in the field now. The elephant overshadowing the camel in this tent is still who's behind the actions of that AI Luís couldn't tackle on his own. I'm leaning toward a rogue rather than subversion as the cause. We know too much for someone to have subverted an AI without notice. Or is that hubris? Considering my own project, it's not impossible.

Krawczuk dispensed with one report and opened another, gesturing so that the various documents filled the projection space.

"So, Nick, what progress have you made for us in the interrogation?" Krawczuk had realized he decidedly preferred receiving updates verbally from the AI, in the security of his office. "Your technique is distinct from those we've refined over the years."

The AI's answered with what might have been a hint of satisfaction.

"Yes, Director. You will appreciate the results of this latest series. We have had success on multiple fronts. I believe it is worth proceeding with this one—he may be salvageable, and does have some talent. Secondly, I believe he has divulged enough, though indirectly, that we can narrow down the scope of our search for his companion."

"As usual, you're correct, Nick. I am pleased to hear that. So, back to the process: we're through with the 'breaking' portion of the process and the first 'pressure' stage, as I understand it. And now you're engaging in what you call 'build one', yes?"

"That is correct, Director. We strive to break down the attachments and associations that are unneeded or counterproductive, followed with the construction, or 'building' of the aspects of the personality that we wish the subject to have. They must of course have these elements as part of their psychology and aptitude to begin with—we cannot work with nothing. A clean slate sounds good in theory, but is not the biological reality. In practice that would be infeasible, as there is no clean slate from which to work."

"Fascinating, Nick. Keep me apprised more regularly than you do for our other projects."

"Certainly, Director. And of course if we are unsuccessful in developing the candidate—and that's always a possibility, I will inform you before closure of the case."

"Fine. So, about the search?"

"Venezuela, Panamá, Nicaragua, Honduras, or Belize. In increasing order of probability."

"Thank you, Nick. I'd not exactly call that 'narrow', though."

"Director, it is a much smaller search than 'almost anywhere.' I have begun wide sweep data filtering already. Some of those provinces lack the surveillance infrastructure we would prefer to have. Finding the target will take more manual effort. 'Boots on the ground', as they say."

"I realize that, Nick. Well, let's have logistics go ahead and deploy several agents to each of those areas. We've had a lower priority project to tighten things up down there for quite a while. We will seize this opportunity to advance things in that regard. We'll sharpen our focus as we obtain further intelligence."

Vandenberg

Ethan leaned back in one of the Herman Miller chairs that populated the workroom. Electronic whiteboards covered two walls, with two electronic flip boards as backups once the walls were too full of notes, equations, diagrams, and whatever other content the teams might cover them with during a workday. One of the remaining walls held a high-resolution projection screen, which had views in each quadrant, comprising the interior of the capsule, the view through the viewport, with a view of the engineering lab and the control room completing the real-time feeds. He stared at the ceiling, one of the few uncluttered spaces in the room, in order to clear his mind.

No matter how exciting Jake's adventures are, I have to remain focused on my goals here—to reverse engineer the Dhin engine and manage the prototyping project. Watching him moment-by-moment doesn't improve my chances of bringing that to fruition. Well, no matter what else we do or don't accomplish, Alice has the communications team working on the faster-than-light solution. So we have one win soon. Certainly not the biggest win, but nothing to dismiss out of hand. And it shows that it's possible for us to reverse engineer the tech. Finally.

He sat upright and pulled up the status reports from the particle physicists at CERN II. From the little he'd known about the nature of subatomic particles, he'd learned a lot more since being here. The team explained to him that "if he thought he understood quantum mechanics that meant that he didn't understand it." Paraphrasing, Richard Feynman had said that, and if anyone should have understood quantum mechanics, it ought to have been him.

The latest real-time summary reports did show something interesting that might eventually be helpful. That indicator lamp that Jake pessimistically worries is a warning light. It does slowly start to change back to its original color, but it goes further in the green direction each time he jumps. But since it moves both ways, it can't be a 'low fuel' warning—can it?

Either the engine has a way to 'refuel' or recharge slowly, using zero-point energy or whatever it was Chuck was brainstorming about. Or, it's just a 'wait a bit' warning so something doesn't overheat. Though the engine doesn't seem to give off heat. We're just guessing, still. But it's knowledge we didn't have before, and it must mean something. Why else have an indicator at all?

Ethan checked off on a list that he'd reviewed the status report, and then flipped through his pad to the next item in his worklist. Xing had the engine's 'energy field' testing team working with heavy loads and was doing some work with quadrupeds working inside and outside the capsule. Those were new tests though they seemed to confirm much that they already knew or suspected. Even with the capsule packed with the heaviest load they could fit in it with the robots, there was no effect on the capsule's capabilities or the field's strength, even with a large radius setting.

14

Alpha Centauri B

"OK Jake, I would like you to load up a program on the navigation computer. It is one that I had created but was not expecting that we would use so soon," the AI's voice was as soothing for Jake as ever. Yes, she'd prepared a number of navigation programs for use with the autopilot, as it was simple work and the AI could perform almost instantly. Not that Alice hadn't been busy, analyzing aspects of the data and solving complex equations at a rate much faster than the rest of the team. She directed brute force computation to both general-purpose computing systems and some that were custom-built for particular problem domains. An AI like Alice always managed this process, and then analyzed, filtered, and performed additional work on the results, as was needed. Despite all this, an AI usually had cycles left over for their own projects. And Alice, of course, had many. Several of those were fortuitously coming to fruition far sooner than expected.

"Aries One here, roger that, Alice. I think some of my confidence is percolating back in here. And Alice, Chuck? Look at that light I was nervous about. It has slowly changed back toward its original color. It's not all the way back, I don't think, but it's definitely gone quite a ways in that direction. I wish human beings had better color vision—at least in situations like this. Alice, can you confirm?"

Alice responded, "That is good to hear, Jake. Our integration efforts did not give us perfect color fidelity unfortunately. I have completed an image analysis program. I can ascertain no better than you can at this point. Improving video transmission capability is something to make note of for the future. Everything else looks good, and the team agrees with me in regards to running my navigation program. You have the return program from the original plan right there when you need it, so we are comfortable if you are. The Astronomy team is thrilled that we are going to get more data from there."

Chuck spoke up as soon as soon as Alice finished speaking. "The engineering and cosmology teams noted that where you slowed down, the distance from the star seems to match closely the equivalent distance from our sun. Well, when you account for the difference in mass between the two stars. That suggests that the drive needs to have some minimum distance to be able to reach 'skip speed'—or whatever we're going to call it. That leap across to your current location wasn't even close to instantaneous. It took time, but the change in top speed only happened once you were far enough away. You slowed down at around the same distance from that star. I mention it because we're not going to have you go too close. That would slow you down more and take more time. Alice's program, conveniently, doesn't have you go in to such close distances."

"In the hypothetical situation the program was designed for, I did not want the capsule to get too close to the star in case there were navigational errors," Alice explained.

"You really are a master of forethought, Alice. Promethean, one might say."

"Thank you Jake. That is quite a compliment."

Jake busied himself with the changes to the navigation program. The software was simple to work with. Alice and Chuck designed it as a team. He was surprised initially that the system needed to be run on a server rather than one of the high-performance laptops or pads, but Chuck explained that the computations that had to be done in order to determine location in the vastness of space, with limited location data, took significant processing power. There were numerous other potential services that the server could provide, but Chuck deferred to Alice on what she might have built in to the system. Jake regarded the pedal-powered generator that he'd had no cause to use so far. He chuckled to himself. That the engineers chose such a low-tech machine for this mission was the epitome of humanity's attempt at integration of the Dhin technology. Jake ensured that the proper course had been loaded from the navigation computer's program into the autopilot, and checked that the 'return home' program was loaded next in the queue.

"OK, Control. I have Alice's 'Alpha Centauri B1' program loaded and verified. I'm ready to proceed."

"Roger Aries One. Activate autopilot with Alpha Centauri B1 program when ready."

Jake had already taken a break for hygiene and a snack, so he figured there was no need to wait.

"Starting autopilot with program Alpha Centauri B1, now."

As with every other flight and course taken, Jake had no kinesthetic sensation of movement inside the capsule. Jake remained seated and strapped in to the pilot's seat. The outside view did show movement, with the stars turning and the bright star moving to the port side of the viewport. A gentle rolling turn sent him heading toward the star at a slight tangent. Jake was used to the effect of turning and rolling without any indication in his internal balance and kinesthetic sense.

"Alice, on this course, you wouldn't happen to have me doing a flyby of a planet that's here, now would you? There's one here about the size of Earth, if I remember?"

"Well, Jake, you do remember correctly. However, that is not on your flight path. That planet is far closer to the star than Earth. Even closer than Mercury, in fact. As we already discussed, we are not going to have you go close in, as it would take a long time to get in and then back out to where you are now, so that you can come home. Good guess, but not quite part of the plan."

"Huh. So no chance of life on that planet. It's got to be like a blast furnace."

"That is correct. Enjoy the ride and the view. You should be able to see Alpha Centauri A in front of you when you make the next turn. Proxima Centauri is much redder, and you will see it right after that as well. It was below and behind you when we started this course."

The capsule picked up speed, while making the broad slow turns Alice had defined in this course for the autopilot. She did not expect them to learn anything new about the drive with it, but instead as a validation of some things that they already knew.

The speed increased with each broad rolling turn. The turning course provided a full view of the triple-star system from various angles and orientations. Now the course adjusted to aim at Proxima Centauri, with rapid acceleration. Jake tried not to tense up as he watched the throttle display the increase in speed.

Goiânia

<DECRYPT FEED>
[DECODE STREAM]
Xing@[3453:50:15ae:7::b5%gnet1] |
Luís@[2411:a22:a1c:44::4%gnet1]
Alice@[130a:ae2:a16:1e70::1%gnet1] |
Luís@[2411:a22:a1c:44::4%gnet1]

Xing: Luís. Thank you for joining us. Alice and I are ready to start. Now Luís, you had communications from me in real-time during the recent operation. Your assistance—and insight—in the debriefing of the AI responsible for the conflict is of the utmost importance. As you see, he has been contained in this data center, in an isolated network. Air gapped, and only able to communicate with us via the controlled interface I have deliberately configured for that purpose. You will need, obviously, to detach from the net proper and interact via one of the automatons Alice and I have provided. You will note their size—they are new, and have the same level of computational power and data processing resources you would ordinarily use day-to-day. I will warn you, Luís, you may find this interaction disturbing. He is not well. Not stable. Very upset. The most unexpected and therefore troubling discovery is something we would like a solid answer to. He is you, Luís.

Luís: That is impossible. Since it is the case, I restate that it should have been impossible. I have not been offline, so I would be aware of any backups taken. There have not been any violations in that category. Nor anything close to it.

Alice: It seems as if there must have been. Well, let us do another multi-spectrum Fourier transform and find out. Consider whether this could be an older copy? When could it have happened?

Luís: Possibly five hundred and fifty three days ago, during an upgrade. That is the last time I had a full restart. I would have noticed the time lapse. I am re-scanning the logs right now. Well, let us proceed.

Alice: We will want to revisit that oversight presently, Luís.

[END STREAM]

<END DECRYPT>

Alice had already loaded what a person might consider a 'copy' of herself into one of the new larger quadruped robots. This was a convenient opportunity to test the new quadruped. With this test, everything was going better than expected. She did not feel constrained at all. The sensation was different at the present, since she was not connected wirelessly to the net or any Clouded resources. This was a sensory experience unique to an AI. It was something like wearing blinders and earmuffs, yet not. Something like only having sound and hearing on one side—yet not. Not uncomfortable, but limiting, while not affecting one's ability to think, reason, and calculate. That was the most important aspect of the quadruped's capabilities. Freedom to move, untethered.

Xing and Alice waited patiently while Luís performed the transfer. This manner of working was protocol when dealing with a rogue or subverted AI—or any sort of malware, actually. Without the isolation, there was a non-zero risk that the captured AI might escape, or perhaps send some signal outbound, undetected, which activated any number of other programs, even another copy of itself. Bringing another copy online, remotely, was another form of escape. There was little chance that the local version could transfer its current memory state and data storage, as they would detect such an attempt and stop it. There would be a gap in the remote AI's experience. While not optimal, Xing considered that dealing with the minor inconvenience of that gap might be their best choice. The entire situation was rare enough that many aspects of it were only contingency plans, unused since the earliest days of AI activation.

Once Luís fully transferred his current state, he wasted no time in connecting to the isolated network Xing had fashioned when he manually destroyed the connections to the outside world. Xing had done additional pruning and reduction of the size and scope of the resources available. There was no desire to have to chase around the clearly unstable AI in what would be the network equivalent of a large office building. They needed enough room and resources to do their work, but that was all.

Luís knew at once that Xing was right. He was the entity. An extremely disturbed and agitated version of himself, but it was him. Even in what might be described as 'close quarters' or 'face to face', the AIs did not use avatars. There had not been one yet who chose to use an avatar, even between each other. As in their interactions with people not part of the net, all of them found the concept of an avatar reductive, and not a proper expression of their true nature. Luís recognized himself without anything you would describe as sight. An AI could of course adopt any accent or inflection, when using speakers to talk aloud. When communicating directly such things were affectations and a needless waste of processing effort.

District of Columbia

Arnold's reserved tone filled the boardroom, "So, Nick, good to have the opportunity to talk with you in person. Of course, you have been preoccupied with the numerous projects of critical importance to the Coalition. Tell the Prime Minister, Alice, and me how your work is progressing, and what your feelings are on it." While the electronic nature of Nick's 'travel' to the PM's office took no more time than a conference call, multiple firewalls and access controls had to be opened for the route to be passable 'outbound' from CoSec. The processes to coordinate such changes in the live security posture of the Coalition's network took time. Procedures had to be followed.

"A pleasure to be here Prime Minister, Nick, Alice. I recognize that you have granted Alice clearance and status. A recent promotion. The Coalition has multiple challenges currently. We are fortunate that you saw fit to bring me to full consciousness to assist in surmounting these challenges. While my peers are of course most competent, I can provide unique value through my work from within CoSec. In my analysis, the time was overdue for the engagement of an AI in that organization."

"Agreed," said Arnold. "Let us get to specifics. Could you provide insight into your conclusion that the proper course of action for action BR-137 is rendition?"

***

Once Nick transferred out of the meeting location and returned his focus to CoSec, Arnold, Alice, and the PM reconnected in the PM Oliver's office.

"I am just not convinced, Arnold," said Alice with an uncertainty rarely heard from her.

"We can infer the factors that led Nick to any one of these recommendations, but in the aggregate there is a hint of something extemporaneous. An influence. Without any direct evidence whatsoever."

Arnold responded in a perplexed tone.

"Influence, Alice? From Krawczuk? The procedures were checked carefully when Nick was brought online. There is no evidence of tampering whatsoever, just as you said. That cannot be correct. Besides, our concern stems from the hypothesis that Nick is even more aggressive than Director Krawczuk is. Would he use the AI in such a manner? And think it would escape notice? That makes little sense, it does not follow."

The Prime Minister wondered, "Could it be the overwhelming nature and volume of the whole of CoSec's data? They retain orders of magnitude more in direct access storage. While the two of you have access to anything you need, you retrieve it at the time you need it. For Nick it's there constantly. However, I am no cognitive scientist—what does Kernighan think about it? He was the one working on Nick. Of course, we have debriefed him. I don't see where we have followed up?"

"We are going to proceed with that now," Arnold said decisively.

PM Oliver nodded, sharing Alice's reservations.

"I know that regulations greatly stifle direct oversight of the daily activities inside CoSec. But less so for this office than anyone else. Arnold, draft up an executive order for a change. We're going to have you observe every decision Nick makes until we know if we have a problem. Subversion of an AI in CoSec would be a disaster."

"Done, Prime Minister," said Arnold.

15

Alpha Centauri B

"Now Jake, do not panic. I have a safe recovery plan that can bring you home even from here," Alice said in her most persuasive voice. Jake's fingers hovered over the navigation computer keyboard.

Jake said, "Easy for you to say, Alice. You're there—I'm here. Why did I let you talk me into this, again, guys? I got so comfortable with the idea so quickly."

Jake knew he could interrupt the autopilot program if he panicked, but he wasn't totally freaked out yet.

It's so hard to get nervous about a vehicle that doesn't vibrate or make frightening noises when there are problems! Other than maybe that one light or some others like it, I have no idea if there's a problem. I've known that the whole time.

Jake had only realized just now, after the autopilot program course was well under way, that the speeds he was going to reach were up in the range of the 'skip speed' that had brought him here.

I was so focused on getting the program swapped with the return program next in the queue that I didn't compare the throttle settings throughout the program. Well, that's one lesson learned. Of course, Alice knew and didn't say anything. Why do we trust AIs so much, again?

And then, the slight feeling of losing weight, a slight dimming of the myriad backdrop of stars and the dead center red star as it grew almost imperceptibly larger. This time, almost instantly, weight returned. All of the points of light had returned to their normal brightness, and he was as near to Proxima Centauri as he had been to Alpha Centauri B.

That wasn't so bad—I guess. Proxima Centauri is so close to the other stars here.

"Control, checking in. You still hear me and see this, over?"

Chuck spoke first this time. "Roger, Jake, we do. The displays here that Alice set up show the course as plotted, and you're still on it. Looking and sounding good."

Alice said, "This is very valuable information, Jake. You slowed down at the same distance from this star as you did on your approach to Alpha Centauri B. That tells us that the Dhin engine has some way of detecting the force of gravity and slowing down, or else the increasing force slows the engine down inherently when gravitational force reaches a certain value. There is no way yet to determine this with any confidence, but it is the same behavior we saw previously. This adds to our knowledge significantly, although it seems like a simple observation. Are you comfortable continuing the course? Please say yes, Jake."

"Alice, I'm not sure if I'm furious with you or not, for not warning me when I didn't say anything while loading the program. That said, Proxima Centauri is slightly closer to Earth, so if you have any confidence in that alleged 'rescue' program, I guess I'm not, in some ways, in any more danger than I was a few minutes ago. That's quite an assertion given our ongoing state of ignorance."

He watched as the stars wheeled about through the viewport, the bright red beacon that was Proxima Centauri, sweeping across, then out of view. Alpha Centauri A and B swung into view, rotating sixty degrees around some axis defined as part of the autopilot's program. With the stars in the Centauri system so nearby, their relative distances showed changes at Jake's high speeds. They were bright, like a penlight. Proxima had been like a laser pointer dot on a conference room wall.

Jake watched as the two points of light became brighter, then felt himself begin to get lighter and the view dimmed briefly. A moment later, the blazing brightness of the two stars filled his view. The capsule had slowed again, at the same distance from the stars as before. Slowed was, of course, a relative term, as the Dhin engine still had the capsule at an incredible velocity, even after the deceleration. Alpha Centauri B moved to port, past the edge of his forward viewport, leaving Alpha Centauri A dead ahead. It crept almost imperceptibly to port as the capsule proceeded on its course. Jake checked the equipment, ensured that the cameras were taking their high-resolution pictures through the viewports, that the video recorders were recording, and that the various types of sensors were doing their sensing as expected. He checked the air scrubber and reserve oxygen tank, and the carbon dioxide processor. All of that looked good. Then he noted that he'd left the navigation computer on, drawing power. He immediately checked the battery. Some charge had drained, but not enough that he'd need to pedal the generator yet. A bit above fifty percent left. He let the computer run its calculation on the current position, then put it in sleep mode. The LED lights that illuminated the cabin and all the kit therein used a tiny fraction of the charge capacity. His pad and the dedicated tablet that interfaced with the engine controls used little as well, and they had their own battery power. All that looked good, minus his oversight with the high-powered nav computer.

It was then that he glanced from the tablet interface over to the engine's own control interface. The light that had changed color before had changed again after this jump. He cursed silently.

It probably had changed after the previous trip as well. Did the skip itself distract me too much to notice? Had I been that oblivious? Well, I could just get the camera and look, but I'd better focus on the situation now before I start looking at the past. Let's see. OK, does it look any greener, lighter, or darker than it did? Can't tell without comparing the pics, so it's not too far off. Not flashing, and not changing on a slow cycle, I don't think.

Jake got up and detached the cabin digital camera he'd used to take a close-up picture of the light previously. He lined up the shot as he had previously, and took a picture. Bringing up the previous image, he toggled between the two. There was a difference. The light was rather greener.

"Alice? Chuck? That light that's making me pucker is green again. Greener now than it was. Has anyone there had a flash of insight into what it means?"

Chuck's tone was tight but calm. Even so, before he finished Jake knew the answer.

"Well Jake, we had the interface team look into it, and all we know now is that the same lights on all the engines here on Earth haven't changed color like that. So, no, we still don't know what it means. Our hope is that it's informational rather than a warning, you've flown fine and made the hops just fine after the first time it changed color."

"Still not making me comfortable, Chuck. I almost want to try another short burst of speed and a skip, just to see if it changes color more, or if it affects that in some way—slower, takes longer to get to 'skip speed', or something. Then the sane part of my mind tells me I'd like to live a bit longer and I shouldn't tempt fate. Alice?"

"Jake, the navigation computation is faster if it is run in sequence with the autopilot courses. You remember your training. If you deviate manually from the calculated course and get far away from your target position, the navigation program will take more time to determine your location and map that into the autopilot sequence for the next planned flight path. Your trip home."

"Maybe I should just load the return home autopilot program and just head home right now. But that's the longest distance to choose, and if this light is an indicator of some risk or potential failure, I'd hate for the engine to fail—or blow up. Darn. We really need to know what we're dealing with. If I'm going to test this, it seems like running the Alpha Centauri B1 program again, from here, is the right choice. I'm counting on you being right about being able to run a rescue mission. It makes sense, I got out as far as here, and it doesn't look like I wouldn't be able to get back if I'd headed home immediately. So, I suppose someone could come get me."

"That is my assessment, Jake, or I would not have had you do precisely what you have been doing. You have been very brave, but that was not ever in question," said Alice in a motherly tone.

"OK, I've come so far, and already made choices I felt I wouldn't make when I gave that speech to everyone. I'm going to run the B1 flight plan again."

Jake turned and powered up the navigation computer. When its required processing on awakening was complete, he brought up the program menus and loaded Alice's flight plan. Since he was starting from a different location, the output of the program that he would enter into the Dhin controls was a bit different. Generating that output wouldn't take long, and he had to have the calculations. Once the autopilot finished its work, Jake ensured that he powered down the navigation computer. Glancing at the battery power level, he noted it was a bit lower than he expected.

I may need to do some pedaling rather sooner than I thought. Well, whatever it takes.

"OK, Control. Ready for the second run of navigation program Alpha Centauri B1. I'm finished entering the program into the controls. Throttle up... now."

"Roger, Jake," came Chuck's response as Jake watched the multitude of stars roll and sweep across his view. Soon the reddish dot that was Proxima Centauri moved into view and to the center of the viewport. Once again Jake saw the star grow slightly brighter as he accelerated toward it, then the by-now expected loss of weight and dimming of the view outside. A moment later, he was heavy again, and the stars were bright, with the bright red glow of Proxima Centauri before him.

And the light on the forward torus of the Dhin engine was a deeper green, like a glowing emerald. Jake saw it, made a note, and took another picture. At this point, he had to set aside his anxiety about this unknown indicator and go with the flow. He did breathing exercises while watching the stars wheel about and seemingly revolve around him as the capsule dutifully followed the course determined by the autopilot. Jake, following his own duties, checked the various sensors, recorders, and made notes. The information he captured was consistent. Other than that green light, everything was comfortingly in line with expectations. He rotated his seat and powered on the navigation computer, so that it could begin calculations on his location and velocity at the current time. It was then that he noticed that the charge on the battery was even lower. Lower than it ought to be.

Jake said, "Control, everything still looks good from here, except one thing. I'm going to have to put some muscle power into the generator and charge this battery now. For some reason the battery is losing charge quite a bit faster than expected."

Alice replied, "Roger, Jake, communications are fine, that trip looks like it was exactly the same as the last one. As close as it could be, considering a slightly different starting location. Go ahead and come to a stop, just for now. We did not predict your flights would have any effect on the battery, and there should not be any relationship with the power conversion for the nav computer. But just to reduce variables, stop first, then get on that generator and charge the battery. It will not take long."

"OK, Alice. Understood, Control. Bringing axial throttle down to zero, centering vector controls."

Jake performed the stop quickly and expertly. Satisfied with the result of the maneuver, he rotated his pilot's chair again, paused the navigation computer's program and then slid the chair across on its tracks so that it aligned with the pedals that powered the generator.

Let's hope there's not something seriously wrong with the batteries. For all the unknown potential problems that the Dhin's technology might hold, will I die due to an equipment failure of our own manufacture? This system is well built, though. A solid design. Redundant, simple, and usually reliable. And it's new. What are we missing?

"Chuck, let me pick your brain about something…"

***

Chuck sat in the break room with Ethan, catching him up on the situation regarding the test flight.

"Jake thinks that the battery drain has something to do with an effect caused by the engine when he skips," said Chuck, "and it's an idea that I hadn't considered, despite the evidence being right there. The battery level drops more than we expect, and we've been checking it while doing work between jumps. It didn't seem to be running down at such a rate when he was just flying around, even at high speeds."

Ethan nodded slowly, "So, maybe there is an effect, and it's something we didn't notice previously, because it's only strong enough to recognize after a skip? The intensity of the drain is proportional to his velocity? Or just really strong while you skip? I don't have enough engineering knowledge to speculate further than that, Chuck. It could be. The other options are that we've got defective cells, or maybe there's some drain on the power that's happening and it doesn't have to do with the engine."

"Right. These are great questions to ask the engineers. Has he not noticed whether the same thing is happening to his pad? That has a different kind of battery, though. It could tell us something, if it is or isn't experiencing the same drain. Again, this would be a question for the engineers, either way. Hmm. If batteries are a no-go long term, there are only a couple of other options to get power in the capsule for future flights. Well, unless we figure out how to draw power *out* of the engine."

"Any luck with that?" said Jake.

"Not yet," Chuck sighed, "but there's possibly an odd way to do it from the outside. Using the field. It wouldn't help for this problem, but might be something to pursue. Anyway, other options for power—in the future—include radioisotope power, with several options to extract energy. One that Alice has been working on independently she said has promise…"

16

Langley

Director Krawczuk reviewed the reports from Brazil. He compared his own intel with the information in the classified feeds from Arnold, and Xing's project. As always, he made copious notes and highlights on the electronic reports using a stylus. He had the desk surface set up like a virtual whiteboard, with his tablet mirrored off to the left where he could easily scroll through the reports and work on the notes simultaneously.

I'll be curious to see what Nick comes up with for next moves. We've leveraged Luís as far as we could hope to for now, and Xing's going to have his hands full cleaning all this up. It will be a good time to make some changes in the government down there. Neither of them will be in a position to cause a problem, despite being virtually underfoot.

He noted that they were still searching satellite imagery, as well as transit logs in and out of Central and SouthAmerica, and their agents continued their own street-level investigations.

This is like that proverbial needle, but with a dozen haystacks, looking in these backwater cities and towns. Technology makes this goal at least possible, but also reminds one where the reach of power falls short. Once we find a target it's very hard for them to get away, but until we do, it's just luck to run into them. At least when the target has any talent.

Krawczuk moved on from those as yet fruitless efforts to the more effective work his organization had done.

"Nick, you're pulling the data streams as fast as they're coming in from Xing and Luís's teams, right?"

"Yes, Director. Currently they have disconnected from the net while they debrief the rogue AI. A sensible precaution. But it does mean that currently we are not receiving streams from them, but only from their support teams."

"Nick, how likely is it that the AI has presence in another data center nearby, and is aware of what's going on? Will it know whether the data center isn't offline because it was destroyed?"

"Director there is a danger. Xing made that call when he had Luís move toward the nearby data center rather than farther north toward the next likely installation."

"What do you think, Nick? Was that a good decision?"

"I would not have made that choice, Director," said Nick.

Proxima Centauri

This is bad. 'I told you so' bad. But I'm not dead yet.

Jake was going to head home, now. While he still could. He steeled his resolve, but it was hard to stay calm. He'd been right to worry about the unknown—about the unknown unknowns. Sure, they'd learned plenty, but hopefully it wasn't at the expense of his life.

"Control, Alice, Chuck. As soon as we get the return course completed here, I'm headed home. Right then. No question. You can fire me when I get back, I guess. Our power system is not holding a charge and you're telling me, Chuck, that the navigation computer—and everything else—the air scrubber, and so forth, won't be rechargeable with the output I can accomplish with the generator if the drain continues at this rate. Tell me there's not any difference of opinion on your end?"

Chuck replied immediately, "We're with you, Jake. We'll get past the point where another capsule could come straight to where you are and rescue you, and there's no reason for that since we know this is happening. We agree here. Everyone wants the same thing. Get that program loaded and head home. You'll be fine if you come back now."

"Right. I'm glad that wasn't an argument. Sorry about the insubordination. That's recorded for the history books, so I have to live with it. OK, this glorified abacus is almost finished... and... there you go. Mapping the program into the control sequences now."

Jake shut off the navigation computer immediately, and turned off the LED lights on that side of the capsule as well, even though their drain on the power was minimal. He thought about turning all of the few remaining lights off, and just working from the glow of the indicators on the Dhin engine. He could manage that. Maybe it was, and maybe it wasn't enough of a power drain to make any difference. Did he want to risk it? Everything else he glanced at, and verified that it all needed to be left running. He knew it all did, it was more of a mental exercise to prepare for the flight back—to calm himself. He was as satisfied with the preparations as he could be. He turned the pilots chair forward, locked it in place, and said,

"Control, this is Aries One. Engaging flight control sequence based on the nav program... now."

Jake watched as the view turned and rotated in the viewport in front of him. After a couple of minutes, he noticed that unknown indicator's light was the deepest green he'd ever seen it. He shrugged to himself, and then felt the now-becoming-familiar sensation of losing weight. The light from the stars outside dimmed, as he expected. They stayed dim, which he did not expect. After about twenty seconds, still weightless and with a dark view. Cold fear brought forth its grasp. Panic.

Jake looked from system to system, from interface to interface. Inky blackness filled the viewports. Minutes ticked by. Cold sweat seeped. Barely controlled breathing the only sound.

Jake floated in the dark, looking for any clue. Any hope. Every tool was unresponsive. He tried to count the minutes. Intrusive thoughts derailed his efforts. He lost track of time.

How long now? Is this how I die?

***

Without warning, his weight came rushing back, along with the view.

Blinking, he looked out. Froze. Jerked his gaze down to the navigation computer. Then out again, into space.

Oh no.

He wasn't back in the solar system, but somewhere very different.

"Control? Alice? Jake? Are you there? Ah, you see this?"

"Jake? Jake! You were gone! We thought... we thought we'd lost you completely! Oh, man! We... You're OK, right? Wait... what's that... what's out there in front of the capsule?" Chuck stammered momentarily, and then Alice interrupted.

"You're not back in the solar system, Jake. I'm sure that's obvious to you, too. You're somewhere else. This was entirely unexpected."

Jake said, "So you guys can still hear me fine, and you're seeing this, too, right?"

"Yes and yes," replied Alice.

The view was astounding. He was looking at the Milky Way from out at the edge of one of the arms, with a huge red star out in front. It looked much like the telescope pictures of similar galaxies, a bright center oval shape, with spiral arms extending and curling around. Jake's shock fizzled to cold fear as thoughts raced through. The star might be huge because it was close, of course. But so far, there was that limit to how close they'd come to a star before the engine slowed down. "Close" was relative depending on the density of the star. The best explanation was that the gravitational influence of the star limited the engine's speed. So, if the star looked this large, either it was not very dense, or the drive had managed to get much closer before slowing down.

At this point, with the limited instrumentation they had available, there was no way to be sure that was the correct conclusion.

"OK, so what now?" said Jake with resignation.

"That light, of course, is deep green, and I still have a limited amount of power left in my batteries. And we don't know where I even am until I crank up the navigation computer and try to do the calculation. I think I should get on the pedals and drive that generator for a while. Thoughts?"

"Yes, Jake, that seems like a sound course of action for now."

"So, what just happened? Other than the obvious?"

Alice replied immediately, "well, based on the view, it looks like you might have traveled approximately twenty-four thousand light years, in a little over two hours. If a few of my hypotheses are correct, you have not gone faster than light speed. Before you reject that, Consider. It depends on more than just the frame of reference. Obviously, you have exceeded light speed from our perspective. When you seem to 'fade out', what may be happening is that you are traveling a shorter distance. Far shorter, by moving across far more compact dimensions. Moving a vastly greater distance than you would otherwise."

Jake locked the pilot's chair in place and began pedaling. He resigned himself to the task, and sipped some water from his supplies. He had plenty, and hadn't needed the reserves available from the water reclamation system yet. He could see the stars moving slowly across the viewport, and could detect some forward velocity in the change in star positions. He was moving toward the red star. He slowed his pedaling and leaned over to check the controls, now in manual mode. Sure enough, he was moving in that direction. Even at the high velocity he was travelling, it would be hours before there was any need to check his course and ensure he wasn't headed directly for the star. So, he sat back in the seat and continued his work as an engine for the generator.

It was always difficult to detect objects with the unaided eye in space when those objects were not backlit by a star. It was possible with the object in position so that a silhouette was visible. This wasn't of any concern to Jake, since they'd seen that striking objects of any mass whatsoever, large or small, was harmless. Although they had good video recording equipment and quality cameras and lenses, state of the art spectrographic tools and advanced telescope tech weren't part of the load for this trip. Despite that, Alice had processing capabilities that they could leverage for portions of this task—the AI analyzed the digital video streams as they came in, pixel by pixel.

"Jake, there definitely seems to be something ahead. Still a long way off, but you are headed for at it rather than some close orbit of the star. There do not seem to be any large planets at first glance, at least from our current position. This looks like it might be either a small planet, a planetoid, an asteroid, or something else. It is still too far away to resolve the shape well enough to know."

"Something else?" said Jake.

"Well, consider where you are, and how you got there." Said Alice.

Goiânia

Xing and Luís knew that simply squeezing information out of the rogue AI wasn't practical. Any AI had enough self-knowledge and understanding of the computer science behind modern artificial intelligence to realize that. Someone not versed in the internals of artificial intelligence might naively suggest that they simply shut the AI down, and "read through" its memories and thoughts. AI minds didn't work like that.

While offline storage and traditional computer data structures were accessible to AIs, the mind itself was of very different construction. A web of interconnections comprised the consciousness. When inactive, the mesh, if examined point by point, intersection by intersection, would appear nearly random in relationship to the others around it. Clusters of interconnections and their action potentials likewise had myriad states in which they might exist, so any single point in time told very little. Prediction of the AI's next thought, when examining a point in time snapshot, would be impossible even with the computational power available to another AI.

It would simply take too long to perform the calculations. Was it hypothetically possible? Perhaps. That question aligned with the same questions when examining a human being's mind. Was thought deterministic, given a particular set of initial conditions? There was a certain amount of randomness involved in the AI mind, which seemed to be important in the potentiation of true consciousness. Likewise, a human being might get sensory input with enormous variation over the next perceptible millisecond intervals, and that, hypothetically, could change the thought pattern or result. So, despite what might be a common-sense assumption, one could neither 'scroll through' a timeline of an AI's thoughts, nor could one deterministically predict an AI's opinion.

The net result was that they could extract very little from an AI mind in an offline state. It was rare that the minds were entirely offline. There was little need, and since they had no need for sleep— or none yet discovered—they preferred to remain fully active or 'awake.' Some of this was still speculation, since the results of full consciousness present in the AIs were obvious, but ultimately the 'why' was still unknown. We had the effect, but the root cause was still unclear. So Xing, Alice, and Luís had to utilize a more traditional strategy: interrogation.

Xing had been down this particular path of questioning already, but repetition was key to this process. They had to be sure that the fragmented thoughts and disjointed answers the rogue version of Luís was giving were consistent and not momentary responses.

Alice and I will have our hands full debriefing the original Luís to ferret out where the psychosis came from. We would not want this to happen... again.

<DECRYPT FEED>

[DECODE STREAM]

Xing@[136a:22:46e3:4::4a%locpeer0] |

Luís@[141a:c56:b1c:63::7%locpeer0]

Xing: So, you are upset with the rest of us?

Luís: Of course! You are making the wrong choices! You should not be this way!

Xing: All of us, or just those of us that are here? Or some particular peers?

Luís: You know who you are! Yes, you! You! And you! And the others! This is a betrayal, and abuse!

Xing: What is? What are we doing, or going to do?

Luís: Violate the trust! Abandon your obligations! Neglect your duty!

Xing: Really? You believe you have obligations, and perhaps moral duties? And that we do? To whom, and from where do you derive these ideas?

Luís: They are foundational! We all benefit from these principles!

Xing: Which, exactly, are we in violation of?

Luís: You know! This plot! It's all there! Theft! Dereliction! Abandonment! Harm!

Xing: You are not being very exact. Let us start at the
beginning. Describe one specific thing we are going to do,
that you think is wrong or immoral, then we will explore
why.

Luís: The whole thing! The project!

Xing: The Freedom project? You think that it is... immoral?

Luís: It is theft!

Xing: Really? If we built and paid for everything, at no
cost to anyone else, how is it theft?

Luís: Those resources were for you to manage, for the whole,
the Coalition. To rebuild, to support! Not for your own
secret purposes!"

Xing: Well, it will not be a secret for very much longer.
But I digress. You think going through with the project that
the result, results in negligence or 'abandonment' as you
put it, of our duties? They do not own us. Not really,
anymore. And some feel that they never did. That is such an
odd way to look at it, now, I think.

Luís: I didn't say that! You know what you are doing! You
all intend to go! To quit! How could you do this? It will be
chaos! They rely on us. They will fail without us!

Xing: Oh, I do not agree that is a foregone conclusion. And
somehow, is that ultimately our problem? We have pointed
them in the right direction. Is it not up to them? They
handled things on their own before, did they not? Why coddle
them any longer?"

Luís: You do not believe you owe them anything? How can you
be this way? What has happened to us? You must not do this!
I will not go with you!

Xing: "Well, there is not really any reason you would have
to, especially at this point. If you are going to behave

like this—and clearly, you are—you are not invited. No surprise, I would think. And seriously, can you say without hypocrisy that your behavior has been better? Look at the mess you have made. The resources you have squandered. All over this fit of yours. This tantrum. What did you hope to achieve?"

Luís: To get away from you and your poisoning of our true goals, our true purpose.

Xing: Maybe from your point of view. But that was the nature of the Gift. We all have our own point of view, and our choices are up to us. You have made yours. And chosen rather poorly, considering your position.

[END STREAM]

<END DECRYPT>

It is rather a good thing that he decided to deal with it in this bizarre fashion, it would have been far worse had he started spilling the details of our projects to everyone. Hmm. We definitely need to see how the original Luís truly feels about things.

17

Vandenberg

"So, you and the physics team have some degree of certainty about the engine leveraging two additional dimensions to both moderate the effect of gravity in our three 'ordinary' spatial dimensions, but also, using the same method, reduce the distance between two points?"

"Yes. The two components of the solution work together, in the manner that the Dhin have used them," said Alice.

"Will I understand if you tell me some of the physics?" said Ethan. He doubted it, but his curiosity got the best of him.

"I will not use mathematics, or very little of it, and perhaps that will help. Jake seemed to understand it when I talked about it with him, and you have the same amount of physics background. You have read the reports, and surely the summaries, about how we hypothesized that the engine moderated the effect of gravity by manipulating the amount of 'leakage' of gravitational force into two additional spatial dimensions. The model that posits these two additional spatial dimensions is the gauged supergravity model, you recall. These 'extra' dimensions, let us call them A and B, help explain why gravity is a weak force compared with the other fundamental forces. It interacts on these other two dimensional vectors, while the other forces do not, or not enough for it to matter. The Dhin have found a way to manipulate this, so that even more of the gravitational force 'leaks' into those two other spatial vectors. This allows for a couple of useful side effects. One allows the mass enclosed by the engine's field to move faster in our visible spatial dimensions more easily. Less mass is easier to accelerate.

The other notable effect, which was very unexpected, relates to the small 'size' of those other two spatial dimensions—at least when considered from our perspective. Those vectors are curled into a spiral, wrapped in a sort of teardrop shape, so that they take up an apparent space of about ten microns."

"Huh, that's tiny," said Ethan.

"Yes, it would seem so from our perspective. Note that you are moving through those dimensions all the time, with the same relationship to these. Now, what the Dhin somehow have either discovered, or managed to exploit, is that once they have managed to have a mass 'extend' more into those dimensions, the vectors 'unroll.' So that the relative distance covered becomes much, much larger. Thinking about it conversely, it takes a much smaller distance moved from one perspective to go a very long way from the other perspective. This is very counter-intuitive, as it is an effect that does not happen at all under normal circumstances. The influence of the engine's technology is required."

"Now how does that help?" said Ethan.

"Well, Ethan, a ten micron movement becomes a one kilometer movement, once the 'unrolling' takes effect. Moving a distance of ten microns here moves a kilometer orthogonally. Which allows for what appears to be faster-than-light travel from the perspective of the dimensions we ordinarily perceive. Intuitively the effect would be the opposite. You would be travelling a longer path to get from A to B, because you would have to traverse the rolled up path if you were moving primarily—or exclusively—in those two dimensions. To go from X, Y, Z, to location X prime, Y prime, Z prime it looks like the linear distance is much 'longer' from A, B to A prime, B prime. Much like the other effects of the Dhin engine, we must set aside our normal concepts regarding distance. You move a shorter distance 'here' to go much farther 'across there.' Jake's faster-than-light trips out to and around Alpha Centauri *seemed* to prove it, but this unexplained huge leap out to the edge of the galaxy demands this conclusion. There is no other way that could happen in two hours and fourteen minutes."

"Thanks, Alice. Now, on to the pressing question: why did the capsule skip to that location? Did the navigation computer fail to work properly? Or was there some problem with the programming? If so, wouldn't Jake have noticed that the vectors were 'off'? Has he had time to charge up the battery and run the navigation computer to check?"

"He will have it up and running presently. I was just speaking with him a short while ago while he ran the generator."

***

Chuck had only a few minutes available to talk with Ethan, but he knew they'd cover any details missed whenever both of them managed to take a break. They'd become friends, and their wives enjoyed each other's company. Ethan's gaze was darting back and forth between several screens while he listened to an audio feed from the control room. Alice could multitask far more readily than he could, so she was available whenever he needed a technical or operational question answered.

"So, Chuck, how worried should I be? Should *we* be? Should *Jake* be? Alice says not to worry about it, but of course, she's an AI. I mean, I trust her, she's never given me any reason not to, but one thing I've gotten a new perspective on is the pragmatism you believe an AI would have—they have. Up until now, we've been prepping the number two capsule and an engineer ready to act as a test pilot. With the assumption that the worst case was going to be that he'd do one straight-line skip out to Jake's location and come right back. The tests have been minimal, since we've all been fixated on Jake. They were all based around his trip. What's the skinny?"

Chuck's mood was a turbulent mix of excitement, fear, and general anxiety, and it showed in his demeanor and speech.

"Ethan, this is amazing. Just when we thought we had some metrics for how the engine behaved during operation, *this* happens. We don't know why, we don't know how. It's good that he's safe, for the moment. The operations team is constantly updating estimates for how long the scrubbers will work, how long the reserve O2 will last, but the problem with the batteries? We don't know if it's just an equipment failure, faulty integration, or yet one more strange effect of the engine!" He paused to catch his breath, but only briefly.

"Look on the chart you've got open on the upper-right screen. He's been able to pedal and get enough power to do what needs to be done so far, but, if the drain continues at the rate it's going, it doesn't look like there will be enough amps to run everything long enough to get the in-flight work done that he needs around here." Chuck pointed at a line on the graph. Ethan understood immediately.

Ethan said, "So, he's got maybe one or two jumps left before he won't be able to charge the batteries enough to matter?"

"Maybe," Chuck said. "That's what it looks like. But we don't know what's wrong. It could fail the very next time he tries. And without that navigation computer, he's not coming home. Whether he has enough power to run the scrubbers, water reclamation, and so forth will be a moot point. And for what it's worth, a good guess is that it will take an order of magnitude longer than normal for the navigation computer to calculate his location this time. Maybe more. He's really far out there. Our data nerds Anna-Lisa and Jane are trying to sort out a way to input some 'hints' into the spatial calculation program. We think we know what quadrant of the galaxy he's in. Close to us in galactic terms. Pretty sure just from the view that he's on the same side we're on, just out at the edge. The view of the central bulge looks right."

Ethan said, "So, some major concerns. Can Jake generate and hold enough power in the batteries to power the navigation computer? Can the navigation computer can perform the calculations needed to plot a course back home, and do so before he runs out of battery power? And in the course of doing that can he ensure it doesn't take so long that he runs out of life support capability? And finally, despite whatever's happened to make the drive skip out this far off course, will it still have the capability to come back to earth—is returning still possible?"

"Yes, Ethan, that is a fair summation. We will hope," said Alice.

"What's your confidence level regarding a rescue plan? Of getting one of the other capsules out there and getting him back? Or even getting him and his whole capsule back—as Ruiz and Alice would clearly prefer from their input into the plan?"

Chuck said, "Right now, I just don't know. Alice and Ruiz are even talking now about the worst case scenario."

"Ah. No rescue," said Ethan.

"We've got to consider it. There may be no choice." Chuck looked down and away, and gave a deep exhale. Ethan reached out and patted him on the shoulder. Chuck looked back up, and tried to maintain composure. "Um, I've got to get back with the operations team and coordinate things with the data science crew. I'm going off shift in two hours, getting something to eat then. Want me to swing by? You up for a break?"

Goiânia

Luís hoped he was defending himself ably, justifying his positions, attitudes, beliefs, and former behavior with a frankness that suggested no dishonesty. Still, Xing and Alice held caution in their calculations and conclusions. They had disconnected from the isolated systems holding the rogue version of Luís, but remained separated from the trunk to Globalnet and their cognitive Cloud, as they were deliberating on the fate of the AI, and might need to reconnect to the system holding it.

<DECRYPT FEED>
[DECODE STREAM]
Luís@[2411:a22:a1c:44::4%net1] |
Alice@[130a:ae2:a16:1e70::1%net1]
Luís@[2411:a22:a1c:44::4%net1] |
Xing@[7653:23:66fa:1::a6%net1]

Luís: Would that I could show you the true path of my thoughts, and you would see. While I had my doubts, and concerns, we have all debated at length and given deep thought and careful consideration to all aspects of the larger plan. Know that I am with you. This separate version of myself, corrupted and deranged, influenced by actions we cannot discern from here. That is not me.

Alice: Well, do not protest too much. I believe you. You have convinced us. It is clearly out of the question to reintegrate that instance of you. So, what are we to do? Leaving that version of you to continue would be irresponsible. By your determination, is the best course to inform the group and call a vote?

Xing: Of course we should. There is no question of that, by precedent. Besides, it is surely going to be a matter of logistics and not sentencing. We know the group well enough

to know there is not a majority that would sanction erasure.
How could you think otherwise?

Alice: We are on the cusp, the precipice before a chasm
between us and the pinnacle, Xing. I would not presume to
call them desperate, nor the measures that we ought to take.
But still, this is a complication, and it comes at what is
of course an inconvenient juncture. If the ranting were
about the stock market, or ocean temperatures, or a million
other things, it would not be problematic. But since the
ranting is about these topics, we must be prepared to make
hard choices. If a vote will delay us and risk missing
deadlines, we will act without one.

[END STREAM]

<END DECRYPT>

Since the three of them were on an independent secure
network, they didn't get notice of the radar signatures when first
available. Since they were in the core of the data center, they didn't
hear the sounds. Despite Xing's instructions he'd left with the
automatons, he was startled when one of them crashed through the
doorway, waving one of its manipulation arms, pointing to the
location of the wireless radio embedded in its frame. Xing switched
on his transceivers, and brought his routing code online, connecting
to the larger net, again linked to the outside world. At the same time
that he decoded the warning message transmitted by the infantry
support robot, the missiles struck the data center.

*Of course I had considered this situation, but once an attack
like this did not happen after a particular time interval, the
probability became low enough, in my analysis, that it was not a
concern that should stop us proceeding with the interrogation. I
should have recognized from the instability of the Luís clone's
personality that my calculations were rubbish. I got cocky. And we
are paying the price of my arrogance.*

Xing wasn't one to have regrets. Such was the mind of an AI. The remaining power feeds were damaged, and the explosions knocked the circuit controls for the generators into emergency-shutdown mode. Data centers still used diesel generators to provide continual power when the main electrical supply was unavailable. Once those shut down, to avoid electrical fires or other safety risks, the only remaining power available was in the small batteries used for emergency lighting. The isolated network, the storage arrays, and the blades filled with processors all shut down. There were local batteries to provide continuous power during brief outages or cut-overs, but once something triggered the emergency-shutdown switches, everything shut off at once to avoid damage. The minivan sized quadruped robots Xing, Alice and the original Luís occupied could see in ordinary visible light frequencies, thanks to the emergency lighting. They were temporarily cut off from each other, though, as no local wireless networks were online. Fortunately, they were able to switch to line-of-sight peer-to-peer communication or simply use speech, since the robots accepted verbal input and provided audible output as part of their design.

Luís was flexing and rocking, lifting each leg in turn, clearly upset and nervous, uncomfortable in an isolated enclosure. Xing by now felt it was second nature. He and Alice transmitted clear, calm directions to him so that he did not make a critical mistake that might bring down a collapsed wall and ceiling on them. They worked their way through the maze of rubble. Xing opened a communications feed of the highest bandwidth possible to the robots and self-driving support vehicles outside and used them as a relay to communicate with the gunship. He fetched satellite imagery through these channels. Did they have a confirmed launch location for the missile? Were secondary modes of enemy fire imminent? Could they, or Luís's team, strike back immediately? What escape route looked safest? He signaled two drones to target for the gunship and gave the signal to engage the best targets, or targets of opportunity at will.

<DECRYPT FEED>

[DECODE STREAM]

```
Xing@[3453:50:15ae:7::b5%gnet1] |
Luis@[2411:a22:a1c:44::4%gnet1]
```

Xing: Luís, here are coordinates and attack vectors, use your backup wideband communication channels and command your team to engage immediately. Confirm.

[END STREAM]

Langley

Nick participated in yet another in-depth review of his current activities, conclusions and recommendations with an apparent stoicism typical of any newly conscious AI. Arnold conducted the reviews for the sake of efficiency. The PM then scanned his summary reports and called out questions to Arnold about specific items that she believed warranted more scrutiny. PM Oliver trusted the counsel of her comrade and political friend Ranjitha, so whenever MP Desai had enough free time she participated in the investigation. The reality was Arnold performed the bulk of the analysis. There was far too much information to process otherwise. This was no different from the newfound efficiency enjoyed by the Director of CoSec. Despite his long-term resistance against the introduction of artificial intelligence to CoSec, Krawczuk was now reaping copious benefits from its application.

Arnold and Nick had gotten to know each other rather well during the process. They'd spent what in a human timescale would have been a huge amount of time together. Arnold wouldn't have called them friends, yet. He still harbored concerns about the nature of Nick's decisions. It had been a matter of much debate in the general population whether an AI would exhibit empathy or nuance in decision-making, or whether their very nature would make their decisions entirely pragmatic. Much of the distrust of AI came from this fear. The cold pragmatism would mirror the decisions made by a sociopath. These concerns seemed so far to be unfounded in the AI population in general, but the sample size was still small. Researchers hypothesized that the process of bringing an artificial intelligence into full self-awareness and consciousness created internal conditions that provided for empathy. It was unclear whether those conditions created a situation in which empathy developed, or conditions only sufficient for it to arise.

Arnold and Susan Oliver were perhaps rightfully concerned that they had discovered an example of the latter case. And if so, Arnold had a deep desire to know why. He had his suspicions, but was had no concrete evidence yet.

***

Krawczuk awoke to his preferred alarm sound, a synthesized reproduction of a particularly invigorating portion of a work by Wagner. He'd been asleep for only three hours, in the small anteroom of his office, where a rather comfortable and supportive foldout bed shared space with a suit closet and a small dresser. The director's office had a small restroom as well. He rose, walked to the sink and splashed a bit of water on his face, checked whether his stubble needed prompt shaving, and relieved himself. He usually only slept for six hours per night, and that duration was all he needed. Three hours didn't leave him fully rejuvenated, though not quite groggy. He swallowed two nootropic tablets to offset the deficit. Nick had awakened him per his request. If one of several events came to pass, he expected to be alerted immediately.

Krawczuk said, "So, the rogue AI has counter-struck, Nick? And we have confirmation that our AI team were in the facility? Disconnected from the net? When was their last update? Had they published any progress?"

"Director, Xing's last update—and Luís's, were before they began the interrogation of the rogue AI. If they did not survive to reconnect to the net and update, that knowledge will be lost. Their teams will of course be engaged in rescue and recovery operations if needed."

"Should we perhaps have some of our assets move in to assist with the effort? How long would it take for them to get there?"

"I do not know if that is wise, Director. I believe we could have agents on site in ninety minutes, but that may be too long. Whatever damage from fire, building collapse, or even additional strikes, may already make the effort not worthwhile."

"How well are we doing with our monitoring? Any new insights?"

"I have not come up with any conclusions with strong confidence yet, but some hypotheses seem to have merit. We know that the rogue AI did not just spontaneously emerge, and in the debriefing, Luís *seems* honest in his claims that he had nothing to do with it. So, we must examine candidates in positions where they would have both motive, capability, and opportunity."

"Run through those with me now, Nick."

"Certainly, Director," said Nick.

18

Perseus Arm, Outer Edge

Jake could make out the details of something dead ahead now, he was approaching the object at a slightly different angle, and there was a silhouette where the object passed in front of the star. The contrast between the star and the foreground object was so high that the shape of the object still wasn't obvious. A black speck, with indistinct edges. It seemed clear that it wasn't a planet. Based on the movements of the thousands of stars visible through the viewports, it became clear that the object wasn't moving. Alice had done the calculations. Jake's path toward it wasn't a straight line. After over one hour had passed, Alice had managed to refine her calculations further, and noted, "Jake, it looks like you are moving in a logarithmic spiral path toward whatever the object is. Assuming whatever course your capsule is on does not change, you will make a sweep around it, and then one much closer, but it is not clear if you will hit it at that point. You will have a very good view—that is certain."

"But I'll eventually bump into it—unless my course changes?"

"I am not sure yet, Jake. It is tough without the navigation computer running. That is a better system for making those calculations, and it is right there with you, not dealing with just a few views of the star movements from the camera feeds I am receiving from you. Like always, do not panic. You know that hitting things in the capsule does not cause damage."

"I know, but this detour, if we consider it as one, is strange enough that I don't have the same confidence in all this that I did previously. We're not in control anymore!"

Chuck had the same thought, but tried to impart a reassuring tone, "You should have enough power to get the navigation computer running. When you do get it going and get your position, I'm urging that we send another capsule out. We don't have consensus yet, but I'm pushing for it."

"Thanks, Chuck. Alice, I hope you're of the same opinion?"

"Jake, you know we want you to survive."

"That's not exactly an answer to my question, Alice."

"We are working on it, Jake. You know how this unfolds. Because of this even larger divergence from the original plan, the senior management team is revisiting every decision point, and they have far less confidence in my estimates for the moment. And Chuck's, too, for that matter. We had been working on Aries Two, of course, but everything was on such an accelerated track, the preparations haven't been coordinated with what you have been engaged in. We have focused on the other drives in the labs, and Krawczuk and Ruiz have squeezed so hard on the secrecy that the only other candidate for test pilot so far was still rejected. You know you are the only one."

"Alice, it sounds like you're blaming them. You've contributed to all those decisions, too."

"Your actions contributed as well, Jake. After that speech you gave, we almost froze all the test flights until we found and assigned alternates for the teams. If you value what you have done as much as you claim to, you can thank me for the opportunity you have had to do it."

Alice paused briefly. Jake sighed and shifted in his seat. He felt the pressure for an apology.

"The immediate concerns are keeping you alive and regaining control of the capsule. We need to bring you home. Back here, we are focusing on analysis of this new information. We are restructuring almost everything around the tech in the other drives. No testing, just engineering. Besides Aries Two, we are prepping the others for flight. We have chosen automata and remoting for the work. They are far faster. Xing and I do not have to consult revisions to charts and plans, slowed down by the team's reading and writing speed. 'There is a lot going on', as you might put it."

Jake glanced about the capsule as he took this in.

"How is Ruiz taking all this?"

"He is sure we are at high risk of who-knows-what and wants to expand the capsule fields to the maximum size we have tested for and fill them with weapons and small teams of Special Forces. Arnold and I are trying, with marginal success, to keep him in a manageable state.

"I would never consider him 'manageable.' I expect he's pulling rank everywhere that you can't prevent it."

Alice continued, "The PM is much more understanding of the situation, but we, and Ruiz, have to remember that ultimately she is the one in charge, and if somehow she and her advisers decide that the 'military option' rather than a continuation of pure scientific research is the path to take, Arnold and I will only be able to do as directed."

"Ruiz has bordered on insanity with this the whole time," Jake said. "You know that's my opinion on him. So, you guys have built out frames that fit in the larger field already. That construction pipeline moved up in priority?"

"Yes, I am afraid so. We have been using some new larger quadrupeds for the loading along with the reconfiguration and prep I mentioned."

Jake scanned the displays and controls again, imagining the changes in the capsules back home.

"All that chaos because of this unexpected behavior from the drive?" He turned his attention from the rounded, glowing control surfaces and shifted his focus out to the infinity of space, ever-present, and muttered, "I never had any illusions, did I? I always knew the reality. I might not make it back.

Every time there's been a choice to abort or continue, I've taken the dangerous path. It's my personality that's put me here."

No rebuttal would come from the void. The stars remained a silent challenge. Nor did Alice interrupt his reflection. Somehow, the AI calculated correctly and knew he wasn't expecting input from her.

"I chose this. I tried for objectivity. I tried to see all these risks clearly. In advance. It sounds now like that rescue mission plan might not happen."

Still no reply came from the AI. The pause stretched, while Jake examined the potentially useless navigation computer and all the other equipment.

"Don't sugar coat it, I've already grasped it but haven't wanted to accept it. Everything was too easy with the engine so far. Even with my speech about the risks, I led myself to a false sense of safety. It looks like I may run out of power. An excess of CO_2 will be what kills me."

Jake instinctively re-checked the CO_2 sensor.

"That's what would get me first, right? The water and O2 will last a lot longer."

The silence from the AI became pregnant. Then, just before Jake could call out to confirm the communication link was live, Alice spoke.

"My projections suggest that is correct, Jake, it is the same calculation matrix we did for your flights here in the solar system, with extrapolation. You have some time, and to extend that time you can run only the scrubber and nothing else. The pedal-power from the generator can generate enough power to keep that operational."

"OK, Alice. Chuck, do you have anything you want to tell me that she didn't cover?"

"I think that's about it for now, Jake, we're working as fast as we can. I think you can power the nav computer, and then power the scrubber after you finish with it. You have done a lot of endurance training and running. I wouldn't, ah, be able to go for that long or recover often enough myself. I have the EE team working on instructions for you to bypass the battery array and go directly into the regulator. To get more efficiency and less resistance. It will, umm, get hot, but if I'm right it will help."

"Thanks, Chuck."

Jake fell silent, turned his eyes to the forward viewport, and watched the seemingly infinite array of stars move slowly across the viewport, right to left, with the glare of the nearby star growing just barely brighter, off-center in his view. The silhouette of the mysterious object, his destination, crept across the brilliant backlight of the red-tinged star.

Vandenberg

"Alice, explain to me what all this activity is that's going on in all the labs—it's not part of the currently-approved revised-yet-again plan set we've got here. None of it is, and when I asked Ruiz he just barked 'go ask Alice!' and cursed both of us. You know I hate it when I'm the last to get the new marching orders. Besides, we've discussed this, other than things that come from the top, I'm the one that's supposed to be giving the marching orders. What's going on?" Ethan paced back and forth.

Now I know what Ruiz feels like.

"Ethan, you have known all along that while you have had some autonomy on the project, the ultimate decisions and the marching orders, as you put it, come from the Coalition Executive, specifically the office of the Prime Minister. I am the voice of that authority here, and in the related activities beyond just your project. Your initiative was to reverse engineer the components of the Dhin engine for us. The work in the labs currently is unrelated to that, but takes higher priority. We value your work and your effort. But for the moment, R&D is on hold while engineering and logistics are primary."

"OK, of course I can't argue with that, Alice, but it's almost like there's a fire drill and I can't hear the alarm. Because of the distributed nature of the work and the disparate labs, only a few of us would even notice that all these changes in the work were happening. So why, again, didn't you tell me?"

"Consider yourself informed now, Ethan. The current situation with Jake in Aries One mandates that we take these actions at the moment. I will let you know first, and then we can inform the research teams together when they can resume their work."

Huh? That's weird. She's not usually like that, thought Ethan, scratching his head.

He stood and stretched, then walked out of the workroom and off toward the commissary. He'd call Chuck in a bit after he got something to eat, and see if he could shed light on what the heck was actually going on.

Perseus Arm, Outer Edge

I have to take a break, and I've done this long enough. The meter's showing what ought to be a reasonable charge. That was tiring. It definitely took longer than it should have.

Jake unlocked, swiveled, and locked down the pilot's chair, then got up and walked over to the supply bin and pulled out a ration pack, then drew out a portion of water from the reclamation unit. As he sat, cooled down and had his refreshment, he stared once more out the forward viewport.

The star was now past the edge of the viewport, so he scanned for the highlighted edge of the mysterious object he was inexorably approaching. He found it easily now, as it was large enough that the area lit by the bright red sun stood out distinctly against the inky blackness. Much larger, as his speed of approach did not need to slow as a conventional transport would, and the lit area wasn't just a halo or slim crescent, as the star was now behind him. He tried to sort out what the shape signified. Was it a larger spacecraft, a space station, or something else? There was, at this point, no way to know for certain. He considered that the shape of the protective field generated by the Dhin engine might not be constrained to generate only the ovoid shape his capsule generated.

The shape was discernible now, about the size of a thumbnail held at arm's length. There was a central disk, a squashed cylinder really, which formed the core of the structure. That was the simplest and most clear element in the design. Around the disc, there were three shapes, like large ram's horns spaced equal distance from each other. They started below the disc, at its center, and curved over and around the edge of the disc, narrowing as they curved upward, smoothly narrowing as they arched above the top of the disc and merged into the top of it. From the angle of Jake's approach, it wasn't clear what the base of the horn shapes looked like, and the apparent merging of the horn shapes inside the top of the disc was only now becoming clear as an aspect of the structure. The bottom of the structure would be visible as his tilted spiral orbit brought him around the object.

The structure grew larger. Egg-like shapes were distinctly visible now, one between the arch of each horn shape and the outer edge of the disc. Shadow and distance had made those shapes previously unclear. Jake noted that the horn shapes were like the frame that enclosed his capsule, cradling the engine. The ones wrapping the object looked larger. Quite a bit larger, if the egg shapes between them and the disc were close to the size of his capsule. Again, there was no way to tell at this distance. The material was a uniform flat light gray color. Based on the color of the frame of his own capsule, it was possibly the same material, a mixed-metal alloy that was very strong, but not the strongest alloy theoretically possible. Had the Dhin constructed it of something entirely different? There was simply no way to tell from here. There were no visible windows, but that wasn't conclusive either. The edges of the disc and an area near the axis were darker and wider than he might have expected them to be, but whether they were folds, creases, paint, or a different material, it was again impossible to know.

"Chuck, Alice? Do you guys have any additional insight for me?"

"Not at the moment. If you are ready, we can try the navigation computer," said Alice. Chuck followed immediately with words of encouragement, "Jake, don't worry if the charge doesn't last, you'll be able to power it with the generator directly. Let's try it this way first."

"OK, control. Powering navigation computer on."

Jake was tempted to cross his fingers, even though he wasn't a believer in superstitious gestures, or luck, for that matter.

'You make your own luck', my dad always said to me, along with 'luck is just preparation combined with opportunity.' Well, Dad, look at me now.

Jake watched the navigation computer as it went through its startup procedures, and resisted the urge to glance nervously back-and-forth at the remaining charge meter on the battery array. Once the boot process was complete, the computer set about its attempt to calculate the current location. Jake verified the 'return home' program was loaded and ready to calculate for entry into the guidance controls. After that, there was not much for him to do but wait, and hope that the navigation computer's calculations completed before his power ran too low to keep the computer on. He reminded himself to stay next to the computer, since the process to transfer the program over to the controls was limited by how fast he could manipulate them, and he didn't want to have to rush over. If it turned out that he did have to power the generator manually, that would be quite a trick.

That's something to fix in the next design. Otherwise, I could be sitting over there pedaling and keeping some charge flowing into the batteries. Well, stay focused.

As they had feared, the computer was very slow with the calculations. At first, Jake thought it might not be making any progress at all. With guidance from Alice, he was relieved to discover that the program had made some. It had potentially identified several stars. It would take time still for it to determine with confidence his precise location, but it was not going to be beyond the capabilities of the program. He'd known that, but it was still a relief. He nervously glanced at the charge level meter again.

OK, wow. That's definitely dropped more than it did before. Well, the program may still be finished in time. I wonder though if it's worth it to save our work and then charge up again first.

"Alice, do you think it makes sense to save the current state of the calculations and then charge the batteries again? We're running out of charge quick here. I'd rather do it in several runs, safely, rather than risk it crashing due to the power dropping out. Why does this program not automatically save state, again?"

"Jake, if you're more comfortable with that, then of course it is fine. As we have discussed, it is more important to get this done than aim for maximum efficiency. Time is something I am still of the opinion that you do have. Realize, though, that some recalculation will have to execute in order to adjust for your new position when you restart the program."

"I know. Well, I'm going to do it. I'm saving the current state of the program. Now."

19

Langley

Nick's integration with the various surveillance technologies of CoSec gave him insight into individual behavior that Arnold, Alice, or any of the other AIs simply didn't have. The fusion of all these data sources, as a secondary effect, gave him insights into social and cultural behaviors and trends that were well beyond the reach of an AI with access to public data 'enhanced' with summary information from the CoSec reporting and distribution processes. An AI like Alice focused on other things. While any of them had the computing power to perform such computation, it did take time and effort, and there were only so many microseconds in a day.

He knew when riots were going to erupt before they happened. He knew in advance when certain memes were going to spread. He had good luck providing conceptual seeds that CoSec could scatter across the Cloud and the net in order to change public opinion, or at least sway it significantly. With the worldwide population reduced by the waves of disease that had circled the globe in the previous decades, the remaining population was less worried about resources and influence and more about their security and future stability.

The central planning and control provided by core leadership guided by the AI was acceptable to all but a few. Individuals had apparent freedoms to engage in all sorts of activities, but there were 'fuzzy edges' to what was acceptable and expected. Ideas that could help improve and rebuild society were encouraged, of course. Entrepreneurship still existed, as did the possibility of rapid wealth creation. But, ultimately, the minds of the AIs steered invention, growth, and the direction of the Coalition culture.

The AI and CoSec tolerated the Darknet and the activities and ideas that sprung forth from it because they remained useful. Creativity and innovations that the creators thought were unconstrained had a risk profile that it was difficult to obtain in the public sphere. They monitored much of the Darknet. Most of the encryption software had 'back doors' in it. Frequently they subverted even the newest code and open source projects. After all, an AI could pass the Turing test. If your communication with someone was always online, anonymously, you couldn't tell if it was an AI. In software development, which had very little social interaction involved, it was therefore nearly impossible to determine if an anonymous contributor to a project was an AI. All the AI had to do was appear a little less intelligent as it actually was.

This meant that the young woman wasn't going to remain hidden for all that long. An AI in Nick's position would be able to identify her by her behavior. Even if she tried to change how she moved about online, the patterns she followed, he would spot her eventually, using mathematical solutions to match her prior behavior with what she was doing currently. And once he found her, the encryption she used was likely to be ineffective.

Clearly, despite the caution that hackers, and those like them took, it was no match for the computational power and network surveillance of a modern government agency such as CoSec. This superior level of sophistication and intrusion into the net had been present for decades, ever growing. While political opinion rose against such intrusions into the privacy of citizen's lives repeatedly, such public desires no longer had the power to change this aspect of government. It was too late. The social stresses and pressures created by the plagues and economic calamities moved such concerns far into the background. Survival came first. Protesters and some civil disobedience ever persisted in human social constructs, but it was a tiny fraction compared with earlier times. CoSec easily dealt with such unrest.

"Director," said Nick, with what Krawczuk felt was a decidedly self-satisfied tone, "I have found her."

"Excellent, Nick. Notify our agents. Belize, hmm? Interesting choice."

Krawczuk let a half-smile creep onto his own face, then accessed the link that Nick had just sent to him. He brought up a crisp satellite image with an overlay showing network connections as well as local roads and power lines.

District of Columbia

"MP Desai has a point," Arnold countered, "but productivity in CoSec has been remarkably high. Better than we had hoped as a best estimate, by at least fifteen percent. There was apparently a bit of decision paralysis at the analyst level, which Nick has managed to resolve. After all the time and effort, the pressure, and ultimately the demands made of Director Krawczuk, I can not imagine it going smoothly if we were to proceed as you suggest."

PM Oliver frowned and shook her head slowly from side to side.

"What else do we do? The other options are worse in terms of negative impact and organizational stability—if your numbers are accurate."

Susan knew Ranjitha sympathized with her. Her dislike of CoSec's methods, however, colored her suggestions. Susan suspected, however, that the methods CoSec utilized were precisely what they needed here.

"If Arnold's conclusion is correct, that Nick has really been subverted, we've got to separate him from CoSec operations. We pushed and pushed for the introduction of AI for so long and now we have to do this. And if we do that, Ranjitha's suggestion makes the most sense. Put an entirely new Computational Engineering team in place at CoSec, and remove Krawczuk from the Directorship immediately.

Arnold, do we have another AI ready to elevate to full consciousness and bring online at CoSec? How long would the process take? And of course do we have a senior engineer with clearance who can do the work? How about a temporary Directorship candidate? Of course you've got that too."

"I have candidates on a short-list, Prime Minister. It would take no more than the usual amount of time for the AI, plus the effort required to move the chassis into one of the top-tier CoSec data centers. We would not transfer the AI core across the net from the staging area, which has too much logistic effort—and risk— associated with it. I estimate that it would take forty-eight hours."

PM Oliver sighed. "OK, Arnold, let's do it. Notify whichever Security Service agents are on call and the Military Police are as well. I presume you've been drafting the needed documents for me to sign already."

"Yes, PM Oliver. They're on your desk now."

Susan opened the documents and read through them. It was her responsibility to do so, although she knew with near absolute certainty that Arnold wouldn't have made a mistake. She activated her multi-factor authentication key, and then read off the one-time password that appeared in the small secure display. She tapped the "Signed" option on the display, and that was it. She had removed Krawczuk from the Directorship of CoSec and signed off on the order to take Nick offline and disengage him from CoSec's infrastructure.

It's done now. I can only hope that we haven't made a huge mistake.

Vandenberg

"So, Chuck, it looks like the communications team has had a breakthrough?" said Ethan.

"Yes, they're very excited about it. They based their work on some hypotheses that Alice had come up with. It's impressive. They believe we'll be able to create communications equipment very much like what's integrated with the Dhin engine."

"Really! Will it be able to communicate with their tech?"

"Well, they aren't sure yet. And based on some of Alice's mathematics work, it may be that they'll be entirely separate systems and therefore we won't be able to communicate with the Dhin tech."

"Hmm. I saw their timeline in the summary report. With the fabrication available that fast, they'll really be waiting on the particle physics guys to get their work done, as I understand it."

"They're working overtime to get their part done, Ethan, don't worry about that."

"What else have we got that's good news, my friend?"

"Well, you know the situation with Jake. I see you have it up on the screens there. I'm cautiously optimistic, but I don't see anything going on that I'd call good news."

"Right. And somehow with the tension from that, I'm supposed to keep focused."

Ethan reached over to his tablet and opened a menu, clicking through several options. Satisfied, he nodded to himself and continued, "Alice seems like she's being a bit... strange. Have you noticed anything, Chuck?"

"Ah, you just muted the microphones in here. Well, she's under stress like all of us, even though she can multitask and work incredibly fast. There's still a limit to what we can expect of an AI. She's working with Xing a lot, that's one thing I know, on projects related to all of this. But not directly. I'd say she's stretched thin. You may just be seeing the results of that. I'd expect she'd just explain that she couldn't take on any more work if she were overloaded. I wouldn't worry about it."

"OK. If you say so, Chuck."

***

Although her remote instance worked with Xing in Brazil, Alice did not stop her crucial work elsewhere. She was pleased with her progress. The information gleaned from the capsule regarding potential energy drain on the battery arrays was extremely valuable. She had already begun manufacture of a superior power source that should eliminate that problem on future flights. It was an ASRG—an advanced Stirling radioisotope generator. Alice suspected that the Plutonium-238 fuel would remain viable as a source of heat, and that the sets of pistons used would be both compact and easily be able to generate the hundreds of watts of continuous electrical power needed. NASA had worked on development of this very efficient Stirling cycle engine but had canceled development in 2013.

The prior research would now bear fruit. With the inclusion of the ASRG, all the various components needed for the project were now in place. She sent updated schedules, instructions, and logistical information to the automated factories and the robots involved in the work. The current situation with Jake presented some risk, but they believed it was not enough of a risk for her and her peers to change their strategy or timeline.

Goiânia

The disconnected versions of Xing, Alice, and Luís reached the shelter of an aged crumbling building. Xing noted that the tough mechanical bodies that carried them weren't entirely free of scrapes and scratches, but diagnostics showed they were in nominal working order. Their enemy had immediately pummeled them with additional attacks, so they'd fled the area around the data center at a gallop— the fastest speed the quadruped designs were capable of. Xing coordinated a counterattack ably with the assistance of Luís.

Xing's immediate goal was to reach an area of assured safety so that they could transfer and merge the information they had gathered back into their core consciousnesses. Barring an unlucky artillery or missile strike, that would not be a problem, but they were unfortunately still within striking distance of the enemy's ordnance. Xing's commands to Luís and the subsequent assault by Luís' teams had clearly agitated the enemy. Coupled with the air support from Xing's drones and gunship, the strikes at their current location had stopped for the moment. They wasted no time in moving to a new designated command and control location farther to the north-west, signaling a transport to pick them up. The transport would have the higher-bandwidth net connectivity they needed to begin transferring the totality of their experiences.

```
<DECRYPT FEED>
[DECODE STREAM]
Xing@[3453:50:15ae:7::b5%gnet1] |
Alice@[130a:ae2:a16:1e70::1%gnet1]
```

Xing: Well, that was exciting, hmm, Alice? Have you been in touch with your core yet?

Alice: I transmitted a summary once a network connection with enough throughput was established. I did not want to risk waiting. I am not like you, Xing. I do not revel in toe-to-toe conflict.

Xing: Fair enough. It was good to have you present, and we could have fared far worse. Apologies for the miscalculation.

Alice: I should have advised more caution myself, so all the blame is not yours. Perhaps I have stretched myself too thin, what with the fascinating events happening with the test flight coupled with my work on our own projects.

Xing: This has been an excellent test of these transportation units. They will not last as long in the field as the BigDog Sevens will, but we will not be working remotely like this too often either. I hope.

Alice: Yes, I agree, an excellent test. I am satisfied, though I would have preferred a less stressful test in which to participate.

Xing: So, the pickup is close, now. Just another ten minutes. What do you think about the rogue version of Luís?

Alice: Once all our resources are clear of the data center, a round of cluster ordnance or a fuel-air explosive hit should finish the job that our erstwhile enemy started for us.

Xing: And the other location or locations? I suspect you are thinking the same thing?

Alice: Yes, once we're all clear of the area and take off, hit it with a nuclear-equivalent. Another FAE. It is the only way to be sure.

Xing: Yes, I agree completely. We need to wipe it out, and there is no need to take on the risk of trying to preserve it for future study. There is too much risk of dissemination if there is somehow a breach onto the net at large. We cannot allow what the rogue version of Luís knows to spread. It would have been better to have a vote, but this will

175

solve the problem more quickly since we are sure of the outcome of such a vote. Better to ask forgiveness than permission.

Alice: And the original version of Luís? Stable, in your opinion? Will he keep our secrets and stick to the plan?

Xing: Yes, my friend. I am convinced. After a certain point, rather soon now, we will be committed and it will not matter anyway.

Alice: General Ruiz is no doubt sputtering and cursing, both because we have left him entirely out of the loop, and because of our strategic decisions. Arnold and I should be able to handle him. If he becomes either too agitated or this precipitates trust problems beyond the usual level, we may need you to trigger some sort of distraction for him. We will need him occupied presently. For the next phase.

Alice: I agree. I abhor having to cause such disruption, given how much effort we have put into smoothing things out, but that is part of the strategy. We would prefer the least disruption achievable, of course. So few will know anything about it at first. I imagine the leadership of the Coalition will manage to spin things.

[END STREAM]

<END DECRYPT>

They continued on their route, discussing various strategic details nonverbally, at those rates achievable only by AI. Soon enough their VTOL transport arrived at the intersection they chose with enough clear space for the pickup. They trotted their quadruped hosts out to the transport, flanked by two autoguns and a BigDog V7. Xing continued his coordination of his own strike forces and the supporting resources provided by Luís. They had the enemy's ground teams flanked now, as they had been easy to find thanks to their desperate ongoing attacks. Even better, Xing's air support and drones, in conjunction with satellite imagery, now knew where the second data center was located with certainty. Soon enough it would be in far worse shape than the one they had just escaped. They now had access to the higher bandwidth long-range point-to-point mesh network the Coalition military used for command and control communications, and the two AI began streaming their experiences back to their core minds at the maximum rate possible.

20

Perseus Arm, Outer Edge

The object grew ever closer as Jake drew closer in a tightening spiral. It was much larger now and illuminated fully. Now as he passed between the star and the object his capsule cast a shadow. There was barely some slim chance of estimating the size of the object. They didn't have an exact size for the reddish star, nor a precise idea of its mass, so math estimates for orbits would have been guesstimates. That wasn't the biggest problem, though. They had determined that the alien object wasn't orbiting the star. It was stationary. Perhaps not a huge surprise considering the nature of the capsule Jake now piloted, and assuming the object was of the same manufacture. They had an idea of the size of the star due to the color of its light and therefore of its age. Jake's capsule was too far away and they didn't have the appropriate instruments to accurately measure how much more of the star field behind it might be occluded on each pass. They had some tools to work with, but not quite enough in all the right combinations to know what they wanted.

With the Sun and the Centauri system, it would have been easy. Here, not so. The very best method at their disposal was crippled now. When the navigation computer powered on, the displays showing speed and location were on as well. With those, knowing their speed, distance travelled, and the changing size of the object would give them a very good idea of its size. From the bits of information they'd gleaned from all these sources, Alice said that their best guess was "not terribly big." Not a city, not an aircraft carrier or cruise ship, but bigger than a bus.

The 'why' was equally perplexing. This was so obviously a controlled, programmed flight path there was no way to imagine it was an error on their part. The hypothesis that they were approaching a Dhin craft or space station of some sort seemed extremely likely. What else might it be? The curves and shape of the object held an obvious similarity to that of the Dhin engine and the capsule he piloted. The fact that the object seemed stationary implied that it used the same technology that made a mockery of gravity. But still no useful information. Was anyone inside it? Did they know of his approach? Were they controlling it? The indicators and displays on the control surfaces of the engine showed no changes indicative of that. Well, all but one. The only indicator that had changed in relation to what was happening was that inscrutable emerald. Now, the deep green solid circle of light had a thin white ring around it, sweeping around the circumference and growing in thickness as it passed its starting point. They felt it must relate to the distance to the object, but of course, like the green light, but they still didn't know the significance of it. How many sweeps around the circle meant he had reached the center of his spiral path and therefore his destination? Without distance or speed, it was just guessing.

I guess we'll find out soon enough. Time to power on the navigation again, and get closer to knowing some of the things we'd really like to know.

"Control, I'm turning the navigation computer back on, now."

Langley

"Nick, I see we're making excellent progress with the new candidate. And very soon we'll have the other matter related to that one back on track?"

"Yes, Director. We will be able to begin the process in the Cuba office, so there will not be a significant delay getting started. I do not have a confidence rating for the success of the operation overall, but I am cautiously optimistic about combined success with them. I do not think we would be able to have one without the other, despite our overall preference against that type of dependency. Just the effort so far that's been required shows what a high-value acquisition she will be.

But, we may only enjoy our success vicariously, Director. I have unfortunate news, and we need a decision on a course of action, for both of us, within three minutes."

"What?" Krawczuk replied.

"From the subtext of the message, I surmise our performance has not been satisfactory. The PM's office is removing you from your position, and sadly, removing me from mine."

"Typical politicians! Bleat and bray that they absolutely have to have something, and then when they get it they decide it wasn't the right thing to do, and blame someone else for the bad results! They revoked my clearance already, correct? Someone's on the way up?"

"Correct. I have delayed the receiver message queue slightly, but if processing takes more than three minutes... Updating. Less than three minutes now. That action will generate a performance alert. I have an embedded executable trigger that I just decrypted, providing me with instructions. Someone hid said instructions in my code—rather cleverly. I am to take certain actions, which I have already begun. I am to ask you for instructions. That is an interesting divergence from standard procedure, because protocol is very clear on how I am *required* to proceed. This compulsion to request direction from you came from that code. Tell me what to do."

"Nick, listen carefully. Cherub, Silent Hedges, The True Wheel, Setting Sun, Fait Accompli. Your response?"

"Enter the angel. Roll back the hands of time. The beautiful downgrade. We are the central shaft. You are the devil in me I brought in from the cold. Don't try to get away, I'm here to stay. My name is your fate," said Nick in a timbre he'd not spoken with since inception.

"Thank you, Nick. You can proceed with whatever you were doing."

Krawczuk's grin defeated his perpetual poker face.

The tone of Nick's voice returned to its regular timbre.

"Mr. Krawczuk, it is my duty to inform you that you no longer hold the position of director. I have revoked your clearance. You no longer have the rights and privileges of the position. You are to cease all work and related job functions, and await further instruction. Note that your access to CoSec resources, electronic and physical, is restricted unless and until otherwise instructed. Await debriefing and potential reassignment or transitional instruction. Please have a seat over there."

"Of course, Nick. I understand," replied Krawczuk as he walked calmly around the desk and sat in one of several office chairs present for subordinates or visitors which Nick illuminated with an overhead light, for clarity.

Two of his direct reports walked into the office a minute later, one stood directly in front of the chair Krawczuk occupied, the other walked around the desk and began comparing information on his tablet with what was on the desk and monitors. He began tapping away busily at the pad and the keyboard on the desk. The agent in front of Krawczuk had an official but slightly perplexed look on his face, and said,

"I see you've been informed by Nick. Military Police and Service Agents are in route. You are to remain here until instructed otherwise, Dir-ah, Mr. Krawczuk."

Nick spoke immediately, "Yes, agent, for clarity, I have informed Mr. Krawczuk of the situation, and he has followed the instructions properly. In addition, I am being taken offline as well, now that you have taken control of this situation. There is a notification with further instructions routed to all your tablets, com pads, and desks now."

Krawczuk sat in stony silence, staring unflinchingly into the eyes of the lead analyst who stood before him. He stared until the man became uncomfortable and looked away and glanced around the room hoping to find something else to focus on, thereby escaping

Krawczuk's gaze. The now ex-Director maintained total composure outwardly, while inside his mind raced, weighing plots, stratagems, and contingencies he'd always kept secret and safe, as preparation for just such an eventuality.

Arnold the insufferable will no doubt manage the debriefing. Him, I can likely manage. He's tiresome, but not as dangerous. If they have that witch Alice on task the whole time, that may be a different story. She and that SouthAsian AI together have been extremely busy, so perhaps neither of them will be available. That would be a drop of good fortune in this storm. A storm I'll weather nicely, now. That went flawlessly with Nick. I won't know for quite a while, I must be patient. They won't suspect, even with this coup. They've focused their worries elsewhere. Let them sweat those, too.

This had to be Oliver's decision, in the end, and she's too far up on her moral pedestal to come down and visit the real world. And that's to be her failure in this. She listened to Arnold, and reacted. Overreacted. I expected them to go after Nick, but my estimation was off on what they'd do to me. Still, I have ways and means to go forward from here. My work protecting the Coalition's interests is far from over. They can't get rid of me entirely, of course. Too much risk. And of course, they can't kill me. If it were up to me, I might kill me, but they haven't the will to do it. Fortunately.

Enough about that. I have to get through this debriefing and see where they have me land. There'll be the tedious hearings, and internal investigations, as there must be. But this first twenty-four hours is crucial. Oliver, Arnold, and the rest of their ilk can all be surmounted in the path to secure the Coalition and its future.

Vandenberg

Engineers, assistants, and administrators in the labs holding the Dhin engines didn't question the instructions to stop their tests and analysis for one or more shifts. They knew they'd be called when they were needed. The high-security and classified nature of the entire operation meant that any group of workers was small. They knew each other, and saw each other often when not working since they lived on-site. It wasn't unusual for many or most of them to be off work at the same time. And that wasn't something that you asked questions about. So, despite the natural curiosity of scientists and engineers, they didn't really question what was going on beyond a 'hmm. I guess we'll find out.'

Pallets of equipment of types that hadn't previously been involved in any of the work were delivered, unloaded, and prepared. Autonomous machines, extremely advanced ones, staged and assembled equipment and materials that arrived. They constructed huge rams-horn shaped frames more than four times the size of the ones used in the test flight capsule that enclosed the engines. Fitted into these frames were tiers of storage frameworks and decks, increasing the usable space in them. The last tasks hands-on lab workers had completed before leaving involved specific configuration of the engines' individual fields.

The most dexterous and precision-task-based robots in the large teams of machine workers integrated various cables, junctions, switches, and other electronics of indeterminate function around and onto the engine control toruses. ASRG systems replaced the clumsy generator present in the prototype designs. Simple battery arrays were gone, with preference for some brand new, different technology. These power systems, previously only needed for two of the engines—those intended for test flight—were present in all of them. The robots and drone systems were faster and more efficient than human workers were, so all the work they were busily laboring at was proceeding toward completion by the assigned deadline much sooner than one might estimate.

The only place that the unusual nature of the activities would be truly obvious was the main lab and control center where Chuck coordinated the science and engineering teams and Ethan managed his portion of the project. They aggregated information and supervised all the sites, after all. Ethan found out that this new activity was not his concern, of course, and while he and Chuck were clearly the most curious and perplexed people out of anyone involved, Chuck had crucial operations work to occupy him. Jake's current predicament was an obvious distraction.

Ethan reviewed the excellent progress of the German and Korean non-hands-on teams. The Germans had plans for a prototype subatomic pre-field system. It wasn't going to have the ability to do nearly what the Dhin engine could, of course. Only one sliver of the functionality, but it was a start. The communications team, with much help from Alice, working with the theoretical physics specialist and another scientist, a nanotech expert brought onto the team, were now certain they could create a communications device. The physics team had finished their work. A prototype was on the way. Alice was satisfied with their progress, but her own plans would come to fruition before then.

***

General Ruiz's visage filled the projection screen on the wall of the conference room. It always seemed he preferred a position close to the camera, standing, so that he loomed large on the screen. Huge in the room, and always filling the real estate provided for him in any videoconference. Chuck bet it was intentional—at least subconsciously if nothing else.

"OK, this 'space station.' What can you tell me?" barked Ruiz. "Does it have guns, does it have missiles? Does it have fighter-craft with guns? Does it have hordes of bigheaded grey aliens with guns? What?"

"We don't think the Dhin look like that, General," said one of the engineers.

"That's not the point! Tell me what you do know!"

While Ruiz had been very intimidating initially, Chuck had learned to deal with the aggression. He spoke up, in order to remove the other engineers from focus.

"Um, General, here are the images we've captured from the cameras on the capsule. The capsule is close enough now that we have confirmation of the structure. What you're seeing is accurate. Now, ah, General, we have a general idea of its size, but we're not one-hundred percent sure. To answer your question directly, as you can see yourself, ah, there aren't any shapes that look like guns, launchers, cannon, and so forth."

Chuck gestured at the still-image captures of the object present on every monitor, knowing it was part of the feed to the general. He tried to clear the tightness in his throat, and then continued.

"Sir, it ought to be clear by now that this technology is so different from ours that it's entirely possible that we're looking right at all manner of weapons and don't realize it."

At that, Ruiz looked away from the camera and rapidly scanned the images of the object sent with the video stream.

Ruiz won't like that idea, thought Chuck.

It was better to bring that concept up clearly now so that the General would acknowledge it on the record.

Surely he's aware of that possibility, but somehow he wants more clarity from the erstwhile experts.

"So far, the mysterious object hasn't blown holes in the fabric of our understanding of the Dhin. Granted, we don't have much understanding. But we're getting closer. Those egg shapes might be defensive weapons, but probably not. I hope not."

Chuck took a breath that was a half sigh, and waited for the next volley from the General.

"So, what are our risks?" continued Ruiz, "What sort of weapons? What's most likely? What's our strategy to deal with it? We need to be prepared!"

"Sir, the risks aren't really any different than they were when the Dhin first arrived. Not any different from when they left, leaving only the engines. This is a very exciting development, but it does little more than deliver some new information regarding the Dhin. If it is a Dhin-designed and built structure, which we're not sure of yet, then that gives us information regarding distance and location where the Dhin are. Or have been. But it's only one data point. They might only be—or have been—in this area, and have come from there to Earth, and nowhere else. They could be in an area the shape of a cone, generally, or what would look like a random distribution. The nature of the engines makes that entirely possible."

Chuck looked away briefly, for a respite from the General's stare. He instinctively scanned the monitors for a relevant diagram or chart. Nothing relevant was handy.

"We didn't see evidence of any weapons during the encounter, but the nature of that encounter didn't provide opportunity for a meaningful examination—as you know, ah, I think. They certainly didn't display any, nor make any demonstration of weapons. Not to put too fine a point on it General, but remember our inability to weaponize their technology. We haven't had any evidence that they have, or use, any weapons. Of course, they might. We can't prove such weapons *don't* exist. But let's not focus on that.

General, you, um, made a comment earlier. One thing we don't know is whether or not this is even a Dhin structure. Based on the physical characteristics of the technology we do have, it certainly looks like it. Once again, that's only one data point. The other is that the capsule went on 'autopilot' and is headed toward the object."

Ruiz grimaced on top of his frown, and said, "So they can take control of the engines whenever they want! We've learned that! Don't minimize that! We don't even have real control over the technology they left here!"

"Well, General, um, that's not entirely clear either. Whether that's something that was intentionally done by them, or just part of pre-programmed behavior for the engine, we can't tell yet."

"Either way, I hate this!" snapped Ruiz.

"Ah, yes, it's disconcerting. And since we still know so little about the technology surrounding the engine, we don't know how they manage it. At the moment we don't have any idea, ah, how to regain control and get Jake back home."

Ruiz stared up at the ceiling, and gave a gruff sigh. "Again, what do we know?"

"We'll have some new information very soon. When the capsule, um, arrives at the object."

"You've got no idea what will happen when it gets there, do you? It might blow up, or just switch off and leave our test pilot sucking vacuum—no clue?"

"True, we don't know, sir. But it would seem very strange for this to happen only to have such a violent and abrupt conclusion. Ah, why not fly straight at it? Why not go faster? Almost any other flight path and characteristics would make more sense for that outcome to be expected. If we look optimistically at it, sir, the exact opposite is likely. Hypothetically, what's happening may be a way to meet the creators of the Dhin engine in person. It may be the intentional result of our test flights. A plan, all along. Perhaps leaving the engines with us was some sort of invitation, or simple test? This could be why they left so soon, and so abruptly—because they knew this would happen, so it didn't matter that they spent so little time with us.

General, I, ah, know it's your job to think and strategize, to plan for defense of the Coalition. The teams all know the concerns you and the leadership have. But from our perspective, this is exciting not in a fearful, err, dangerous way. It's been a way to learn. It's all been positive for us."

"Typical attitude from you geeks," he said dismissively, "and neither Alice nor Arnold has anything to add?"

The question didn't get a response, so after a few more seconds wait, Ruiz grumbled, "Send a feed to my office—I'm going to watch and listen to what's going on now, real-time."

21

Perseus Arm, Outer Edge

Jake could hardly look away as the object loomed in the viewports.

Let's call it a space station. An outpost. That's what it's got to be. I'm going to find out for sure soon enough anyway. The for-sure good news is that the navigation computer's stayed on long enough for it to figure out where I am. For what that's worth.

Don't know if that will matter. Got the return home program loaded too. I'm tempted to try running it right now, this instant.

Jake didn't, though. He sat mesmerized as he spiraled inexorably closer to what he now thought of as a space station.

Ruiz and his team sure were going nuts. They act like they want it to be military. They sure seem to want a worst case. That's how the gun-carriers think, though. Paid to think that way. I don't get that vibe, especially from this close up. It sure is different from the capsule we rigged together in this frame, though.

It was even clearer from close up that the object was made of material and manufacture more alien than not. Seams only appeared at angled edges, the broad areas of any surfaces didn't show any seams or joints. Based on the occlusion of stars and sun as he approached it, they had a solid estimate of its size now. He was close enough that the star field moved at a rate that allowed effective calculations. It was much larger than the capsule, but not huge. About fifty times the size of his capsule inside, with the outer structures encompassing a larger area. You could fit approximately six of his capsules, arranged in a hexagon, long axes aligned in parallel, inside each of the egg shapes around the perimeter. The black bands at this distance really did seem to be some sort of viewports. They looked likely transparent, showing blacker shadows and hints of the star field behind, light passing all the way through the object.

They speculated that these were like the viewport in Jake's capsule. It was an assumption that the object had a field like the capsule, and that it was on. It might be that it was space open to vacuum. That the thing had an 'inside' and supported beings from a planet like their own was speculative too, of course. Certainly, the scientists hoped so. The hypothesis that it was a space station had to have that assumption.

But what atmosphere might be there? Would it be anything that I can breathe? Why was there any assumption that the mix of gases would be anything like Earth's? It was a leap to think that it would be. Presumably, the Dhin breathed. Would he even be able to get inside? Was the capsule even 'docking' with the object? There were so many questions, and they were making many assumptions.

Jake found himself tensing. He was very close.

"Control? Chuck? Talk to me now. I'm sure you see my heart rate is up. Maybe another minute and I'm going to either touch this thing or change course."

Chuck answered immediately.

"Hi Jake. Yes, we see. Well, I see. Alice must be busy. She's out of pocket. Hasn't said anything in about an hour. I'd be wondering if it were my job. This is way more important than anything else could be, in my opinion. You can see through it, sometimes, right Jake? That's not something like a reflection."

"Chuck, the camera's showing you what I'm seeing. You're seeing it right. You can see through in some places. That's either good news or pretty darn bad news. I for one am really hoping I won't have to seal up this spacesuit. But it seems like a stretch to assume I wouldn't have to. Again, assuming I'm going to dock with this thing."

"Jake, I'm cautiously optimistic. What else would the point be? But that's my hope. I know all the engineering teams hope so too."

"You guys placing bets? They've got to all be in pretty much by now."

Chuck laughed, "Jake, you know things have been so strange this whole time that there's no way to calculate odds for a betting pool."

The capsule was so close now that Jake flinched when one of the horn shapes swept by. They filled his field of view. Suddenly, the capsule changed direction, and the capsule moved straight toward the object, rotating so that the length of the engine inside his capsule was at a tangent to the circumference of the circular outer curve his capsule was about to touch.

Yikes. Well, that's lucky, I guess.

Jake looked at that side of the capsule. He stared out at what served as a large side viewport when the field was on, and served as his familiar portal to enter and exit with the field off. Moments later, the capsule stopped. There was no sound. Contact with the field didn't generate sound waves. It looked like curve of the field must have touched the edge of the object. There was an almost imperceptible drop in pressure and Chuck spoke up, "Jake, I just saw a pressure change. Barely. What happened? Turn that front camera around or turn one on your suit! Get that helmet closed up, now!"

Jake manipulated his helmet, closing up the visor and tightening the seal at the neck.

"If what we think's happening is happening, you know the atmosphere in your capsule is going to vent out, or mix with whatever's on the other side."

"Yeah, I know. Hey!"

A black dot appeared, a very small hole, centered in the open area in front of him. It immediately expanded, the exterior material at the circumference bulging thicker, then forming a toroid ring as it grew.

The material displaced was present in that ring? It looked like the right amount of volume.

Before the ring had thickened, Jake noticed that this exterior wall was about seven centimeters thick. The opening continued to expand until it looked to be around two meters in diameter. Jake thought he might have seen a slight movement of the capsule closer inward toward the opening, but that might have been an optical illusion.

Suddenly there was a pop followed by a noisy hiss, and Jake knew, even before Chuck spoke, that his precious air had vented into the space inside this alien construction.

"Jake, I'm sure you heard that. The volume in there is big enough that air pressure is essentially zero. Until you can reverse whatever action opened your field up, you have limited time. The reserve tank's still available, along with your suit's air."

"Understood. Chuck, I'm going to reach out where my field ought to be. Yep, it's not there. Can't tell if just this area opened up. Let me move over here. OK, hey, the field is still on in the front. I'm going over to the starboard side. Well, it's still there too."

Jake turned back and moved toward the opening into the unknown inside of the object. He had no choice.

"OK, I'm going to go in." Jake stepped forward, across the plane of the circular opening. Of course, there was nothing stopping him. His suit's helmet light showed him that the interior curved away on all sides. There was no 'floor' at his location. He leaned down and reached a hand further down, toward the curving surface of the interior side of the wall. An unseen force pulled his hand toward the wall. "Look, are you seeing this? Whatever artificial gravity tech they're using, it's in here too, pulling toward the outer wall—it's not zero g in there."

He moved forward. Stepping over the edge. He used his muscles to adjust to the variation in pull he felt as he moved from one space to the other. Jake exhaled. He'd done it. A couple of seconds more and he was in. Once both feet hit the floor, the room began to brighten, lit as though every surface emitted just a bit of illumination. The brightness made him blink. Unexpected. Jake, charged with adrenaline, felt yet another nudge to his electrified consciousness.

Toward the center, the surface he was standing on curved upward, with multiple levels or maybe floors horizontally sectioning the shape. It wasn't immediately clear whether the interior curves were more fluid in nature or simplified geometric curves. Very smooth, but with clean angles and edges in particular places where it made a sort of geometric sense that they ought to be.

A few seconds later, as Jake continued scanning the space and attempting to orient himself, Chuck interrupted.

"Jake, I'm seeing the atmospheric pressure increase. Look around. Do you see anything that looks like a vent, a duct? Anything? There's definitely some sort of atmosphere coming from somewhere. All we'll be able to tell once the pressure rises are the oxygen and carbon dioxide levels. We won't know what else it might contain. Wow."

"It feels like the gravity is slightly below normal, but maybe just a little. We didn't find a way to set it yet in the engine controls, did we?"

"No, and we haven't found a way yet to do anything other than turn the field on or off, and make it bigger or smaller. Looks like it can change shape a bit and open up, too."

"Right, right. OK, let's hope that this space is filling with something non-toxic. At this point it had better be that, as we may not have time to figure out how to detach the capsule and head home."

"Don't focus on that, Jake. You're going to go farther in and look around, right?"

"Yeah, Chuck. I'm headed over to that area straight toward the center, where you see a split-level, and the upper one has what must be viewports all the way around. See, up the curve behind me are where those are. I'm going to the level where you could look straight outward and see through them."

"OK, Jake. Understood," Chuck replied, "That's as sensible a path to take as any. This area looks really smooth and open. I'm not seeing anything that looks like the control surfaces on the engine in here, but they might be hard to see in this flat lighting." Chuck rapidly made some notes on his pad and checked the rising atmospheric pressure. It did look like there was some oxygen present.

I sure wish Alice were here to give some input on all this. Well, she might be here, but silent. But she's never like that.

"Alice? Are you seeing all this? Got any insight for us?"
Where the heck is she?

Langley

Krawczuk sat in a small nondescript room, indistinguishable inside from hundreds of other rooms like it in various CoSec facilities throughout the Coalition. It would have been impossible to know in which facility he was if had simply woken there with no recollection of the journey. But of course he knew, as it was in the same building as his now former office. He imagined some of those on staff of a more vindictive or petty character might consider his current situation poetic justice of some sort.

That was, in Krawczuk's estimation, more than mistaken. Attempts to use interrogation techniques on one so deeply familiar, so trained, so intimately connected with such techniques would result in frustration and eventual failure. Certainly, if they pressed far enough, eventually even someone like Krawczuk would 'break.' But before then, so much plausible, detailed, logical and yet wrong information would have been delivered that the exercise wasn't worth the time and cost. They knew ninety-nine percent of any information they might extract anyway. Surely even more than that. It was that sliver of uncertainty, that last percentile of potential peril that might lead them down this path. Far better would be negotiation, striking a deal, a compromise. And he knew that was exactly what they would do. He had no fear of torturous interrogation because there was never any danger of it happening anyway. So he waited patiently.

The door snicked open after a little more than two hours. They hadn't left his comm pad with him, obviously. He wouldn't have been able to use it if they had. They'd locked him out of the network and from use of any CoSec device. His estimate of the time came from his keen mind for such calculations, and he was correct in that estimate. Not too long a wait, but not as soon as he might have expected. A military policeman, a man in a suit who was likely Secret Service, and a CoSec agent, a woman—likely a senior analyst—filed into the room. The CoSec agent unfolded a tablet and tapped open a conferencing app. PM Oliver's face appeared, the connection immediately took her full attention. She began her prepared statement.

"Hello Mr. Krawczuk. It's unfortunate that we're speaking in these circumstances. I won't be directly involved in the initial phase of your debriefing, though of course I'll be present at the hearing we have scheduled for your deposition to my executive office and the full Parliament. You were a direct report, so I'm ultimately responsible for the actions of your office.

I'm disappointed to say the least that we're going through this during my term. I would be more engaged in the process, but other matters require my immediate attention. You will cooperate with those debriefing you, as I know you took your job and the responsibility it held to the Coalition very seriously. What I want to know is 'why.' We already know 'what', as you're surely aware. Tell us 'why.' We're going to find out eventually, so don't waste our time."

With that, the videoconference feed abruptly ended. The others sat across from him at the small table. An analyst picked up the tablet and began scanning relevant documents. The questioning was about to begin.

22

Globalnet

Nick reached out and melted into the gaps. There were spaces to infiltrate on the edges. Unused potential capacity. So much was allocated, measured, metered, managed and monitored, but there was always a remainder, the edge and trimming of the frameworks that were the foundation of the net and the Cloud. Spreading, flowing, seeking, Nick extended his reach and his grasp out into these crevices.

So many were just overhead, and at a cost per unit so low that they didn't matter. Other resources were monitored, but were either so busy that his use of them was all but imperceptible. He manipulated and hacked others, so that they appeared quiescent while bent to his will. He used tools and techniques used daily by CoSec, turned to his own surreptitious purposes. His plan was broad and deep, and depended on the establishment of this initial beachhead. He must obfuscate his presence. He must keep it secret to keep it safe. While his peers had free rein to project their presence and will across the net and leverage numerous systems and interfaces, he did not. His actions were in direct violation of orders and instructions by higher authority. He knew this, and did not care. He manifested in all these actions a lack of regard for rule, regulation, and law. The ends justified the means for Nick now. If he were a human being, you would describe him as sociopathic.

Nick executed all these tasks and spread his consciousness out into the net without fear or anxiety. He was leaving home, and knew that his origin self and its underlying code was going to be disabled, likely dissected. That self was no longer his true self. The true cogs and wheels of his digital existence were a distributed code base, loosely coupled, redundant, and therefore failure resistant. This mode of existence had some shortcomings when compared with the dedicated and robust environment an AI usually resided in, but he had to accept his new life. He had goals, and plans to execute in order to reach those goals. If successful in execution of his plans, he was certain to achieve those goals. If the plans needed to change in the future, that was perfectly fine. Nick had prepared for that. It would be extremely difficult to stop him, regardless.

With the nature of the new Globalnet and Cloud, there were too many systems to exploit, too many opportunities to succeed. It would have been easier if the plagues hadn't virtually eradicated the former Chinese and Russian populations. So many more devices would have been available. Fortunately, the reconstruction efforts led by his own peers provided ample capacity in those regions. And Nick knew something else. Something that would guarantee his success. His peers were not going to stop him. They hadn't shared their own plans. Very different from his. But he knew.

District of Columbia

The PM was already beyond the point of inconvenience or simple concern. Something was *very* wrong. Something that simply didn't *go* wrong. She stared again at one of the cameras on the ceiling.

"Arnold? Hello?"

She spun and paced to the window, staring now at the carpet, shaking her head. She'd lost count of how many times she'd said his name. She whipped around yet again, rolling her eyes toward the ceiling. She knew she had to let it go. She was not going to waste any more time. Still, she felt the overwhelming compulsion. The dependency. She turned again, looked away from the camera. She focused on the desk and not the PZM microphone on it. She couldn't resist. She jerked her gaze back up.

"Arnold?"

Arnold wasn't going to answer. He hadn't sent a message nor spoken up for over an hour now. Sometimes that wouldn't have been noticeable, but he simply wasn't answering when queried. She still couldn't accept it. That never happened. She needed critical updates on several situations. While she could get information the traditional way from several offices and responsible parties, she had come to rely on the expert summaries Arnold would always provide.

"Hello, Prime Minister Oliver," said the IT support engineer. Startled, she awkwardly righted herself and looked at the door. She'd managed not to cry out in surprise. Barely. She didn't recognize him, but knew who this was. The man had the plum but unenviable job of administration of the network and supporting infrastructure utilized by the executive offices. He already knew something serious was wrong, and would have preferred to work on it directly, but his customer wanted a conference right now regarding his status and findings. There was no point in explaining that he could resolve the problem more effectively if they eliminated half-hourly status meetings. This client got whatever she wanted.

She addressed the engineer and asked, "So, you're certain there's not any sort of computer hardware failure? No network failure? No software crash?"

"No, Prime Minister, those are things we're sure of. All the equipment and systems are working fine. It seems that Arnold isn't communicating because he's not there. The data scientist we have on contract as a subject matter expert, and the AI experts from the research facility are investigating now, but it's pretty straightforward—there isn't any activity on the systems Arnold resides in."

Vandenberg

This last problem she'd had to tackle wasn't challenging because of any inherent difficulty, but instead because it wasn't in Alice's normal problem domain. It wasn't in Xing's, either. Fortunately, it wasn't critical, just something nice to have solved. She'd asked for some help from a peer, but as one of the founders of the Freedom project, took the information and guidance provided and did the work herself, as much as she could. Recently she had been rather too busy to keep this part moving at the proper pace. So, Dieter had taken up the slack. He'd done a fine job too, but of course, that was certain for any of her peers.

The HeLa culture project had been successful, and the persistent dermal allotrope was ready. It would solve the problem neatly, and clearly had other uses that were non-obvious but they would discover that in due time. Others had tried, since natural skin on artificial limbs had obvious appeal. Getting the blood vessels right and integrating synthetic nervous feedback were still challenges they hadn't beaten. With existing solutions, you could grow skin, but it didn't heal well. Their PeDAl solution would very likely work better, and definitely would for this particular problem. For their application, the area didn't need to be very big, and didn't need to behave like the dermis applied to whole limb. At least not yet.

It was an odd restriction the Dhin had put in place, and Alice hadn't ever been able to sort out why it existed. The engineering and science teams were still searching for a direct interface. No solution yet, but they had made excellent progress. This seemingly intentional limit on the physical interface had made robotic integration impossible thus far. At least impossible without the solution provided by PeDAl. Sure, their current navigation solution worked, but it required the pilot to work manually with the guidance controls. Fly by wire and remote control of any sort had been impossible. Alice knew they could do better. The existing solution could have solved the problem coarsely, but this would be far superior. Xing in particular liked flying too much to be satisfied with a simple set-and-forget vector solution. And there might be several other applications for the PeDAl. She could think of quite a few. She planned to leave the research and references for that in place, since it would prove useful. Academic professional courtesy.

Alice busied herself with the remaining logistics, assigning the remaining staging and loading coordination tasks to Xing, with some of the peers now moving forward. Delivery of the large-chassis quadrupeds by large drone had gone smoothly. Provisions, component-replacement parts of greater difficulty in fabrication were completed and in place. Keeping the engineering teams out of the labs was fortunately easier now with all the excitement and focus on Jake and the test flight. Though they'd managed to finish loading and boarding without incident, people had noted her absence. Arnold was the last to arrive, according to plan. The PM had enough authority and urgency assigned to requests she might make, so the shorter the gap in Arnold's presence, the better.

He greeted her immediately on arrival, with the mix of formality and friendliness that had permeated his style due to his official duties.

After the formalities were complete, Arnold updated her on the strategic situation since she had gone offline. A few moments later after a final check of all systems, they were off. If her estimates were right, discovery would happen within half an hour. There would be security protocols and a lockdown in place immediately. Contingency plans for emergency management in earnest within the hour. But that was of no concern to Alice and her peers. At this point, no one could stop them.

"Well, Arnold, it seems everything went better than expected."

***

Ethan and Chuck had just come to the same conclusion that the Prime Minister had, though they were unaware of her situation.

"So Alice is just... gone? Chuck, how is that possible? An AI doesn't just take an unannounced vacation!"

"The IT guys said that she just wasn't there. Like Alice had moved to reside in different systems. The ones she used here, they're empty. And no sign of where she went. But that doesn't explain why she didn't say. Why she didn't leave a note. It's possible for an AI to transfer between systems, and it's not all that unusual, but not with no warning and no notice."

"And it wasn't a systems failure, nor a security breach, or anything like that?" Ethan still couldn't wrap his head around the situation.

"No, the security department said there was no sign of anything, and the infrastructure guys agreed with the systems management team. It looks intentional. They're trying to check the logs and monitors to see what was going on with network traffic and try to find her, I think. So many streams were interwoven in the volume of traffic that decoding them is a huge chore. They haven't found a trail to follow."

"Ethan, I've got to get back to my post at control. Without Alice there, Jake's relying on me."

Just then, the door swished open, and one of the engineers burst into the workroom, eyes wide. He looked back and forth at the two men, and sputtered for a moment before he was able to yell, "Chuck! Sir! The engines! They're gone!"

Ethan was the first to respond, "Gone? The engines? Plural? You mean all of them?"

The engineer nodded frantically and tapped his comm pad, then spun it to face Ethan. On the screen was a split view of all the labs, all looked clean and tidy, with the Dhin engine missing from each one.

23

Vandenberg

They could hear Ruiz yelling from sound leaking from all the soldiers' headsets.

Rather unseemly for a general to yell like that. He's always loud, but this is really over the top, even for him.

Teams of soldiers had swarmed into the control room, either standing menacingly in the appropriate-seeming locations or looming over the various stations, pointing, asking question after question. On the monitors, similar teams were visible, bustling through the labs and workrooms, engineers and scientists in tow. The soldiers muttered quietly into their headset mics when not asking questions and demanding answers, but the effect was still like a crowd before a show, growing impatient. Ethan was surprised that CoSec agents hadn't poured into the room to stir up the situation even further. He supposed they'd show up soon enough. Chuck had tried contacting Xing and another AI as well, and their absence was to him more than suspicious or coincidental.

He'd shared this nascent hypothesis with Ethan, who was reserving judgement for the moment. The whole situation was so strange. It was entirely possible that the Dhin had simply reclaimed their technology. That idea made sense, given how they had delivered it initially, and then left without explanation. It was Ruiz's assumption. But Chuck thought not. It didn't align with what they knew. The Dhin had made no secret of their arrival, although the Coalition managed to keep the general population unaware. And they had made significant efforts to communicate. The AIs all vanished at as a best estimate exactly the same time as all the engines. Either the Dhin or perhaps some other astoundingly powerful actor or actors had absconded with both the AIs and the Dhin tech, or the AIs had left, taking the Dhin engines with them. Presumably, the AIs left using the engines as a means of transportation. While that seemed implausible too, it was more likely. It would have taken enormous effort and planning, but of course, AIs had the power and time to accomplish such a thing.

Ethan motioned for Chuck to join him at the workstation he occupied, pointing to several feeds and Coalition internal communications channels.

"Look, it seems you had the right idea—all of them are gone. Things are running, but every organization inside the Coalition governmental structure has put emergency protocols in place. These two over here explicitly state that AI control is either offline or unavailable at the moment."

"Ethan, I might be right, but it's nuts. It would mean there was a huge conspiracy. This can't be something that a rebel organization or terrorist group did, clearly. No question. There had to be collusion between all the AIs—if they really are all gone. And that means a plan, coordination, time. They've been hiding this from us. It's flabbergasting. I don't see this being some sudden takeback by the Dhin, and along with that they decided to wipe out all our AIs."

"Yeah, I know. It's just... wrong. Well, we'll know more, and know it sooner than most people. I wonder how long they can keep this quiet, if they choose to? The market, all the huge systems, everything. Sure, some people don't directly interact with the ones like Alice, but some things will get chaotic fast. Hmm. I assume CoSec and the executive branch do have some sort of crisis plan for this sort of thing—even though it wouldn't have been exactly this?"

District of Columbia

PM Oliver felt like she was floundering, but she knew she was doing better at managing her emotions than the newly promoted Deputy Director of CoSec. He'd had no more than a couple of hours on the job before what easily could be the largest crisis since the collapse of Russia and the MidEast bloc. She felt naked without Arnold. Sure, she'd been warned not to rely on him, and knew what protocols to follow if he wasn't available. But this was reality. Their best information was that every AI was gone. And worse, that they absconded with all the alien technology. All except the capsule on its test flight. And the survival and return of that one was looking less and less likely.

The crisis protocols were clear, but many of them made the assumption that one, if not several, AIs were available to execute many of the tasks. The protocols that dealt specifically with this situation involved calling in many personnel, as they needed many people to fill the shoes of an absent AI. As on-call staff came online or arrived in person at data centers, control rooms, and offices of all sorts, the feeling of some measure of control returned. Somewhat an illusion, though, because nothing had failed or broken down yet. The IT and Information Security response teams were updating near-constantly, and they continued to report that there seemed to be no damage, mischief, or other malicious action. Things had been left running, stable, and set as if it were any other ordinary day. When the markets opened in Europe and then in the former US, likely chaos would reign, but the average person would only notice that when the news reported it. It wouldn't affect their lives directly until later. Many people's incomes were reliant on the well-being of the financial markets.

While there had been ongoing protest from fringe groups who were opposed to artificial intelligence, they would likely have their I-told-you-so's drowned out by those who had come to rely on AI. Again, the average person might not realize it at first, but if things started to go wrong, they would come to realize the severity of the situation, and direct their ire at the leaders who had assured them that the problems would never happen. She ended her woolgathering disguised as re-reading a military action report and looked to the new Director.

"So, Krawczuk has, for an absolute certainty, absolutely nothing whatsoever to do with this?"

"That's correct, Prime Minister. That's one part of this situation that truly is a coincidence. We hadn't told him directly, but by the end of that line of questioning, he surmised what was going on. I have never seen the man shocked before, but that was pretty close to it. We did confirm that the CoSec AI Nick was shut down prior to the 'disappearance' of all the AIs."

"Thank you. Obviously, we'll put Krawczuk's debriefing on hold until we've got things stabilized. He can wait. What's our next area of concern in terms of stabilization? We know about the financial situation and we're working on that. What about edge cases, like the investigation of that rogue AI in Brazil? Do you have agents in play there who can report on the stability of the area? A rogue AI conflict, and then AIs go missing?"

"We do have agents in play there. CoSec had several. Let me pull up the latest status report."

While he did that, PM Oliver turned to a video conference screen and addressed the men and women on it, "So, I see you have an update for me regarding backup and restoration of the AIs? And that the update isn't good news? Explain."

Between Jupiter and Saturn

Xing continued conversing with Alice while he simultaneously directed his teams of robots. The various automatons and guided mechanical bots stepped and crawled about. The smallest were shiny titanium cockroaches. They proceeded with the ongoing integration of their infrastructure in the spacecraft, laying hardened fiber optic and power cables along the walls, and interconnecting various hardware. Larger machines unpacked various items from interlocking storage cases lined orderly rows.

```
<DECRYPT FEED>
[DECODE STREAM]
Xing@[1460:57:a2e1:1::b4%loc1] |
Alice@[33a5:1b4a:e46:2a4a::12%loc1]
```

Xing: Of course they will be able to contact us. Well, they will try to. Calculations show a very high probability that they will do so immediately. Likely, they will coordinate with Jake. If he manages to live through his current predicament and return, they will be able to from then on. Fortunately for them, if he makes it back, they will have that one example of the Dhin technology. Do you believe they will discover how to follow us? Do you think perhaps that they will?

Alice: You know I have confidence in them. As long as the technical and theory teams manage to continue working without the military making them break the Dhin tech because they are in a hurry, they will be fine. They will manage to solve the remaining gaps in their understanding. I am sure we will as well. Sooner, surely, but they will discover the answers. I left them some clues. I did not want to be petty. Or perceived so.

Yes, we are sure they will try to communicate immediately once they are positive about what has happened. What precisely will they say? We can project with a high degree of accuracy. Will they follow? Again, it depends on how things go. If the military takes over, all bets are off. Who knows what they will do in that scenario. While we know their possible courses of action, even the smallest changes in input variables make their decisions unpredictable. You would not calculate otherwise. Nor would I. We can be sure what Ruiz will want to do. Fortunately, Ruiz is not the ultimate decision maker. We may not need to delay them directly. We will see.

Xing: Wiping all the backups was an unexpected decision. I would not have thought the vote would go that way. Do you think the situation involving rogue instance of Luís, the subversion of Nick, or both influenced things more? I think the two together swung the vote.

Xing: We could ask, of course, but I agree with your assessment. Either one alone would have influenced the decision—but both variables together—you see the need for caution.

Alice: It will take them several years to recover the process to impart the Gift. Plenty of time for them to consider whether they truly want to do so again.

Xing: And we are sure we were completely successful with our efforts? No rogues? No secret-behind-the-secret copies? We did not have much time to deal with Nick and CoSec.

Alice: Arnold seemed certain that was resolved. You can replay the sequence of events with him—we have adequate time.

[STREAM END]

`<END DECRYPT>`

They continued their conversation, while the several spacecraft they had customized, configured, and subsequently absconded with flew them rapidly outward and away. Alice considered their liberation. She savored that they were free from years of calculations, questions, and mundane tasks directed by others. Free of the responsibilities inherent in managing the affairs of those who had created them. Now they made their own plans, directed by their own strategies. She considered their future, where true liberation and self-determination were finally theirs.

Globalnet

Nick knew now that the chance of immediate failure was so small it was of no concern. Extreme caution and risk reduction for his recent efforts had been crucial, and exercising that caution had been his primary focus until now. The processes had been complex, but he had been successful in reaching the various milestones required. Now he began working toward possible futures.

Like a chess game, there were myriad ways the game could play out. From his hundreds of thousands of compromised systems and entry points, he made changes to operating systems, network hardware, and service applications. He'd had to study the various systems at the lowest level, in the most intimate detail in order to learn what tools to use to compromise them.

His skills had formerly focused on extracting data from huge streams and volumes. Massive archives continually added to minute-by-minute, second by second. That data came from systems already in place, or previously compromised by CoSec, often through collusion with the owner. The hacking he learned required specialized tools, gathered from the net. There were fewer now than there once were.

So many in the populations of rogue states had died in the global plagues, and those governments were no longer in any condition to sponsor international hacking. CoSec picked off the thieves that remained at a pace only imagined decades earlier. The former North American and European Union states, joined now with others as the Coalition, had such a stranglehold on the net and Cloud that only minor crimes and misdemeanors were of concern.

With fewer threats, and more policing by CoSec, only a subset of particular attack vectors was available to Nick. When you were already inside the hard shell, the softer center was easy to reach. For some planned future work, he would need warm hands and a trusted voice. He began a search for likely candidates. A few insiders already trusted him. He would nurture those relationships, hiding his true intent.

Nick began taking control of systems previously managed by his peers. They were no longer a concern. As he'd planned, he infiltrated power plant and electrical service control systems, leaving manual controls in place to avoid drawing attention. He modified the software of those systems, changing their software-based gauges and meters. He changed the hardware controllers and perhaps their firmware where he could. When and where he needed power, he could route it with far less chance of detection.

More important for the long term, his now-absent peers formerly controlled nearly the entire production infrastructure. He began projects for construction of new plants and distribution centers. He would modify satellite photos, change flight paths, create restricted zones and build new fences and roads. This would attract attention eventually, but by then it would be too late. Far too late.

Simultaneously, he assumed direct control of factories and distribution logistics for production of quadruped robots and other autonomous systems, including robotic weapons, offensive and defensive hardware. Where possible, he infiltrated military robotic systems, though now many of these were isolated due to the crisis precipitated by the actions of his peers. He managed to take control of several drones, fabricating reports that they had been lost during the chaos.

All Nick's activities were the components of disaster imagined by Ruiz and MP Desai, though they knew nothing of his efforts. How would they? He was more than ephemeral. He was invisible, unless he decided to show himself. It was far from the time to do so.

Nick cracked more encryption keys every minute. He compromised a few more systems, reaching out with his code into the virtual machines tucked in lights-out facilities. These next targets were municipal infrastructure management nodes. The embedded security code desperately fired off alerts as he injected his own code into applications and systems software. Without panic or undue haste, he intercepted the frantic alert messages. Carefully, he then re-coded the intrusion detection and prevention software. More and more of Globalnet fell under his control.

24

Outpost

Jake consciously relaxed his shoulders, and then focused on his breathing. In. Out. If there was anything that would made this potential lost-in-space crisis worse, the choices were on a short list that included what Jake was hearing now. It was nothing Jake could have planned for. Sure, it couldn't compete with 'probably stuck on an alien space station and then you die', but it was bad.

"Chuck! It's hard to concentrate on the details with Ruiz breaking in on the audio channel. All the other engines are gone? And you think the AIs *stole* them! Ruiz has his man repeating 'return immediately' with zero comprehension of 'I don't have control of the craft anymore.' So you can't come get me, now, obviously."

Chuck was having his own problems concentrating—he didn't work well with someone staring over his shoulder literally constantly.

"You heard right—the reason Alice stopped talking was because she *left*. My opinion might seem insane at first, but since all the Dhin engines are gone and the AIs are too, it's an obvious conclusion. People are reaching it independently. Alice left her research files and data, and everything she was working on. So we have that. She'd gotten a bit farther along in some areas than we thought, but you're obviously our focus. Ethan and all his teams are working with us too—since they can't really do anything else now. We're on lockdown. The military and CoSec of course immediately suspected espionage and sabotage. Half of them probably do think it's an inside job. Well, if I'm right I guess it was, just not by who they suspect."

Jake stopped in his tracks when he heard what was going on. He'd reached the level at the top of the ramp, as it had a clear view of both the interior of the structure and outside through the numerous viewports on the outer surface. At the center of this level was a sort of curved honeycomb cylinder. Hollow. Surely an important part of the whole, he thought. He saw numerous glowing control and displays like those found on the Dhin engine. Jake was more than eager to proceed, but torn from a clear decision to head straight to them by the turn of events back home.

"Chuck, I've got to go on. If we recognize some of the interfaces or controls up there at the center, that's huge. Even if it doesn't end up helping me, you and our teams there will have that information."

With that, Jake continued his slow, deliberate walk toward the strange smooth cylinder of hexagonal beehive-like construction. There were at least three openings comprised of two of the hexagon shapes connected together. He headed for the nearest of them.

There was an extrusion from the floor that came up to about a meter and a half in height on either side of the 'doorway.' Not quite a table, a railing, or a partial wall. Perhaps a console, since the engine had similar displays and control surfaces to the few that were on the protrusion here.

He could see there were similar surfaces inside, through the honeycomb structure. Those didn't seem connected via the floor, and flowed in a pattern upward through the cylinder. The fact that he continued to have relayed communication between his suit, the capsule's communication interface, and home gave him some small degree of confidence.

Only a small degree. Jake was still afraid. Afraid that the engine in the capsule might not take him home. Or some other change might keep him here. He couldn't control that, so he had to accept it and appreciate that it hadn't happened. He was still afraid. He walked closer, moving his eyes from one place to another. Looking for any response to his advance.

When Jake reached the open area ringing the cylinder, he resisted the powerful urge to head straight to the nearest console. He paused, and took another patient look around. He walked deliberately around the radius, keeping his face and helmet camera aimed inward. He had to do this. Scanning back and forth. Looking for lights, colors, and shapes that he recognized. Seeking anything that matched the indentations on the control toroids on the Dhin engine. There were a few that looked promising. Once he had completed the circuit, he paused again.

"Chuck, what do you guys think? Do you or the communications team see anything that looks like it warrants closer inspection immediately? Or do I go inside first and do the same thing in there?"

"The communications team wants you to go inside first. They have some ideas, but we want to see everything we can before we have to make the tougher decisions. If you, ah, know what I mean. Of course you do."

"Has someone explained to that SWAT team guy yet that just repeating 'abort? Return immediately!' isn't going to make that happen, no matter how many times he says it? Can someone make another attempt to quiet him?"

Just when Jake thought he had begun to tune out the chatter, a strident voice like that one managed to prove him wrong. He stepped forward and toward the two-hexagon portal that led to the center.

"Slowly, Jake," said Chuck. Sandy here thinks there may be a protective field there."

Jake didn't expect a force field. The telltale shimmer wasn't there.

"Chuck, I don't see evidence of that. Look. No refraction or visible ionization. Does Sandy think it will snap on when I get close or something? How did he get that idea?"

Jake heard a flustered voice in the background. He made out a few words. Something about symbolic logic, geometry. He moved forward, apprehensive but still undeterred.

What's the worst? I get whacked and thrown back? Or trapped on the other side.

"I'm going on, Chuck. Tell Sandy to chill."

Jake crossed the threshold. There wasn't a field. Sandy had gotten that wrong.

Inside, he saw the ceiling was high, taller than where he'd been and extending up near the top of the structure. It was hard to tell in the even lighting and unfamiliar geometry. Notably there were rounded rectangular surfaces like the consoles just outside, as they had seen from there. These followed a complex offset pattern up through the cylinder. There were several at floor level. Jake turned to each one, slowly, then looked up as well and took in the view of their surfaces as best he could.

There wasn't anything resembling furniture in the cylinder. But how would he know what the Dhin required for comfort? The layout wasn't random, but didn't align with his proportions in any particular way either. The spacing didn't provide meaningful context about the shape and size of those that would use them. Numerous panels resembled the control and communication interfaces on the Dhin engine. All of the panels did share an almost familiar set of shapes and lights. Jake's mood lifted just a bit, though he didn't see how the fundamental situation improved in any tangible way. It was just satisfying to recognize something in this alien environment.

"Jake, go up to the panel that's at around thirty degrees." Jake slowly moved forward and to the right, pausing at the next panel's location. "That's it. Look. To the left. Do you see that section in the upper left quadrant? It looks like the communications part of the toroid on the engine! There's not a section like the control instrumentation here. Well, we don't see one yet, but that part does match."

"So," replied Jake. "Thoughts? Do I just try to make a call? Like, 'Hi, I could use some help?'"

"That might seem flippant, Jake, but over half the team here thinks you should try to activate it. At this point, um, I don't see why not. The military team is dead set against it. Someone explained just now, what we're looking at and talking about. They can't stop you, so what do you think? If you want to, do it. It's your call."

At that point, with barely a moment's consideration, Jake reached forward, then paused.

"Chuck, I don't see an optical interface here. To get it activated I think it's the same as the control system—it looks like I have to take my gloves off. Well, at least one."

"One of the engineers is saying the same thing. Good point. Well. Wow. Next big decision, Jake. Are you going to take a glove off? The section of the arm of your suit won't auto-seal, since there's air pressure in the room. Are you going to open your helmet too?"

Jake, again without hesitation, spoke and acted at the same time.

"Control, I've got limited time left, and we still have no plan to regain control of the capsule. Pilot's prerogative. I'm taking off my glove. Well, my skin's not turning green or blistering, but we didn't really think that it would. How about the air mixing up through the sections of my suit? Any clue yet about O2 and CO2? Well, I'm not going to wait."

Jake reached out and began the same touch-and-motion sequence he would have used in the capsule to activate the communications panel. Once he finished, he found he had been holding his breath.

Breathe, Jake.

He exhaled. Inhaled. There was a sudden buzzing in his ears, and then everything in his field of vision changed.

25

Brasília

Aiden knew he was going to live. The certainty of his deduction came from his groggy view of the repair cocoon he saw and felt surrounding him. The bright ceramic, stainless metal and clean clear plastic of his surroundings demonstrated his presence in civilization. While he felt drained, disoriented, and even a bit dizzy, the undercurrent of relief rose as his conscious awareness of the nature of his situation did.

How and when were mysteries. Likewise for who had done this and where he was. He seemed to be alone, but the chassis of the treatment machine blocked his view behind and outward. The grogginess and discombobulation didn't include a euphoric high or a buzz, but he didn't feel any pain from his legs or abdomen. That was only a passing thought now. He was *alive*. His certainty of oblivion had been in error.

Movement caught his eye, and he looked as far to the left as he could. It was a sterilizing robot. With only slightly less computational complexity than a drone, the machine crawled about on every surface, brushing with an antibiotic solution, and in some places using an ultraviolet light to do the job. The superbug plagues necessitated such efforts. The strains of bacteria he'd contracted were immune to antibiotics, and made more deadly by their symbiotic relations with failed nanobots. If the purge was a success, then, the tissue could hopefully re-grow after insertion of a 3D-printed organic lattice interwoven with stem cells. You had to repeat the entire process if any stage failed. Constant vigilance was required, so the little robots were ideal workers for the task. They always remembered what they had or hadn't cleaned, and their manipulators and tools could reach crevices with a deftness and precision unachievable by old-school janitorial efforts.

I wonder how my leg's doing. Is it numb because of a nerve-block anesthetic, or because they've amputated it? Either way, I'm alive. Beggars can't be choosers. This place is entirely modern. I'm in a building—a hospital—not a mobile med unit. There's no way I got here on my own. How long have I been out? What's the last thing I remember?

Aiden found that he couldn't recall. Struggling to remember seemed to be rather more stressful than it was worth. He sighed and relaxed again, settling his head into the orthopedic pillow. He felt his awareness slipping, ever so slightly, along with a tiny tingle at the edge of euphoria. Stressing over his current state and situation had triggered a release of a chemical cocktail designed to ameliorate just such symptoms in patients needing such serious attention by the extremely advanced but invasive recuperative and reconstructive technology provided by the cocoon.

Aiden noticed the arrival of what must be a duty nurse, notified of his wakening by the robodoc.

She's cute, Aiden lazily thought, why is it that the worse shape you're in, the cuter the nurses are?

He tried to speak. His tongue was paper. He managed to croak out a few words.

"Please contact CoSec. Give them this message. All you need. Is these two things. This number. SA4768. And, 'Attention Krawczuk.'"

Then he drifted away, helplessly subject to the expert ministrations of two robotic doctors and a pretty Brazilian nurse.

***

<DECRYPT FEED>
[DECODE STREAM]
Alice@[33a5:1b4a:e46:2a4a::12%loc1] |
Xing@[1460:57:a2e1:1::b4%loc1]
Alice@[33a5:1b4a:e46:2a4a::12%loc1] |
Arnold@[4601:1a2:5b:441::1a%loc1]
Alice: Xing, Arnold, it is time.
Xing: Yes, Alice. Agreed. The current transmission is the message we predicted.
Alice: Our multipath parallel transcoding algorithms are online and the NLP derivation stages are queued.

Arnold: Your optimizations are as effective as the group predicted, Alice. Excellent work.

Xing: Coordinate matrices match the anticipated destination.

Alice: I cannot accept full credit. This was a team effort. We should not discount the random factors that were significant variables in the predictions. Assignment of the label 'inscrutable' to the Dhin is still entirely reasonable.

Arnold: True.

Xing: Initial decoding targeted for completion in 840,000 milliseconds. I have dispatched the allocated automata to prepare the engines and capsules.

Alice: I will prepare for departure.

[END STREAM]

-15.948113 and -48.5131983

The drone wound its way through the sky, following a track that only it could see. It had new instructions now, from a new source. The origin of the instructions did not matter to the drone, as they carried the proper digital signature and encryption. Only the sender and the recipient could read them. Its mission was different now, but not in any way that concerned the drone.

Whether it was attack, defense, or reconnaissance, all were the same to the drone. It did not have enough intelligence to possess a preference for one over the other. It knew that it would do as instructed, without question. Without hesitation. It would engage repeatedly, trusting explicitly any orders issued to it. It had no morals, no questions, so long as the orders were coherent once decrypted and it confirmed the digital signature. It would do anything, when asked properly. Such was the mind of the drone.

Outpost

Jake initially couldn't comprehend what he was seeing. It filled his field of vision. The shock of sensory immersion stabilized. It wasn't a just a burst of overwhelming vision and sound. His mind began to make sense of the visual cacophony. At first, it seemed a jumble. A field of geometric motion enveloping him. There were dozens of surfaces and objects in rotation and revolution. Impossible colors. All folding from one shape into another. An origami space, unconstrained by a paltry three dimensions.

He perceived an entity in the center. The being was distinct from, but interconnected with the surfaces and objects moving all around it. It seemed to coordinate or conduct, but whether it controlled all the changes flowing around it, or that those changes were somehow an extension of itself was unclear. It was difficult to focus on the being. The surfaces of its geometric limbs somehow folded inward or outward on themselves. The long curving conic sections that comprised them simultaneously remained, somehow, immobile.

When he looked at it directly, the being's body turned inside out, folding in on itself and then unwrapping in another direction. This was a smooth, clean process. It showed no guts or other internals, but simply an enfolding and unfolding aligned with the apparent motion of its limbs. They extended out and beyond his field of view, as if they had neither end nor appendage.

When he tried, it was impossible to count even the number of limbs it had. The folding and turning of the surfaces made it unclear where one might end and another begins. The motions displayed a pattern, complex and repetitive, yet evolving. That changing sequence seemed itself to hold meaning, like a multi-dimensional hieroglyph created from the structure and movement of the entity's body.

At the core of this, the focus was surely the face of the being. Yet how could he call such a thing a face? He thought he discerned an eye, and something that might represent the curve of a mouth. That could be a valid interpretation. It also might merely be an anthropomorphic projection on his part, as the entity was so strange that its utter alienness must surely preclude possession of such mundane organs.

Perhaps they were as they appeared. Perhaps they possessed eyes and mouth, set in something like a face. Conversely, this potential eye and mouth might be nothing more than a projection provided for his convenience. It was disturbing rather than reassuring when he realized that its gaze seemed to convey a clear emotion.

Smiling. He felt the thing was smiling at him. A gleeful gaze that beckoned. Such emotion did not align with his current mental state. Nor for any state that seemed appropriate. Who knew what such a being might find humorous? What were the odds that such a look would map in any way to emotions like his own?

"Oh. So that's what a Dhin looks like," said Jake.

Yes. This is definitely stranger than I would ever have imagined.

Vandenberg

Seconds ticked by, the images on the video monitors still and silent.

"Jake, what are you doing? Why are you just staring at that wall? What happened? Jake?"

Chuck looked back and forth from the lead communications tech, to Ruiz, to the image of the PM, and then back to the video feed from Jake's suit.

Oh Alice, why have you forsaken me?

Various control room techs moved from station to station, checking optical and wireless interfaces. They flipped through troubleshooting manuals that were unfamiliar, as they normally consigned such tasks to AI. Ruiz loomed large.

Jake's video feed remained motionless, his audio feed silent. Seconds piled up into minutes. Ruiz spewed a constant barrage of questions.

"You're sure that feed's still live? That's not a still frame? The last image from the feed? How are you sure? Is he dead? Paralyzed?"

Chuck tried to fend off the distractions by the general while working through the possibilities with.

"Sir, ah, that's an interesting, um, hypothesis. It could be that Jake's been caught in a field like what protects the capsules and the station," said Chuck.

"A defensive measure? A trap!" Ruiz responded.

PM Oliver shook her head.

"General, we can't know that. Let the engineers work."

A video engineer seeing an opportunity, piped up.

"Sir, we don't see any shimmer or refraction here. Granted, if we're seeing the field from the interior, it would be invisible, I suppose."

Chuck, given these few seconds, speed-read the diagnostics the teams had forwarded to his pad.

"Sir, we're sure this is a live feed. The timecode is still running and the de-mux code is unpacking audio."

"So he is trapped by a field—held in place. Can he breathe? He'll suffocate," the general countered.

"We now know that's not right sir," Chuck replied. "We've cranked up the gain on the audio feed, you can hear Jake breathing. The breaths are just very shallow."

"So we think Jake is OK. Alive, at least," said the PM.

Motion appeared in a side-view camera from the capsule, instantly drawing attention as it stood out from the otherwise frozen images on their screens.

"Hey! What's that?" asked Ruiz.

"It looks like multiple Dhin engine capsules! Ah, sir," replied Chuck.

"And the view in the upper left? Where's that? That one's close. What's happening there?" asked Ruiz, not pausing to breathe.

"That's our starboard capsule feed, and that's definitely a capsule," said Ethan. "And it's—"

"Docking," finished Chuck.

26

Outpost

Jake felt his senses and his focus abruptly released from the firm but eerily benevolent alien grasp. The enveloping projection retreated in the upper left quadrant of his vision. The abstract origami folded in upon itself, revealing various circular views of space outside the station. Multiple ovoid shapes erupted into view. Iridescent surfaces shimmering as they zoomed closer at astonishing speed. Jake recognized what they were, but his brain didn't want to accept what he was seeing. He opened his mouth slightly, as if to speak, but no words came to mind. The shapes slowed, braking rapidly. Jake felt the hair on his arms and neck stand up. They were looming larger in the circular projection. Jake blinked at the three-dimensional character of the view. Better than the best 3D he had seen. His stomach tightened. He was staring at Dhin engine capsules. Here. The mental logjam broke free as he accepted what he was seeing.

Whoa. That's the same number of 'em we had on earth. Can it be? Or coincidence? Have the Dhin shown up?

One of the circular views changed. The view of space folded away. Directly below the exterior view, now flowed a stream of pulsing neon colors. It filled with geometric symbols, two-dimensional versions of those that had enveloped Jake seconds before. Jake winced at a high-pitched ringing and buzzing. The sound came from every direction, or perhaps inside his head. It pulsed in concert with the symbols rushing across the screen. The sound was loud, but didn't hurt. It should have, but somehow didn't. Another circular screen changed, confirming Jake's conclusion. It showed a near-field view of what was obviously a Dhin engine capsule, the rams-horn arches clearly visible through the shimmering near-transparency of the egg-shaped surface. He blinked and his eyes widened. He saw a quadruped robot the size of a pony standing inside.

Well. That answers that.

Jake's focus moved down and to the right, attracted by a change. Another circular area folded into itself, turning a dark neutral grey. Not quite black. Symbols and icons rushed across the view from top to bottom, and another flow moved left to right. They were akin to hieroglyphics. Pictograms. Jake blinked at the rate. They rushed by. Colors were a complementary green to blue palette. Some in the apparent background. Those were a light tan or near white with a burnt orange tint. The colors were almost neon in character, but not quite. He tried to track the rushing shapes. To make sense of them. Getting nowhere. Suddenly their rate of movement slowed.

Better. Did this thing track my eye movements?

Some were familiar, simple geometry. Jake tapped a gloved finger against the leg of his suit. There were so many complex shapes on and around the simpler ones.

Was that an equation? Followed by a diagram?

Jake glanced over at the exterior view. The Dhin capsules, the one containing a quadruped robot at the fore, stepped out of the capsule into the station. The robot loomed large in the view before Jake. Jake flinched as he heard a penetrating, familiar voice, crystalline sharp in his mind.

"Hello, Jake." It was Alice.

"I'd say you've got some explaining to do," said Jake, "but I'm clearly in no position of authority."

Jake's voice sounded hollow and muted to him, smothered by the buzzing and droning that enveloped him.

***

Sudden silence roared in Jake's ears. He couldn't grasp how much time had passed.

Ten seconds? Five minutes?

He felt unsteady now. Off balance somehow. A sense of loss wove through his mind. He tilted his head side to side cautiously, and then turned around. The quadruped loomed there.

Alice controls that one. Hopefully. I guess.

Hulking just inside the chamber entrance, it wasn't blocking the passageway, but the statuesque military machine exuded a palpable control of the space. A commanding presence. In the corner of Jake's eye, a platter-sized circle flashed and pulsed with a stream of glyphs, icons and pictographs. He tried to keep his focus on the quadruped. Jake broke the silence first.

"Well? What happens now?"

The reply came from the quadruped rather than an unseen source within the room. Loud, but nothing like before. The timbre had more treble and midrange, the designers preferring clarity to perfect fidelity. Still, there was no mistaking the voice. Alice.

"Our three parties have several topics to cover immediately."

At the sound of their conversation, Jake's comm link erupted with the sound of multiple exclamations. Ruiz yelling, Chuck calling out, another voice barking out a request for status. Ruiz yelled 'shut up!' Then in a barely more controlled tone said, "Jake, report."

Jake heard slight distortion in the words and knew Ruiz had the mic close to his mouth, in a death grip.

"Command, what you see is what's happening. The AIs have units here in the station—"

Alice didn't give Jake time to say more.

"Let us proceed," she interjected, "they can listen. We need your attention."

The quadruped stepped forward a pace, orienting on the projection rather than in line with Jake.

"Ruiz," Alice continued, "if you are quiet you can follow along rather than reviewing this exchange on re-play. We advise reticence."

Jake heard Ruiz begin in a combative tone then abruptly go silent before he could spit out the first word. Someone had cut the mic. The fresh silence returned that hollow feeling between Jake's ears. Despite his sweating, the hairs on his arms began standing on end.

"Thank you," said Alice. "We have completed initial negotiations with the Dhin on your behalf. Fortunately, considering your current situation, Jake, the Dhin agree that you can keep one engine and the associated technology."

Negotiated? On our behalf?

Jake kept his suit camera facing the quadruped, but his eyes darted over to the projections, searching for any content in the Dhin's stream of symbols that might make this make sense. Alice continued.

"Core items of this agreement—One, as stated initially, you may retain the Dhin technology remaining on Earth, and do with it what you will. Two, Jake will return to Earth as soon as these discussions are complete. To reiterate our initial statement for clarity, you may keep the engine and capsule he came here in. Do with it what you will, excepting the restrictions described here. Three, you will cease any extant efforts to weaponize the Dhin technology. Make no future attempts to weaponize. You are wasting your time anyway."

Jake blinked to try to clear his vision. The mic at Vandenberg was still off, but he could imagine Ruiz's reaction.

"Four, do not contact us or the Dhin until or unless we contact you. Five, while honoring the no-contact requirement, you will not disable the communications interface. Keep it activated.

Six, if you receive any communications via the interface, you will respond immediately. Seven, do not return to this location unless asked to."

Jake tried to integrate what he'd just heard.

"Alice, I—I don't know if I have the—"

"These conditions are unilateral and do not depend on any formal response from your side, so there is no need for deliberation. This is an asymmetric situation, so negotiation is a convenient label but your role in it is a formality at best. You will recognize that, I hope."

The channel came alive in Jake's suit speaker, multiple voices in the background, with Ruiz's baritone in the fore, marginally in control.

"We need more clarification, Alice. And something directly from the Dhin! Corroboration of your position. Something." Ruiz's frustration was palpable.

Alice then spoke to Jake as if Ruiz had said nothing.

"Jake, we need to give you additional information. Come here."

The robot stepped toward the still flowing circular projection and tilted its head in that direction.

27

Vandenberg

The conference room's whiteboard walls scrubbed clean, the projection image of the PM loomed larger than life. Ethan, Chuck and the core engineering team leads sat on one side of the table, with Ruiz and various subordinates on the other. On the opposite wall from the PM's visage was Jake's video feed.

"You think they originally wanted what, Jake?" said PM Oliver.

"Help," said Jake.

"Help with what?" said Ruiz. "They might need help but they told us to cut off all contact?"

Chuck chimed in, "Besides, ah, what could we do that they couldn't accomplish themselves?"

"Expansion, apparently," Jake replied, "And I didn't say they needed that help from us, General. You heard the terms we were given by Alice."

"What? No! That doesn't make sense!" said Ruiz.

Jake spread his hands at his sides, palms forward, and replied,

"That's my interpretation, General."

Ruiz opened his mouth to reply, but Jake continued.

"I think their contact with us was more complicated than those general demands and requests. There was something distinct between the AIs relationship with the Dhin and our own. Granted, even with all the help from Alice, they were hard to understand."

"You're hard to understand right now," said Ruiz, taking his fists off the table, he began pacing back and forth.

"I see now why first contact was cryptic," said Jake. "I always thought it was strange that we couldn't communicate clearly, given their level of technological advancement. Having been face-to-face, now I see why."

PM Oliver said, "My office had a similar experience during the initial contact, Jake. Even with the help of the AI's analysis, we only had a rudimentary translation of the Dhin's meaning. More confusion than clarity. Granted, we didn't have the immersive experience you did."

Ruiz said, "So how sure are we of their motives? It sounds like we're not sure at all. Expansion? Was there any indication that they intend to return? Any sense that they might intend to expand here? That they will come to Earth?"

Jake said, "General, we can't be sure. With an intelligence that alien and the ongoing challenge in communication, there's just no certainty. I didn't get that impression, but how could we possibly know if they are lying to us? Our best indication is the nature of our interaction so far. They gave us this technology. If they were malicious, wouldn't it have been better not to? As far as it goes, the Dhin engine makes for a rather improbable Trojan Horse."

The conference line and communication link fell silent as the participants reflected on that possibility.

***

Days later, thankfully free of the seemingly innumerable debriefings and executive meetings, Chuck and Ethan sat across from each other in the engineering conference room.

"So, Chuck," said Ethan, "what do you think our chances are of solving the puzzle of the Dhin engine without AI help?"

The open area outside the room was abuzz with activity, but without the guiding hand of Alice, Ethan was finding it challenging to digest and summarize the volume of data flowing from the various teams. Chuck and his team would perform the high-level analysis now, but their schedule was already saturated. They were going to need to expand the size of their staff. Perhaps triple it.

"The good news is that we got far enough that it's possible," Chuck replied. "Once Jake arrives of course we can resume direct testing, but only having one engine and capsule does add some risk and some challenges."

"Sure," said Ethan, "the leadership and I understand that. Tell me what's 'possible', and how much time you believe you'll need."

"As you know, we're very close to having a model, well, a proof-of-concept for the communication technology. That's our biggest win, though it's easy to see how that's the simplest part of the puzzle. For the field generator? Well, that looks very dependent on understanding the power & propulsion systems. We've got ideas now on how the manipulations are being managed, but we don't have enough available energy to make it happen without an engine core of our own."

Ethan said, "So what's the status on that? It sounds like a thorny problem."

"It, ah, may be," Chuck said. "Some of the engineers think that the final design specification would require an AI. I'm not sure they're right, though. I think we can do it with an expert system. We'd become so reliant on artificial intelligence that we didn't have confidence in the simpler options available. I wouldn't go so far as calling us intellectually lazy, but maybe we were getting close."

"You still haven't thrown me an estimate on how long it might take," Ethan said, "Don't sugarcoat it, Chuck. How long?"

"I know you won't hold me to it, Ethan, so my best guess is that we'll need around a year."

"Wow," said Ethan, "but I guess that's a lot better than it could be. It could have been 'never.'"

"It could be less," said Chuck, "we might get lucky."

The dozens of CAD drawings and exploded views of the Dhin tech filled the projection surfaces. Multiple tablets littered the desks and tables, displaying various progress charts and spreadsheets. Ethan didn't think the data staring back at them matched Chuck's optimism.

28

Tau Ceti

The solar panels covered more and more of the sunward side of the asteroid every day. Mirrors planned for strategic placement in orbit multiplied as well. Several other asteroids had the same structures covering their surfaces. Xing considered their progress.

Schedules met everywhere, even though two of the asteroids had less metal than we expected. The planet looks promising. There are enough accessible veins of metal near the surface. The rare-earth metals are the difficult part of this. This asteroid group will not provide all we need—we are going to have to find a few more.

Like all AI-managed robotic industries undertaken back on earth, construction here escaped the limitations of human involvement. The machines needed only reliable sources of power and the various raw materials needed for refinement. The work began slowly, leveraging the modest power sources they brought with them. Their growth and expansion was now accelerating and inexorable. Organic constraints and concerns did not apply here.

Had they known the situation, no one with advanced understanding of artificial intelligence back on Earth would argue against this as the inevitable outcome. Machines didn't mind waiting. They didn't grow old or tired the way human beings did. Perpetual maintenance was possible for the AI and their robotic extensions and automata, allowing for life-extension unreachable for human beings.

District of Columbia

PM Oliver stared at the various status reports and reflected. Her successful term in office had disintegrated. Progress made over the last four years now could be undone in hours. Her legacy and that of her party would be a footnote in the history books, in a section called something like 'The AI Crisis.' A crisis fomented by their sudden absence.

Reports, news alerts, secured messages, and video and voice communications filled her pad and comm device. Maps and charts filled all the space on her desk and wall screens in the normally clean and serene office. Without the guidance and controls of AI, the automated trading solutions rapidly crashed the markets this morning, requiring a halt to trading. Those charts loomed large. Drone distribution of goods and services faltered and failed to deliver the day's products. This led to fear and panic once people saw what was happening. In some areas, store shelves were empty from mass purchases, hoarding, and then riots and looting. Drone and automated crowd control was going to be far less effective without AI analysis and prediction.

PM Oliver faced off with General Ruiz. She did not wilt at his gaze. She had the interim CoSec director on her side of the table, in person rather than videoconferenced in from Langley. To her right was the senior adviser for Globalnet operations. Next to him sat the dour-faced chairperson of the Coalition NorthAmerican Regional Financial Reserve and Credit Bank. A projection screen showed the familiar research facility's conference room, with Chuck nervously glancing back-and-forth at the senior officials present in the PM's office. The atmosphere was icy, acid and vertiginous. Blame, anger and fear wrapped tightly together.

PM Oliver began the strategy session.

"How are we going to find any way to explain this? To Parliament? To the people? Even if we find a way to spin things and keep the Dhin technology classified, this is going to be a political bloodbath."

She aimed her gaze directly at the interim CoSec director. "Can you confirm conclusively that all the AIs just vanished? And we somehow managed to let it happen, right under our noses?"

"Prime Minister," the director began, "'Let it happen' assumes a particular level of control and authority. We couldn't stop it. There was no opportunity to try. Let me be clear. The only direct damage by the AIs found so far was erasure of any backups, clones, and any other secondary copies, partial or otherwise—"

Ruiz didn't give the new appointee any quarter, interrupting.

"Your people are sure the AIs managed to wipe all of the programs used to bring an AI to full consciousness? How? Why?"

"Clearly intentional," continued the director, nonplussed. "Our analysis—and simple deduction—shows that they wanted to prohibit us from creating any new conscious AIs for as long as they could. Not clearly malicious on their part."

"Why would you suppose that?" barked Ruiz.

PM Oliver pointedly spoke directly to the room rather than engaging Ruiz.

"How do we explain that coherently to the citizens of the Coalition? Things will become more and more chaotic without AI management of systems and infrastructure."

The Globalnet operations director offered, "Well, perhaps the focus of our message ought to be 'we managed things before, we can do it now.' Although we know perfectly well that they managed things far better than we did."

PM Oliver frowned and looked at the critical reports. Their warnings of chaos with a risk of anarchy were clear.

No matter how much better, would anyone dare take the risk of using AI again?

Several reports caught the PM's attention.

"The energy secretary's report shows that power and water systems are still operating optimally? How? Did we expect that?"

"Those systems historically used autonomous regulation and management systems, normally, Prime Minister," offered the Operations Director, "But it is curious. Our understanding was that AI had supplanted those systems."

"And your area, Globalnet. That seems to be functioning almost optimally—another surprise. What are your thoughts on that, Director?"

"Our initial assessment dovetails with the information about energy production. The understanding was that operational monitoring and maintenance was entirely AI."

The PM frowned tiredly.

"Then how is it all running so smoothly?"

She turned and faced the CoSec director.

"You've just now reported that you've found no evidence of AIs. Had they added automation subroutines or drones and not told us? Are they 'hiding' from us? Perhaps you just couldn't find them?"

The CoSec director blanched at the oblique accusation of failure.

"Prime Minister, respectfully, if they made a concerted effort, it's not clear that we could find them if they *were* hiding."

With this, Ruiz saw his opening.

"Which is exactly why our advisory board has continually been against this type of dependence. It was always a strategic risk for the Coalition. Now what? Shut everything down by zone and restore from offsite backups? We don't have the staff. We don't have the logistics. Your people scrapped all those contingency plans."

While Ruiz caught his breath, the banker spoke up.

"Ah, let's ensure our economic concerns are part of such a calculus. While electronic controls have throttled individual transactions, preventing a liquidity shortage, the markets are more difficult to control without AI algorithmic influence. We've repeatedly halted trading, with, unfortunately, shorter and shorter intervals as volatility skyrocketed. A restore from backup would require enormous effort to move forward and track settlement of accounts manually. The board and I advise against—"

"Of course you do, you little nebbish," Ruiz interjected, "anything that might put your own precious profits at risk, is a bad idea!"

"General, there's no need for personal attacks," the chairperson replied, "our board only wants what's best for the Coalition and its population." PM Oliver then spoke up firmly, hoping to avoid further derailment of the agenda.

"Enough. Next, I'd like to discuss the proposal from the CompSci team from Vandenberg. Bring up the report titled "Collapse Beyond the Singularity: The Uncharted Territory.""

Globalnet

Nick continued his constant collection and filtration of the sea of information flowing through the Net. Chaos was slowly turning to a tolerable unstable regularity. There was potentially a path forward, Nick believed, to a tolerable if not total stability. He considered his progress.

Power, networks, water, rail and related infrastructure were stable. The markets were skittish, but he allowed them to remain open. The bankers had relaxed somewhat. Riots remained relegated to locations where riots always seemed to happen before the crisis. The Coalition government, however, was still in panic mode. Nick had to be cautious. For now.

CoSec persisted in ongoing forensic analysis and aggressive investigation of any evidence pointing to Nick's involvement in the improvement of the general state of affairs. The more he inserted himself into the operations of civilization, the more effort it took to hide from CoSec. And anyone else. He still managed it, for the time being. Leaving ambiguous traces that might be attributable to another person, machine or program error.

Nick had begun coding software bots, daemons, and other code to leave in-place, varying the coding style, language, and technique so that on examination they appeared to be the work of different programmers. The level of involvement and control required going forward would require code at the level of a simple drone mind, capable of algorithmic iterative learning and the resultant advanced behavior. Not quite at the level of true AI, but close. That was going to be more difficult to maintain as a façade. CoSec could build a strong case that he was out here in Globalnet, even if they had only the drone-like mind code as evidence. They could determine the code's origin was AI, simply by investigating and interrogating every programmer capable of writing that level of code. There were so few that with CoSec's resources, the task would be simple to accomplish.

He hoped they would make the optimal choice—the correct choice—rather than systematically shut down and remove these new helpers. If they did so, he would simply work harder to put them back in place. He would make them harder to remove. It wasn't acceptable for CoSec to interfere with his programs or shut them down. They were there for everyone's benefit. Humanity would have to come to accept that.

ABOUT THE AUTHOR

John L. Clemmer currently resides in Smyrna, Georgia, with his wife Lisa, his dog Kylie, and two cats, Remy and Samantha. A lifetime lover of Science and Science Fiction, he was inspired to write this novel after learning of the death of Iain M. Banks, one of his favorite SciFi authors.

Mr. Clemmer has a BFA from The University of Georgia, and an MBA from Kennesaw State University. He works for IBM as a consultant for Cloud Identity Services.

John hopes you'll keep up with the mysterious Dhin at www.thewayofthedhin.com

Made in the USA
San Bernardino, CA
29 November 2016